DESTRUCTION

Forgotten Colony, Book Four

M.R. FORBES

Chapter 1

"Paige, stay here and keep an eye on whatever that is," Caleb said, marking the incoming lights in the distance on his HUD. It was airborne, a ship of some kind, moving slowly—but not too slowly—toward the Inahri city-ship.

Tentative. That was the right way to describe it. Up until a few minutes ago, coming near this place would have triggered the artificial intelligence protecting it to activate a signal, a quantum waveform that acted like a targeted, ultra-powerful electromagnetic pulse. The ship and everyone on it would have been knocked out of the sky.

But that was a few minutes ago, before the Guardian Intellect had been destroyed, blasted with an odd energy weapon that did not affect organic matter or the wiring that ran through the Guardians' standard Space Force Marine Advanced Tactical Combat Armor. It only affected the node-to-node systems of the Intellects, the creations of the Axon, a race that was hundreds of thousands of years humanity's senior and whose technological advancements were all around them.

It was too bad it hadn't made them any smarter when it came to preparing for war.

They'd had thousands of years to get ready for the coming of the Relyeh, a race of aliens even older than the Axon. The Relyeh had created the trife, the demons that had conquered half the galaxy, including Earth, and who the Axon claimed were expanding at a suddenly increasing rate.

The best they had come up with to deal with the trife was to give humans their own technology to see what kind of toys they could create, and then force them to fight genetically engineered demons until they were deemed superior.

The idea would have been over-the-top ridiculous if Command hadn't come up with the very same idea when they let Riley Valentine change the navigation computers onboard the Deliverance to bring it here. Here, where the trife infesting Earth had originated. Here, where she was supposed to unleash human-trife super-soldiers with massive healing factors, enabling them to survive almost any encounter.

And here, where the trife weren't the most dangerous alien they would have to deal with.

Humans were.

Caleb still couldn't believe how all of this was unfolding, starting with the shitstorm they'd had to fight through before the Deliverance ever left its hangar. Things had only found a way to get worse from there. Valentine was slowly mutating into the same human-trife hybrid she had created. He and his Guardians were stranded on a city-sized starship made by humans with technology given to them by the Axon. Unfortunately, Caleb and his Guardians had no clue how to use it, or even how to get from one part of the city to another.

And the humans, who the Guardian Intellect had named the Inahri? They seemed to be on their way, well aware that something was going on in the city. They had to know and were testing whether or not the Intellect was no longer operational.

And Flores was dead.

Caleb felt it every time he lost a member of his team. Whether he had known them for years or for only minutes. As soon as they fell under his command, they were his responsibility to keep alive. Flores had given herself up to save him, trying so desperately to make up for the worst decision of her life, when she had run from a fight and gotten her squadmates killed. It wasn't an offense he could forgive her for — only God could do that — but he hoped the courage she showed at the end had helped her find peace in whatever came next.

"Roger, Sergeant," Paige replied. She moved closer to the transparency in the wall, eyes fixed on the incoming lights. Caleb's ATCS estimated the range at ten kilometers and their speed at one hundred kph, giving them six minutes to prepare.

Of course, they had more than six minutes. It would take time for the craft to do whatever it came to do, and the city-ship they were standing in was massive. It was possible they could avoid the strangers altogether.

The real question was...should they?

That was the sticking point. Both he and Valentine believed the Inahri were a threat. But they diverged in the second part of the equation. Valentine thought the best way to manage the threat was to attempt to ally with them. He wasn't sure. There might have been a time when he believed negotiation was the best defense, but the trife had put a dent in that belief, and Valentine's duplicity had punched a hole straight through. He had expected Hal's betrayal, but it hadn't made things any easier.

Still, if the ship wasn't a drone and there were people on it, he was sure it would be better to confront a smaller group. Then again, how were they supposed to communicate? The Inahri were descendants of humans who had been taken from Earth over ten thousand years earlier, but they had evolved on a different world. There was no way they spoke English.

Too many options, not enough time. And he was wasting it.

"Guardians, let's go," he said, breaking back down the long corridor at a run.

He was at least half a minute behind Riley. Was she planning to try to meet with the Inahri? Had she seen the lights coming their way? She didn't care about the colonists. She had admitted as much. She would gladly turn over the energy unit to get on the Inahri's good side. She would gladly give up all twenty-six thousand people in the colony for the chance to convince these humans to help free Earth.

He wanted Earth back too, but at what cost? And if the Axon were right about the Relyeh, to what end would winning Earth back from the trife matter? The demons were their front-line soldiers. Their grunts. What kind of damage could their masters do? Even if Riley was right and she got what she wanted from them, would she free Earth only to lose it again, and kill their next best hope of continuing their race?

They ran down the corridor, back to the quantum teleporter. The device was their next challenge. Hal had set it to bring them up here. Caleb had no idea how to use it. None of them did.

There was a small rod implanted in the floor beside

the platform; it had to be the controls. Caleb came to a stop in front of it, with Washington and Dante flanking him and Kiaan hanging behind them. He reached for the rod, only to have it begin emitting a soft light that formed into a hologram. It had strange symbols on it, clearly an alphabet of some kind, but he had no idea how to read it.

"I wonder if this thing comes with a manual?" Dante said.

"We wouldn't be able to read that either," Caleb replied.

"I wonder where the power is coming from if this place doesn't have its energy unit."

"Backup batteries, maybe," Caleb guessed. "Do you think they have emergency stairs?"

Washington tapped him on the shoulder and pointed toward one of the other exits.

"Okay, but don't go too far."

The big Marine gave him a thumbs-up and dashed down the corridor on the left, vanishing within seconds.

"When in doubt, start mashing buttons, I guess?" Dante said.

"That could be dangerous. We could wind up teleporting ourselves to the trash incinerator or something."

They spent the next minute puzzling over the controls. Caleb checked his HUD a few times, watching the lights continue their approach through the camera on Paige's helmet and the mark on the shared tactical grid. The vessel had become more defined, and he could make out the sleek shape behind the lights. It was large enough to carry at least four humans if it was occupied at all.

And it would be there in four minutes.

Washington reappeared from the left branch, going ahead of them and rushing down that path.

"Sergeant Card," Kiaan said. "Do you mind if I take a closer look?"

"Do you have an idea?" Caleb said, moving out of the way.

"I'm just studying the symbols. There's a pattern to them. And look." He pointed to one set of symbols. "Those look like numbers to me. They say math is the universal language."

"Algorithms," Caleb said. "The Axon communicate completely in math. Maybe the Inahri do too?"

"It's possible. These symbols are heavier. I don't know if I'm reading them right, but my guess would be we're on Deck Sixty-one. What do you think, sir?"

"Given the height from the base, I'd say that's probably about right. Give or take."

"So all we need to do is find Deck One, right?" Dante said.

"I hope so, Colonel."

"Please, call me Sheriff Dante, or just Sam. Colonel was Governor Stone's mockery. The Marshals were a joke. I'm sorry, Kiaan. He sent us out here to die, and you don't deserve that."

"We aren't dead yet, Sheriff," Kiaan said.

"That's the spirit," Caleb said. Washington returned from the forward corridor, swinging around to the right side. "Wash, anything?" He shook his head on the way past.

"I guess they don't have emergency stairs," Dante said. "When you have something like an energy unit, you probably never expect the power to go out."

"Or they have something like it, and we just don't know where to look," Caleb said, glancing at his HUD again. Three minutes.

Kiaan continued studying the hologram. He put his

hand up to it and swiped to the right. The symbols moved with the motion.

"The digit symbols aren't changing," he said. "I think that means this would be lateral movement through the ship. Same deck, different teleporter."

"Logical," Dante said.

Kiaan swiped down.

"The numbers are increasing," Caleb said, starting to get a feel for the symbols.

"Other way," Kiian replied, smiling sheepishly. He ran his hand the other direction, and the numbers started going down.

Washington came back from the corridor. He had a panicked look on his face, and he started waving frantically toward the teleporter.

"Wash?" Caleb said. A bolt of energy sizzled past the other Marine, hitting the ceiling across the room. What the hell? "Paige, we need to go. Now!"

"Roger," Paige replied.

"Get on the teleporter," Caleb said, looking back the way Washington had come. He didn't see anything yet, but another flash of light preceded a second bolt, which missed Kiaan by centimeters. "Paige, hurry!"

He looked back at the holographic controls. They had figured out how to work the settings, but how the hell were they supposed to activate the device? He tried to remember what Hal had done, but it all happened so fast. Damn it.

Paige reached the room at the same time the enemy came out of the shadows and into view. Caleb wasn't sure whether or not to be pleased their attacker wasn't human. It was similar to the Basic Intellect whose capsule Hal had claimed, except it was more metallic, and its movements more stiff. A robot of some kind?

It fired at them, forcing Washington to pull Kiaan to the floor of the platform. Paige and Dante got down too.

Caleb looked back at the hologram. Swiping changed the target. So to activate it…

He slapped his hand through it. A white light appeared at the top of the teleporter, suggesting it was active. Of course, it would give the user time to board.

He glanced at the Guardians, and then back at the robot.

"Stay on the teleporter," he said, moving away.

"What are you doing?" Dante asked.

"We have a gun that's effective against Intellects. I want one that's effective against everything else."

Dante tried to protest, but the bottom of the teleporter flashed, and then the Guardians were gone.

Chapter 2

Caleb moved to the corner of the room, out of the attacker's line of sight. He pressed his back against the bulkhead, listening. His ATCS had the enemy on his tactical, and he was able to monitor its movement toward him. It had slowed a little, suddenly cautious. It knew he had stayed behind, and it wasn't sure why.

He was dismayed but not surprised to see he had lost the link with the rest of the Guardians' combat network. They were too far away to get a signal through the alien alloy.

"I hope this wasn't my worst idea today," he said to himself. He didn't think it was possible. Not after he had let it slip that the Deliverance had an energy unit on board. That was probably the worst mistake he had made in his entire career.

He stayed at the corner, waiting for the robot. He heard its slow footsteps. Then he heard a soft clink. A small round device rolled into the room.

There was never anything good about anything rolled into a room by an enemy. Caleb turned away from it, covering his helmeted head with his armored replacement arm as the ball detonated in a blindingly bright flash of light. His filters were too slow to adjust, leaving white splotches flashing in front of his eyes.

He heard the robot coming at him again and turned toward it, trying to gauge its rate of approach. He swung his arm out in a tight clothesline that caught the bot directly across its blank face. The clash of metal meeting metal echoed across the room as the robot skidded off its feet, onto its back.

Blinking rapidly to get his bearings, Caleb caught the movement of the bot's servo-powered arm and dove away just in time to avoid a blast from the weapon it carried. Then the robot paused the attack to get back on its feet.

He followed the grid on his tactical, using a small corner of his vision to guide him. He threw himself at the robot, shoving his shoulder into it. They clanged together again, the force pushing the machine sideways and into the wall.

He grabbed the robot's gun with his human hand, trying to skew the robot's aim.

Instead, the robot used it to yank him sideways, turning the weapon to shoot him in the chest.

Caleb reacted instinctively, snapping his replacement hand down on the robot's arm and forcing the gun groundward. It fired into the floor, and Caleb drew his arm back to throw it forward, punching the bot hard in the head. The blow was enough to break its neck, but not enough to stop it.

The robot kicked him in the leg, trying to take his feet out from under him. Caleb moved with the blow, planting his weight on his other foot and stepping to the side, closer to the bulkhead. The weapon fired past him, again barely missing him. He took the robot's arm in his replacement hand, using all the strength of the synthetic limb to force the machine's arm up and back toward its chest.

The robot punched Caleb with its other hand, the blow powerful enough to strain his ribs through his SOS. It hit him again and again. Caleb winced under the pain of the blows, but stayed focused on getting the weapon turned away from himself. He was stronger overall than the bot was. All he needed, now that his eyes had begun to clear, was time to take it down.

He finally maneuvered the bot's arm in position and then quickly dropped his human hand, putting his finger over the robot's finger on the trigger. As he struggled to force the trigger down, the robot continued to pummel him in the side. but he wasn't about to give in. He stayed with it, shoving the machine back into the wall.

"I'm so damn sick of fake people," he grunted, giving one last push. The weapon went off, the bolt firing directly into the machine's chest. It burned deep, finally cutting through something important in the tin man's innards and shutting it down. It tilted forward and Caleb stepped aside, letting it fall directly onto its face.

Caleb knelt beside it, grabbing the weapon and pulling it away. It bore some similarity to the P-50, though it was more of a carbine than a rifle, with a shorter stock and a small square muzzle. He would have thought the alien weapons would be more exotic but then again, how many ways could you make a practical gun? It was about functionality, not form.

He ambled back to the teleporter controls, reactivating the platform. His ATCS flashed, and he saw there was another target incoming. He checked the time. The unidentified craft should have arrived a minute ago. Was it the Inahri?

Armed or not, he wasn't sticking around to find out.

He tapped the hologram to activate it and climbed onto the platform. The teleporter blinked, and he was somewhere else.

The Guardians were still there, waiting for him.

"Caleb," Dante said, rushing to him as he stumbled off the platform. She wrapped her arm around his waist, helping to hold him up.

"Got it," he said, showing them the weapon.

"Are you hurt?" Dante asked.

"A broken rib, maybe," he replied. "I'll live."

"The alien craft should have landed by now," Paige said.

"I know. I think they were already on Deck Sixty-one."

"Through the teleporter?"

"Not the one we used. But maybe using it locks it out? I can only imagine what would happen if two teleporters tried to go to the same place at the same time."

"Ewww," Paige said.

"Exactly."

"That was a stupid thing to do, Sergeant," Dante said.

"Probably. But we can't run around in here without being able to defend ourselves. I think that bot proved it." Caleb looked around. He could see they were in a much smaller room with only one exit. "Where are we?"

"We don't know yet," Dante said. "We were waiting for you."

"Not where we came in. Kiaan, do you think you can get this thing set to the entrance?"

Kiaan made a face. "Probably not, sir."

"It's okay. As long as we're on the right deck, we should be able to find our way out."

"Yes, sir."

"Wash, you should take this. You're the best shot we have." Washington shook his head and pointed at Paige.

Caleb turned back to her. "How'd you get so good? Metro didn't have any loaded guns up to a few days ago."

"Games," she replied. "And a natural talent, I guess."

"Good enough." He handed her the weapon. "Don't shoot unless I give the order."

"Yes, sir."

Caleb activated the hologram for the teleporter, keeping it lit and hopefully locked out. "I'm not sure how much time this buys us, but something is better than nothing. Let's move."

"Sir, can I ask a question?" Kiaan said.

"What is it?"

"Where are we going?"

"We need to get back to the Deliverance."

"Sir, I know. I mean. We lost our transport. How are we going to get there?"

Caleb hadn't thought about it. There were so many other things to worry about. "What do you suggest?"

"This used to be a city, filled with people. They must have vehicles?"

"There's a craft of some kind right outside," Dante said.

"If we could reach it," Paige said.

"You think we should take a look around first?" Caleb asked.

Kiaan nodded. "I don't mean to step out of line, sir. But, if we go on foot, it'll take days to get back to the ship. Maybe even weeks. You saw the mountains we crossed over."

"Not to mention the trife," Paige said.

"If Metro is in immediate danger, getting there a week from now isn't going to help," Kiaan continued. "We could go for the ship we saw, but that's also risky. We don't know how to control their craft, and making a quick getaway would be unlikely."

"Agreed," Caleb said. "On all points. But, we have no way of knowing if this ship has anything we can use, and we also have no idea how many of those bots might be patrolling it. Not to mention there may already be Inahri here, and we don't know if they're friendly."

"Don't forget about Valentine," Dante said.

"How could anyone forget about Valentine?" Caleb replied. "She might already be talking to them and telling them about the energy unit."

"Maybe they'll plant a bolt in her rear."

"She would heal from it."

"It would still hurt for awhile ."

Caleb smirked. "Here's to hoping. But we need more than hope." He tapped on his helmet, trying to think. "We saw part of the ship during the Guardian Intellect's story-time. The Axon, Rex, had a lab near the center of the ship, where the energy unit was placed."

"On this deck?" Dante asked.

"Who knows. We're flying blind right now." Caleb closed his eyes, trying to remember what they had seen. So many corridors and so many rooms, and they all looked similar. "We'll head for the center, and see what we find on the way."

"Won't any hangar be on the outer perimeter," Paige asked.

"Normally I would agree, but considering the Inahri seem to have mastered teleportation, that's not a given. If we find the lab, we might be able to stumble through their systems well enough to at least get a map or something."

"That's a long-shot, Sarge," Dante said.

"Tell me about it. But it's the only shot I can think of. We're not exactly in our element here. If this were an oper-

Destruction

ation against a terrorist cell, once we took out the bad guys, I'd be searching for data on potential targets. There's at least some correlation here. Paige, you've got point. The rest of you, stay alert. I don't want anyone else dying on my watch."

Caleb tapped the teleporter controls one more time to ensure it would stay active. Then they moved toward the wall in front of the device, which spread into an oblong opening at their approach. Paige went out first, her alien weapon leveled and ready to fire. The dark alloy corridor seemed to stretch out forever.

"Maybe walking would be faster after all," Dante said.

15

Chapter 3

Caleb had gone through the teleporters twice now, and he was still only barely able to believe they were real. It seemed like magic to step onto a glass platform, watch a bright flash and wind up somewhere else quicker than he could blink. It seemed like a trick. A sleight of hand. That it wasn't a trick reminded him how far in over their heads they were, and how low their odds of survival were. Not only was this planet hostile, but the entire universe was more populated and more hostile than he'd ever imagined.

The teleporters seemed almost bland in comparison. Caleb had seen enough action in the last two weeks to last ten lifetimes. He would have given anything for the rest of this one to settle down into something nearing normalcy.

But he would settle for another teleporter.

The corridor they were traveling felt endless. The Guardians spent half an hour moving along it, setting a brisk pace so they could be as far away from the room they had landed in as possible. They had no idea if the Inahri could track their movements so they kept their eyes peeled between the corridor ahead and their tacticals, watching for the combat network to pick up anything out of the ordinary and relay it to the group.

Fortunately, the way forward remained clear. There were no robots in the corridor, and the Inahri didn't appear behind them. It was a welcome break, though the lack of confrontation made Caleb wary. There were too many unknown variables surrounding the city-ship. The Inahri, the robots, the trife, Valentine. Guardian said it was the only one of its kind, but what if there were more of the Basic Intellects? The dark, faceless artificial intelligences had the technology to make them hallucinate. While they did have the anti-Intellect gun, it would only take one neural disruptor to stop them dead in their tracks, and the enemy didn't need line of sight to affect them.

Caleb felt both surrounded and alone, his senses on full alert with every step he took. He assumed there were rooms on both sides of the corridor, but the alien metal hid the passages from anyone who didn't know they were there. It kept the Guardians moving straight, continuing along the passageway in search of anything that would help them better understand the city-ship or give them a quicker way back to Metro.

Information was their ally.

Time was their enemy.

They didn't have enough of either.

The end of the corridor came into view as a slightly sloped, dark wall. The edge of the city, or at least the edge of what they were calling Deck One. There was more to it beneath them, subdecks leading to other parts of the city, beneath the channels and structures they had seen on their way to the central spire. Caleb imagined there had to be more passages there, probably an entire network of tunnels like the inner maze of an anthill. He smirked at the thought. This place did remind him of an anthill. Did the Inahri live like ants? Or was that the Axon culture at play?

They didn't know anything about the Axon. Guardian had spoken of the scientist, Rex, but had never shown what it looked like. The Intellect hadn't shown any Axon. Only humans. Unless the Axon were human? Was there a physical differentiation between the species? It seemed impossible that every intelligent life form in the universe would look like humans. Unless God really did exist?

That idea was too much for him to wrestle with right now. He had a job to do.

"It would be nice if we could make some actual progress," Paige said. "I'm getting bored."

"You sound like Sho," Caleb replied.

"Who?"

"She was one of my Vultures. Back on Earth, and then on the Deliverance."

"What happened to her?"

"She died trying to kill the Intellect we called Hal. We buried her in the jungle. She was a top-notch Marine."

"I'm sorry, sir," Paige said. "I hope I can live up to her memory."

"You're off to a great start."

They spent another ten minutes walking, closing on the outer perimeter of the deck. Caleb used his ATCS to activate the lamp on his helmet, shining it into the alloy ahead. The metal seemed to thin out in response, creating a transparency and allowing them to see outside. He could see the slope of the central tower beneath them, spreading out to the rest of the city. From this angle, he got the impression that the spire would be able to break away from the larger form like it was a starship in its own right.

"I'm still trying to get my head around all of this,"

Kiaan said. "The scale of it. How can something this big have enough thrust to get out of the atmosphere."

"That's why they need the energy unit," Caleb replied. "According to David Nash, it's power output is nearly limitless."

"It must have a limit if the one they came with burned up," Dante said.

"Which tells you how much power the Intellects used fighting the Inahri."

Caleb looked up from the slope, toward the distance. The clouds were still hanging over the plains. It was still raining steadily. He could see the other cities around them, hundreds of dark monoliths rising from their base. He counted the other spires, only able to see three from the position.

"I think I found the unidentified ship," Kiaan said.

Caleb looked to his right. Paige had turned her helmet lamp on, and Kiaan was looking down over the city. A small, lighter-colored craft was resting in one of the channels. A human-sized figure was standing beside it, a weapon cradled in their arms. Based on their size, they were wearing armor of some kind. The helmet looked unusually large.

The helmet shifted, the Inahri looking directly at them.

"Lamps off!" Caleb snapped, shutting his down and backing away. Paige did the same.

"They saw us," Dante said.

"We need to move." Caleb looked to his left. The passage continued, following the rounded shape of the spire. "That way."

His ATCS beeped softly. He checked his tactical. It had picked up a sound behind them, at the far end of the corridor.

"They're coming," he said.

"Maybe we should stay and introduce ourselves?" Kiaan suggested.

The statement brought Caleb back to his earlier thoughts. Maybe it was wrong to assume the Inahri were their enemies?

He couldn't risk losing his entire team to find out, and they had no way to form any kind of decent defense in this position.

"No. If we're going to confront them, we need to do it on our terms. They're too advanced to not get every advantage against."

"Yes, sir," Kiaan replied.

The tactical zoomed out, showing four marks a klick away. They were moving fast. Too fast to be on foot, though the ATCS was able to pick them out. If the armor they had seen was like a hyper-advanced version of their SOS, it was possible they were running that quickly.

"We don't have much time," he said. "We need to find somewhere to hide."

A teleporter. That's all he wanted.

Right now he'd settle for a closet.

Chapter 4

The Guardians ran down the passageway, following the curve. Caleb watched the tactical out of the corner of his eye. According to his ATCS, they were moving around fourteen kilometers per hour, slowed immensely by Kiaan. The Inahri were traveling at nearly triple that and would close the distance between them in less than ten minutes.

"Wash, get Kiaan on your back," Caleb said. "He's too slow without armor."

Washington adjusted his course and speed to meet the pilot, who couldn't hear the instructions over the comm. He was surprised when the big Marine scooped him up, easily lifting and depositing him on his back. Kiaan didn't argue, holding on tight as the Guardians' pace increased.

They sprinted down the corridor, searching desperately for a doorway. The doors were part of the alloy of the city-ship, seamless and invisible, making their escape all the more challenging. Caleb kept glancing at his HUD. They had nearly doubled their speed, their feet skipping off the floor and carrying them forward at a breakneck pace. The

Inahri were steady, still moving faster than they were but not gaining quite as quickly.

"We need to find a door," Dante said.

"Agreed," Caleb replied, reaching across his body to slide his replacement hand along the bulkhead as they fled. He knew the hatches worked through proximity and pressure, but his metal fingers grating across the black metal produced a screeching that almost made his teeth hurt. He went about twenty meters before he tripped something. He heard the light swish behind him and pulled to a sudden stop. The others reacted instantly, and they turned back to the newly expanded hatchway as one.

He retreated to it and looked inside. Another corridor, this one leading across the city descended below what they were calling Deck Zero. "In here. Paige, take point."

"Roger," Paige replied, slipping by him and raising the alien weapon to her shoulder to sight down the barrel.

"Dante, left flank, keep an eye out for Intellects."

"Roger," she replied, holding the anti-Intellect gun in front of her. Caleb moved to Paige's right while Washington took up the rear with Kiaan still on his back, knife in hand. The hatch automatically closed behind him. "Do you think they'll know we went this way?"

"I'm betting on it," Caleb replied. He put his hand out again, running it along the wall. "But hopefully having some metal between us will dull their sensors, just like it killed ours."

The marks were gone from his tactical, the barrier between them too much for the ATCS to overcome. He didn't mind. Better blind than caught.

They followed the passageway as it dipped downward, forty meters until Caleb discovered another door. This one led to a third corridor, a shorter passage that finished in what looked like a dead end.

Caleb stood at the entrance, staring at the dark alloy a hundred meters away. What if it was a dead end?

"Sergeant?" Dante said.

"You know what I'm thinking," he said.

"Yes. It's your call."

Caleb nodded. "Let's chance it." He led them down the passage toward the wall. His pulse increased as he neared it. If there was no door here…

He reached the end, stretching his hand out to the wall.

It didn't open.

"Damn it," he said.

A dim blue light illuminated the face of the bulkhead in strange symbols none of them could read. A beam reached out, quickly washing the front of Caleb with light. Then the whole thing shut off.

"If I didn't know any better, I would say it just did a biometric scan," Dante said.

"We don't have clearance for this door," he replied. "Great. Back the way we came, knuckle-up and stay alert. We just lost a chunk of our lead."

They ran back to the sloping corridor. Caleb's ATCS responded the moment the alloy shrank away, allowing them through. The four marks re-appeared on his tactical. They had slowed too, unsure of where their quarry had gone. Now it seemed their sensors were active again because they suddenly sped up once more.

"Come on!" Caleb snapped. He could hear the Inahri in the passage, their feet pounding the metal floor in a rapid cadence. He moved in position behind Washington, offering his back to protect Kiaan as they ran.

The slope increased, dropping them further beneath the city. The air cooled with the descent, the smell becoming more musty and stale. There was little fresh air flowing through this part of the city-ship, the filters likely shut down to preserve power.

"Faster!" Caleb barked, looking at his HUD again. They had lost a lot of ground, and the Inahri were still quicker on their feet. They were gaining and had closed within a hundred meters. Still a long distance to make an accurate shot against a moving target, but close enough to—

Something hit Caleb in the back, sending a jolt through his armor and immediately taking it offline. His arms and legs straightened and locked, and he immediately collapsed forward, landing on his stomach and just barely avoiding a hard knock to his chin.

The other Guardians noticed immediately, stopping and turning back. Caleb cursed, rolling sideways just in time to avoid another blast, which hit the floor beside him as a nearly invisible wave of disturbed air.

Then Paige was shooting, firing back at the Inahri , a steady stream of bolts which stopped their attack at once. He had no idea if she was hitting them, or if her assault was causing any harm, but it bought them enough time for Washington to help him to his feet. Then he could feel the big Marine manipulating the back of the SOS, opening an access panel and tapping the emergency reset button.

Nothing happened. The armor was dead.

So was his replacement arm. It dragged at his side, an added weight he couldn't manipulate, the control ring that connected it to the flesh displaying a small red LED to indicate it was out of power.

Washington grabbed him and tugged him aside as a shot of moving air flashed past them and hit the wall, causing a spray of sparks when it did. The Inahri had identified they were wearing armor and had responded accordingly. Did that mean they were ready to fight Space Force Marines?

Or did it mean they were accustomed to fighting one another?

"We need a door!" Caleb shouted, loud enough for them to hear him through their helmets. "Kiaan, help me find one!"

He moved to the side of the corridor while Kiaan dropped from Washington's back to search the other side. Paige continued firing, keeping their attackers honest and holding them at range.

Caleb ran forward as best he could in the dead armor, looking for an escape. He heard a shout nearby and looked in time to see Kiaan collapse. His jaw clenched, and he rushed across the corridor, glancing back the way they had come. He could see the enemy now, advancing in a well-organized fire and movement pattern. He smiled when he saw one of the white bolts from Paige's gun hit one of the armored Inahri, but the smile vanished when he saw the weapon had little effect.

"Fall back!" he shouted. "Fall back!"

But there was nowhere to go. They couldn't outrun the enemy. They couldn't outgun the enemy. They were stuck. Hard.

Caleb knelt beside Kiaan and put a hand on his neck. He found his pulse immediately. Kiaan was still breathing, shallow but steady. The rounds their opponents were using were meant to stun, not kill.

He didn't know if that was better or worse.

He stared down at Kiaan. He wanted to lift him and get him to safety, but he couldn't. Not with one arm. The Inahri continued to gain, moving from one hundred meters to eighty, then sixty, then forty.

A pair of rounds hit Washington, sparks flying from the front of the big man's SOS when he was hit. He fell to his knees, putting a hand down and using it to try to pick himself back up. Four more blasts rocked him, and he tumbled to the floor and didn't move.

"Damn it!" Caleb cursed. He had to find another door. He had to give them another way out. He went for Kiaan again, only to find himself a target. He could barely see the rounds coming toward him save for the small distortion of air-like waves of heat. He dove aside, away from Kiaan, crossing the passage again and getting to his feet. "Dante!"

He screamed to get her attention. She turned to look back at him, and he pointed to Kiaan. She flashed her thumb in her best Washington impression, running toward the stricken pilot.

Enemy fire followed her, the Inahri becoming bolder as each of them fell. She fired back with the anti-Intellect weapon, knowing it wouldn't hurt them but hoping they would evade it out of instinct. They didn't, showing they knew exactly what the gun was. Dante was hit twice and fell to the floor a meter short of Kiaan.

"No..." Caleb groaned. They were down. Hard. With Paige the only one still up, and she wasn't going to last like this.

Caleb's heart felt like it was going to burst from his chest, and he struggled to stay calm. In all his years fighting the trife, he had never been in a situation as hopeless as this. He wanted to do something, but he was virtually helpless and at a loss at what to do about it.

He knew what he didn't want. To be a coward. To leave his team behind. He took a deep breath and started forward, dragging himself toward the enemy as Paige was hit three times and collapsed. A few rounds came at him, and he managed to swing his dead arm, catching it with his left hand and using it as a shield. He blocked the displaced air bursts with it, expecting the weapon to be ineffective against already inert, powerless alloy and finding he was right. He caught almost six rounds that way before one finally got past him and struck him in the chest. It sent a tingling sensation through his whole body, and he fell to his knees.

He didn't let that stop him. He kept moving, crawling toward the oncoming Inahri . He could almost see them clearly now. Their armor was bulkier than his, made of a different kind of alloy than both the city-ship and the Cerebus armor. It looked powerful but less agile, equally more and less technologically advanced than a Space Force SOS. The helmets were almost as wide as their shoulders, the transparency at the front large and tinted blue. He could see alien symbols reversed behind them, and the marks of each of his Guardians reflected in their HUDs.

He could see faces too—male and female faces. They were human, though their bone structure seemed much more delicate, their forms smaller and lighter overall. Their eyes were large for their faces, noses broad and flat, mouths small and full. Human, but alien too. Nobody would mistake them for Earthers, just like nobody would mistake him for Inahri .

They stopped shooting when he kept crawling. They stopped moving too. They formed a line a few meters away and waited while he covered the distance still between them. There was no way to win this fight, but he wasn't going to show them any weakness.

Their expressions remained serious. Their eyes were almost kind. He could sense the respect in them, along with the surprise. They obviously hadn't expected him to keep coming.

He came to a stop less than a meter away, looking up at

them. He moved slowly, reaching up with his good hand and grabbing his helmet, twisting his neck to pull it away. He dropped it to the floor.

"So," he said. "Do you surrender?"

Chapter 5

"Move, move, move!" Governor Jackson Stone shouted, heart racing a million kilometers per hour as he watched the figures descending from the hilltop.

The hangar lift was slow. Too damned slow. It had taken nearly five seconds to stop its downward momentum, and another five to start moving up again. They were lucky whoever or whatever had decimated the DDF soldiers on the ground hadn't fired at them, but their luck wasn't going to last forever. The enemy was advancing, charging down the hill in a group nearly a dozen strong, moving so fast it was as though they had rocket-powered boots.

"Jackson?" Beth said beside him, her voice thick with fear.

He glanced over at her. She should never have had to see the carnage they had all just witnessed. The bodies all over the ground, both intact and in pieces. His stomach churned at the thought, his eyes tearing with fear of his own.

"Can't this thing move any faster?" he shouted.

He had a squad of soldiers around him—his personal

bodyguards. They were supposed to be helping him head out of the ship. He was supposed to be one of the first to set foot on their new world. He had decided it was safe to do so. Days had passed without incident, and they had an entire armory of weapons and vehicles at their disposal. Enough to outfit an entire army.

That's what they were supposed to be. That's what Space Force Command had planned for them. They were to be an army of genetically mutated super-soldiers, sent here to fight. Only things hadn't happened that way. Things had gone wrong. Up until this very instant, he was grateful the Space Force plans had failed.

Now, he wished for that army of super-soldiers. And he wished he were one of them.

He hadn't been able to protect his daughter, Orla. He wouldn't be able to defend his wife. Not out here. He had made a mistake thinking it was safe. The drones had flown multiple sorties over the area where the enemy was approaching. They hadn't seen a thing.

How was that possible?

"Lieutenant Hind, as soon as they get in range I want you to open fire," he said, turning his attention to the ranking DDF officer on the lift with him.

"Yes, sir," Hind replied, forcing some strength into his voice.

But Jackson could tell the man was scared. He could see his hands shaking, his rifle rattling in his grip. The rest of his guards were the same. It was one thing to defend him from unarmed civilians. It was another to have an alien army rushing their way.

Jackson looked up. Their lift was finally approaching the hangar. They were only ten meters away. They were lucky it hadn't descended further. If they could get back into the ship, if they could close the hangar blast doors, that would buy them some time. The enemy would need to find another entrance or take the time to penetrate this one. Everyone outside the city could retreat to Metro while they did. Then they could seal the entrances again, focus all of their firepower on a half-dozen doors, and wait.

But for how long?

"Who are they?" Beth asked. "What do they want?"

"I don't know," Jackson replied.

"They didn't even try to negotiate. They didn't even try to talk to us."

"Maybe they're as scared of us as we are of them?" he offered, even though he didn't believe it.

Beth didn't either. She put her head in her hand and sobbed. "I wish those damn Marines had never disturbed us. They should have let us stay in the city and be happy, the way we were before. Now, we're all going to die."

Jackson put his arms around his wife. He was doing his best to navigate these treacherous waters. He had already lied about the Marines to the colony. He had set them up as the cause of all of their problems. It had kept the colonists on his side, which was good. But was he leading them to ruin? His father, his grandfather—they had been good leaders. They were respected and admired for their evenhandedness. He knew what the citizens whispered about him. The more he tried to control things, the less control he seemed to have.

He was doing the best he knew how to do. That was all. Maybe it came across the wrong way at times. Maybe it required making hard decisions and hurting people. But his responsibility was to all twenty-six thousand people of Metro. He didn't want to be the one who failed them.

He didn't want to be the one who got them all killed.

"It's going to be okay," he said, kissing his wife's head. "We'll get back to the city. We'll be safe in there."

Hind and his guards started firing at the same moment he finished the sentence. The loud echoes of rifle-fire hurt his ears and made Beth wail in fear. Jackson forced himself to look out over the edge of the lift, down to the approaching enemy. He could see them more clearly now. They were humanoid, two arms and two legs and close to two meters tall. It looked like they were wearing body armor or an exosuit of some kind, matte black and bulky. They cradled weapons in their arms like the MK-12s his guards carried but nearly twice as thick and much boxier.

The rounds hit the enemy's armor, throwing up short sparks and bouncing harmlessly away. The squad of aliens stopped almost beneath the lift, looking up. They couldn't jump thirty meters. They would have to find another way to get onto the ship.

As long as they didn't decide to blast the lift instead.

"Cease fire," he said. "Ceasefire." The guards stopped shooting. "We're wasting ammo. Hind, as soon as we get to the hangar, I want a full red alert. I want the blast doors closed and then everyone back to the city asap."

"Yes, Governor," Hind replied.

Jackson glanced up again. A few more seconds and they would be—

Something hit the bottom of the lift. Jackson heard it before he felt it, a loud, whooshing hiss followed by shaking and heat. The mechanism groaned in response to the attack, followed by a pop and whine before the lift stopped ascending. The violent vibration knocked him to the ground and took one of his guards over the edge. He heard the man crying out on the way down.

"Jackson!" Beth shouted. He looked up, finding her also dangling from the edge. He pushed himself up, scrambling to her. Hind got there first, grabbing her arms and pulling her up.

A bolt of energy hit Hind from below, catching him in the chest, and burning through his body armor like it was nothing. It passed cleanly through his body and out his back, eliciting another scream from Beth as the Lieutenant tumbled from the lift to the ground.

"Down! Stay down!" Jackson screamed as loud as he could. He wanted to crawl into a hole, pull it over his head and disappear. He couldn't believe any of this was happening. Five minutes earlier he had been so full of hope.

Now it was all gone.

Beth was right. They were all going to die.

"Governor!" Someone said from beside him. He looked to find Sergeant Urias waving him toward the back of the lift. They were only two meters now from the top.

Jackson grabbed Beth's arm. "Stay low," he said, getting to his feet and crouching to pull her along behind him toward the sergeant.

The lift shook again, hit a second time. The blast tearing off the edge of it, Fire licking up from below, the metal twisting and grinding in a deafening whine.

Jackson stumbled forward, making it to Urias, who grabbed Beth's other arm and tugged her forward. She screamed again as he grabbed her waist and practically threw her up onto the main deck, where a pair of soldiers caught her. A bolt hit one of them and he fell backwards. The other fell on top of Beth, protecting her from the continuing fire.

Jackson rushed to Urias. " We need to stay low," he said. The sergeant nodded, cupping his hands, and giving Jackson a boost. He climbed onto the deck, staying as flat as he could. Urias came up right behind him.

"Where the hell are the drones?" Jackson shouted at Urias. "We need a Dagger in the air, now!" He looked across the hangar. Stunned soldiers and engineers stared back at him. "Get the damned blast doors closed!" he screamed.

The engineers sprang into action, rushing toward the manual controls near the front.

"No, wait!" Jackson screamed, bringing them to a stop. If they went to the controls, the enemy would gun them down. "Back up. Forget it. We need to retreat."

He went to Beth, putting his arm around her waist and getting her on her feet. They ran bent over at the waist to keep the enemy from targeting them. The enemy seemed to know the lift was clear because they had stopped shooting at it.

"Governor," Urias said. "Johns is on his way to the secondary hangar. First Platoon is on their way from the city."

"Good, good," Jackson said. Johns was one of their new pilots. He had decent scores on the simulator. "Did you tell First Platoon to bring plasma rifles?"

"Yes, sir. It's going to slow them down. Most of them are still in the armory."

"The Mark-twelves are practically useless against their armor."

He started across the floor with Beth at a fast jog. He could smell urine, and when he looked down, he saw the front of her dress was wet. He checked his pants. Somehow he had managed to keep himself under control.

They made it to the inner blast doors. The engineers were already there with the rest of the soldiers. The whole area had gone quiet. Was the attack over? Had the enemy seen fit to give up after he and Beth had escaped?

That seemed unlikely. But where the hell were they?

"Governor, what's happening?" one of the engineers asked.

"Isn't it obvious? We're being attacked," he replied,

quickly realizing the impact of his tone. "But it's going to be okay." They had made it this far. The enemy had the element of surprise, but once his defense forces recovered, they would at least be able to fight back.

"Governor, Johns is in the air," Urias said.

"That was fast," Jackson replied. He heard the fighter a moment later, screaming across the sky. For a moment, he was tempted to head to the ship's bridge to monitor the situation directly. He didn't want to get cut off from the city if things worsened again. He didn't want to be trapped outside. He didn't want his people trapped outside either. "Call the bridge and tell them to evacuate. I want everyone back in Metro. And I mean *everyone*."

"Yes, sir," Urias replied. Jackson could see the sergeant's lips moving when he switched to the combat armor's internal comms.

"Come on, dear," he said to Beth. "We're safe now. We'll head back to Metro and lock down the city while the DDF takes care of this."

Now that he had a moment of calm to think, he remembered he had only seen twelve or so of the alien attackers. How could a dozen armored insurgents defeat his three hundred soldiers? Especially now that they had a fighter in the air.

"Go, all of you," he said to the engineers. "Back to the city. Hurry!"

The engineers turned and ran.

"Urias," Jackson said, glancing at the sergeant again. His eyes landed on Urias' faceplate just in time to see a bolt slam into it, piercing the transparency and obliterating the man's face, right before he crumpled to the floor.

Jackson turned his head back to the open blast doors.

Three enemy soldiers stood at the edge of the hangar.

Chapter 6

Jackson raised his hands, showing them he was unarmed. There was nothing else for him to do. A glance at the rest of the hangar told him the other guards were already dead, gunned down in an instant by the aliens.

"We come in peace," he said. "We don't want to fight you."

The enemy didn't respond. They moved almost in unison, efficiently sweeping their rifles across the area and ensuring the hangar was clear. Jackson heard a rapid-fire whooshing noise from outside, and he glanced at the open doors to see the Dagger flash past, its front-mounted cannons belching fire. Then he heard a shriek like a human scream, followed by an explosion and a lower-pitched whine from the air, followed by a hard crash. He didn't need to see the action to know the Dagger was gone.

One of the aliens stepped forward and barked something in a language he couldn't begin to understand. Jackson didn't move, keeping his hands raised while tears streamed from his eyes. He clenched the muscles in his abdomen, desperate not to embarrass himself before he died.

The lead alien spoke again, louder and more forcefully. He took a few more steps forward, leaving Jackson able to see past a blue-tinted faceplate.

He stopped breathing, caught completely by surprise.

The face behind it was human.

The alien shifted its rifle as though it were taking aim.

"Wait!" Jackson shouted.

A pair of plasma bolts angled down at the alien from the hole in the roof of the hangar, hitting the alien in the side. The superheated gas dug into the metal, doing enough damage to get the attention of the enemy soldiers. They whirled on the position as one unit, raised their guns and firing three rounds. Three Deliverance Defense Force soldiers fell out of the hole.

Jackson didn't wait to get shot. He broke for Beth and his escape the moment the soldiers pivoted back to raise their guns at him. He grabbed her again and dashed away, knowing they only had seconds to put something, anything, between them and the enemy.

He instinctively dove to the right, pushing Beth ahead of him as they fell against the wall, behind the small lip of the blast doors. Two bolts hit the floor where they had been a moment earlier, digging into the metal.

Jackson put his arms around his wife. They would have seconds at best before the enemy came around the lip and finished them for good. It was too little, too late.

"I love you," he said, staring down into her eyes.

She looked at him, too scared to speak. He held her tighter.

A series of bolts launched from down the corridor and into the hangar, crossing them in a solid barrage. Jackson felt the heat of them as they passed and then watched the return fire head in the opposite direction. He saw one of his DDF soldiers fall, but then the two squads charging their way seemed to get the upper hand, pushing the aliens back.

"We're saved," he said, looking into Beth's eyes. "Come on." He picked her up, staying tight against the bulkhead. The soldiers ran up to him, one of them staying behind while the others spread into the hangar.

"Let's get you out of here, sir," the soldier said.

Jackson passed Beth to the man, and the three of them started running the other direction. Jackson could hear the fighting in the hangar. His soldiers were dying. He didn't need to see it to know it. They had charged into the hangar with no cover, and the more experienced enemy were quickly cutting them down. His people had guns and armor, but they had little to no training. They were dying bravely like soldiers, but they weren't soldiers.

He had blamed the only soldiers they had for their predicament. He had forced them out. And then he had sent Dante and a team to try to kill them.

What the hell had he done?

The main blast doors to the city were already swinging closed ahead of them. Made of thick steel, it would take some work for the enemy to break through, though Jackson knew they would sooner or later. He was more concerned with the fact that they were too far away to get in before they scaled.

"This way," the soldier guiding them said, leading them down another corridor. They broke parallel to the city, taking the passage fifty meters before rendezvousing with another squad from First Platoon.

"Governor," the squad leader said. "It's good you're

safe, sir. We're sealing all the entrances to the city, save for one like you ordered. This way."

The sergeant and his squad surrounded Jackson and his wife as they ran down another corridor to the stairs and began to climb.

"What's happening at the hangar?" Jackson asked.

"They're gone," the sergeant replied. "Whatever is out there, they know how to fight. Better than we do."

"They're human," Jackson said.

"What?" the sergeant said. "That's impossible."

"I looked one of them right in the eye. They're a little strange looking, but they're definitely the same species. Either that or evolution is a lot less random than science assumed. He tried to talk to me, but it sounded like gibberish."

"Yes, sir."

"Are the people evacuating the outer portion of the ship?"

"Yes, sir. The rest of the troops are gearing up and assembling. We're getting the defenses ready as we speak."

"Is the bridge locked down?"

"Yes, sir. Deputy Klahanie reports the terminals are securely locked. Blast doors are closed and sealed. Your identification chip and the backup password are the only two ways to get back in without destroying everything inside."

"Who has the password?"

"Right now, only the deputy."

"Good. I'll make sure he knows to keep it that way once we're safe."

"We're almost there, Governor," the sergeant said.

"Sarge, we've got company," one of the soldiers said. "Coming up fast."

"Get them out of here!" the sergeant barked. "Defensive line, plasma set to stream. These bastards aren't getting through."

"Affirmative, Sarge!"

The original soldier led Jackson and his wife away again, while the rest of the squad turned and brought their P-50s to bear, switching them to stream mode. If they all fired the weapons at once, they would create an impenetrable inferno.

Jackson continued down the corridor, glancing behind them. He saw the first alien come around the corner, and then the squad opened fire. The alien vanished in a cloud of superhot gas, only to appear a moment later, inside the defensive line. The armored soldier kicked one of the guards, grabbed another by the head and broke his neck. He picked up a third by the armor and smashed him into the wall, punched a fourth hard enough to lay him out, and grabbed the fifth, holding him up while he picked up a P-50 and fired it point blank into the guard. Then his head turned toward Jackson.

"How far?" Jackson asked.

"Not far," the soldier replied. They turned the corner, running ten meters and turning again. The blast door was another ten meters ahead. Nearly fifty soldiers were positioned behind it, weapons ready. "Go!" the soldier yelled, pushing Jackson forward. He took Beth's hand and dragged her toward the blast door.

A few seconds later, he heard the soldier behind them scream. Then the defenses started shooting, sending bolts of plasma whizzing past their heads. They made it to the hatch, each of them pulled past their group.

The hatch now was only a few seconds from sliding closed and sealing. Three more steps and they slipped through the narrow opening. Jackson looked back. The enemy had cleared the corridor, deciding not to face the brunt of the defenses. Behind him, the hatch slammed closed.

They had made it.

All of the strength drained from Jackson, and he fell to his knees, leaning over. He suddenly felt sick. He coughed and vomited on the floor, tears streaming from his eyes. Beth slumped to the floor ahead of him, crossing her legs and putting her head in her hands.

"Governor," Colonel Ross said, hurrying over to him. Jackson had known Ross for a long time. He had been the head of his security detail.

"Ross. Are all the hatches sealed?"

"Yes, sir."

"What about the secondary hangar? The Daggers?"

"It's sealed, sir. But I don't know how long that will hold them back."

"Why didn't the drones see the enemy coming? We had eyes in the sky. How did we miss them?"

"I don't know, Governor."

Jackson leaned back on his knees. "Help me up."

Ross took his arm and helped him get to his feet. His body was weak. Exhausted. He used the colonel for balance while he made his way to Beth.

"Beth, honey. We made it." She didn't look up at him. She didn't react to him at all. "Beth?"

Nothing.

"I think she's in shock," Ross said.

"Get Rathbone out here, immediately," Jackson said. "She needs treatment and care."

"Yes, Governor."

"Beth, can you hear me?" Jackson asked.

She didn't respond. Her head stayed in her hands, covering her face.

Jackson drew in a somber breath. How could everything have gone so wrong, so fast? He ran his hand across his eyes, rubbing them. He had to think. The enemy was right outside, and as long as they remained there, this whole thing was far from over.

"Have one of your people take Beth to the hospital," he said to Ross. "Let's head to the mansion. We need to try to keep up with their position inside."

"Yes, Governor," Ross replied. He said something into his comm and a pair of soldiers came over. They each took one of Beth 's arms and gently lifted her to her feet. She didn't resist.

Jackson turned away. He hated to leave her like that, but he had an entire city to think about, and right now they were in serious trouble. He glanced at the hatch. At least they had a few minutes to breathe and regroup.

Only they didn't have a few minutes. They had less than a handful of seconds. The hatch surprisingly began to rise again, revealing too many armored feet at the bottom that became too many enemy soldiers.

First Platoon never had a chance. Nine aliens burst into the access corridor, a wave of death that washed over the DDF soldiers before they had a chance to think about shooting. The aliens were clean and efficient killers, and Jackson stood fixed in place, frozen in shock, motionless while his people died in front of him.

The same alien from the hangar moved ahead of the group. Jackson raised his hands a second time. The leader tried to speak to him again. Jackson shook his head. He didn't understand. The alien thrust his gun forward, pointing it at Jackson and waiting a few seconds. Then he smoothly swung it to his side, attaching it to his armor. He pointed at Jackson. Then he pointed at himself as if to say, "you're mine."

Jackson didn't try to argue. He didn't try to resist.

There was no point. It would only get him killed. The sealed hatch had been useless. The security cracked in seconds. The rest of the locks on the ship would fall just as easily.

In barely an hour, the colony had gone from freedom to imprisonment.

Chapter 7

When Caleb came to he was propped up on a padded bench seat in the front of the Inahri transport. An Inahri woman was positioned on his right, and two men were across a narrow aisle. Another man and woman were further back on the seat, facing away from him.

His hands were bound by a pair of bracelets that he couldn't pull more than a dozen centimeters from one another before meeting futile resistance, even with the strength of his replacement arm. His head hurt. His eyes were a little blurry.

But he was still alive. That was a good sign.

He didn't speak. He took in the rest of his surroundings. To his left, the back of a pilot's seat and the viewport out of the transport from the cockpit. Through it, he could see the edge of the mountain range they had crossed over.

Southeast. They were headed southeast. How far had they gone? How much farther did they have to go?

The pilot was facing away from him. His head was

small and narrow and speckled with a dusting of fine hair. He had his hands up in front of him which he appeared to be using to control the ship, his fingers tapping slightly and his palms changing planes in sync with the transport. A band around the back of his head suggested he had goggles over his eyes.

Caleb faced straight again. The Inahri men across from him had noticed he was awake. When he looked at them, they looked back. They didn't speak, and their expressions didn't change.

He glanced to his right again, past the rest of the Inahri , realizing that the rest of his Guardians were on the transport with them. They were shoved into the rear of the craft on the floor, pressed together in a small cargo space and still unconscious.

Why had they given him special treatment? Because he had attacked them?

The woman beside him noticed the men, and then she pivoted on the seat so she could look at him. Caleb drew back when he saw her face. It was so alien, and at the same time so human.

Her eyes were too big, her nose too small, her cheekbones too delicate, and her lips too full and red. She had cropped reddish-blonde hair and an olive complexion. She reminded him of the way advertisers distorted models in magazines, elongating this, shrinking that, and trying to make the most perfect, beautiful woman, instead arriving at something that didn't exist.

The face he looked at now fell somewhere in the uncanny valley between the two extremes and looking at it unnerved him.

"I don't suppose you speak Earth English?" he said with a smile, trying to appear friendly.

The Inahri had to know the Guardian Intellect was gone. They had to know the city-ship was theirs again for the taking. Did they know it didn't have an energy unit? Did they know the Earthers did? How could they?

But if they were that interested in the city, why had they left already? He couldn't believe that he and the Guardians were enough of a prize.

She smiled back at him, and responded in a tongue he couldn't understand either. It sounded like Chinese spoken with a thick French accent.

Caleb shook his head. "I don't know what you're saying. And you don't know what I'm saying either." He forced a laugh.

She laughed at that. Maybe English just sounded amusing to them. Then she looked at her companions and said something. They all laughed.

At least they were capable of laughter. They couldn't be all bad, then. Could they?

Caleb pointed to his people in the back of the transport, and then at himself. "Mine."

She raised a light eyebrow at that. He repeated the process a few more times, but she didn't seem to get it.

This was going to be impossible.

He looked the other way, back out the forward viewport. The ship was rising over the edge of the mountains, revealing the jungle and river valley on the right. He craned his neck, trying to find the Deliverance in the distance. He couldn't. They had to be too far south.

He would have checked the time on his HUD, but his SOS was offline, and he didn't have his helmet anyway. None of the Guardians did. The headgear was piled beside them, along with their rifles.

He put his head back against the side of the transport and closed his eyes. Everything was happening too damn fast, and none of it made much sense. He hoped the Deliverance was still safe. For all the Guardian's words about how the Inahri had destroyed the Axon, they didn't seem irrationally violent. Maybe they had just been pissed about being used?

In a lot of ways, they were no different than the people of Metro.

He opened his eyes again when he felt a hand on his replacement. The woman beside him was running her fingers along it, and looking questioningly at him. He couldn't even say hello. How was he going to explain a prosthetic made from an alien alloy he shouldn't have access to?

He pointed at her arm, and then slowly reached over and tapped her armor. She seemed tentative about him touching her, but she had five armed soldiers with her.

She nodded in understanding. If that's what it was. He had told her the arm was armor, but that wasn't true. It was the best he could do.

The woman removed her hand and looked up out of the front transparency, and then she snapped something to the pilot. He replied quickly, affirming her direction, and then the transport turned fully south.

She was in charge. He had already guessed, but her orders confirmed it.

"Caleb," Caleb said, getting her attention again. He pointed at himself. "Caleb." He did it a few more times.

"Caleb?" she said slowly, as though forming the word was painful.

Caleb nodded. "Yes. Caleb."

The other soldiers grunted humorously. She smiled. "Caleb."

He pointed at her. She stared at his finger while he repeated the motion a few more times. He assumed she had a pronounceable name, not an equation like the Axon Intellects.

"Za Tsi," she said, pointing at herself. "Za Tsi."

Caleb smiled. "Za Tsi."

She nodded. "Chi."

Was that yes? He figured it probably was.

"Za Tsi," he said again.

"Caleb," she said.

They smiled at one another. He was developing some kind of rapport with the Inahri woman. He was still alive.

Definitely a good start.

He opened his mouth, pointing to it. "Hungry." He wasn't hungry, but it was the next thing he could think of to establish some small measure of communication. "Hungry."

She let him repeat the motion a few times. Then she leaned over, pressing on the bottom of the bench. A drawer slid open, revealing a small, dry square. She picked it up and held it out to him.

He took it. "Food?" he asked. She stared at him. He pointed at it. "Food."

"Food," she said. "Yinai."

"Yinai. Food."

She laughed, so he laughed. Then he put to his mouth and took a bite. It tasted as dry as it looked, only it melted in his mouth after a second, becoming soft and slightly sweet. He chewed and swallowed. Not bad at all.

"Mmmm," he said.

Za Tsi laughed again, her eyes lighting up in approval. The light faded as quickly as it appeared, her entire expression suddenly turning dark. For an instant, Caleb wondered if he had offended her. Then she started yelling at the pilot, leaning and reaching across him and putting his face right next to hers. She smelled sweet and clean. He didn't expect that.

She grabbed a small device and put it to his stomach. As soon as she did, he felt like he was being pressed down into the bench.

Then the transport made a soft hissing noise and began to fall from the sky.

Chapter 8

The motion of the descent was unsettling in a way Caleb had never experienced. He had jumped out of airplanes plenty of times. He had been on a C-130 that stalled and almost ditched in the Pacific. This wasn't that. This was faster, harder, and smoother than anything he'd ever felt, and his body had no idea what to think of it.

The Inahri craft sank toward the edge of the mountains and the top line of the jungle canopy alongside. He felt a light pressure against his abdomen where Za Tsi had positioned the unique device, and he felt a sensation of dropping, but it wasn't close to the g-force he was expecting from the sudden dive. He looked back at the Guardians still unconscious in the rear. They were shoved back against the wall, the movement pushing hard on them. He looked at Za Tsi. She seemed unconcerned by their fate.

"What's happening?" he asked, turning back to the viewport just in time to see something blue flash past them and hit the trees, igniting them instantly. "Oh. Shit."

He didn't need an answer now. They were being attacked. By who and what?

Not a Dagger. The fighters didn't have a weapon like that. Another alien? There was some question about whether or not the Relyeh had ever arrived on Essex. But he didn't get the impression the Relyeh used energy weapons either.

The transport banked hard right. Caleb barely felt it in the traditional sense, but he could see how the others shifted, their bodies feeling the strain even if their minds weren't able to connect the action.

"You're hurting them," he said, pointing at them.

Za Tsi glanced back at the others, and then at him. She didn't seem to understand what he meant.

"G-forces? You obviously know what they are, since you made these things." He grabbed the device on his lap. She snatched his hand and yanked it away. She didn't want him to turn it off. He pointed at the Guardians again, and then at himself, making an angry face. "They're mine, and you're hurting them."

The transport changed direction again, hissing louder as it ascended into a nearly vertical climb. Washington fell on top of Dante, likely suffocating her beneath his mass.

"Damn it!" Caleb shouted. "You're going to kill them!"

His anger caused the two soldiers opposite him to start reaching for something, but Za Tsi snapped something to them, and they straightened up. Then she looked at Caleb, pointing at him and then at the Guardians, and then toward the viewport. The transport was out of its climb and diving again. Caleb looked in time to see a dark shape flash past, and white bolts fire from their craft. The bolts missed the attacking ship, sinking into the jungle and starting small fires where they hit.

Caleb clenched his teeth. He knew they were in the

middle of a dogfight, but what good would winning do if all of his teammates were killed?

The ship banked left and right, having maneuvered itself into position behind the enemy ship. A slight upward tilt brought the opposing craft into view. It was similar in size, shape, and material, though it had a few cosmetic differences that made it appear more menacing.

Was it an Axon ship?

Caleb had still never seen an Axon. He got the impression they were humanoid because their Intellects were humanoid, but he had no proof of that. For all he knew, an Axon could be like an amoeba or a t-rex. But the only other option was that Inahri was fighting Inahri .

Was that so far-fetched? Earthers fought one another all the time. The Guardian had said the struggle for freedom had made the Inahri more violent and unpredictable, and with the Axon gone and no way off the planet, it seemed almost logical that they would start taking their aggression out on one another.

The dogfight didn't last much longer. The enemy craft tried a bold maneuver, attempting to flip over and fire on the chasing vessel. The move took too much of its momentum away, and it left half a second where it was upright in the air on its way over, offering a full target for the pilot. Caleb watched the Inahri 's hands shift, thumbs tapping the air and the weapons firing in response. The rounds hit the enemy ship, tearing through it and breaking it into pieces, which were pulled toward the surface in a smoldering mess of debris.

The pilot whistled with joy, and the other Inahri matched the sound, whistling back. The transport banked again, returning to its southeasterly heading and climbing back to a reasonable altitude.

Caleb grabbed the device on his lap, tapping the same

spot Za Tsi had hit. It powered off, falling onto his legs, surprisingly heavy. He moved it aside and stood up, half expecting the Inahri soldiers to shove him back down. They didn't. They let him go to the Guardians. He grabbed Washington's arm and pulling him off Dante. Then he leaned in over her, feeling for her pulse. She was alive.

He whipped his head back toward Za Tsi. "If any of them are hurt, you'll be next."

She didn't understand the words, but she understood the tone. She glared back at him, unhappy with the way he was talking to her, but also accepting it. Whether it was because he had stood up to them or whether it was something else, they seemed to have a level of respect for him.

He checked on Kiaan and Paige, making sure their pulses were strong and steady as well. Then he sat each of them up, arranging them more comfortably. He picked up the inertial dampening device and brought it to Dante, putting it on her legs and turning it on. Then he held up three fingers.

Za Tsi said something to the other soldiers, and three of them deactivated their devices and passed them back to him. He secured the Guardians, and then returned to his seat. Za Tsi stared at him as he sat there, studying his expression.

"I wish we could communicate better," Caleb said.

She kept staring at him in silence. He leaned his head back and closed his eyes again. As if the Axon, trife, Relyeh and a unified Inahri weren't enough to contend with, there had to be multiple factions engaged in some kind of civil war.

Caleb never would have imagined that would come next.

He wished he was back on Earth.

Chapter 9

There were nine enemy soldiers in all. They wore identical battle armor, large and bulky, with oversized helmets and large faceplates. The faces behind them were human, but not exactly human. Their eyes were a little too big. Their chins were a little too narrow. Everything about them seemed slightly exaggerated. Jackson found their looks both terrifying and beautiful at the same time.

Their leader was the tallest of the group, and even he didn't reach two meters. He had wispy light hair on his head and a small ring of scruff around his mouth that was just thick enough to cast a soft shadow. He spoke with a raspy, quiet voice in a tight cadence of language the Governor couldn't begin to understand.

What he did understand was that he was a prisoner, and Metro belonged to the aggressors. It had taken only nine of them, with superior weapons and far superior training, to kill almost two hundred Deliverance Defense Force soldiers, break through the seals, and lay claim to the city.

When Jackson surrendered, he surrendered for everyone. Second Platoon had come up the engineering passage from South Park, and he had ordered them to stand down and drop their weapons. It hurt his pride to do it, but there was no choice. As soon as the soldiers' rifles left their hands, their lives were saved.

The enemy rounded up the discarded weapons, stacking them near the seal. It took a few minutes of back and forth for Jackson to understand what was expected, but he wound up sending the soldiers back to their homes and families. It didn't take long for him to understand that the attackers had come for a specific reason, and the more he cooperated, the smoother everything would run.

They knew he was important. He guessed it was the only reason he was still alive, out of all the people who had been on the lift and beyond the city seals. The enemy had seen how the soldiers defended him and tried to get him to safety, and they knew he had power and control. He was just thankful Beth had gotten away, escaping down the passage and into Metro proper before the enemy arrived. The soldiers would bring her to Doctor Rathbone, and hopefully she could alleviate her shock and return her to some level of calm.

He had so many other things to worry about, but he couldn't stop thinking about his wife. She had already been through too much in too little time. He worried that witnessing so much violence would push her over the edge and she would never come back.

He was drawn out of the thought when the enemy leader barked something at him. Jackson sat up stiffly against the bulkhead, looking up at the man. Despite the city's surrender, their conquerors didn't seem to have any interest in going deeper into the ship or even entering the populated areas at all. Jackson had seen at least twelve run down the hill, but there were only nine here now. Had his people managed to kill the others? Or were they already busy searching the rest of the Deliverance for whatever it was they wanted?

Probably the latter. He had seen the enemy walk right through a plasma stream unharmed. There was nothing they had that could hurt them.

"I don't know what you're saying," Jackson said. Of course, the enemy knew that. But they had to get his attention somehow. It was better to be yelled at than kicked.

The soldier spoke again, this time to the two others flanking him. They took his arms and held them out to his sides. He shifted in the armor, and then manipulated something inside so that it clicked and spread open from the front, allowing him to climb out of it.

Leaner than Jackson had expected, he was dressed in a simple tunic and pants that seemed out of place inside the armor. The material was light and loosely woven, transparent enough that Jackson could see the outline of flesh pulled tight against muscle and bone beneath it.

The two soldiers moved the armor back, folding it in such a way that it remained upright when they let go. The leader stepped toward him, reaching into one of the folds of his tunic and removing a small cube from it. He crouched in front of Jackson, offering the cube.

Jackson took it between his thumb and forefinger. As soon as he did, a hologram appeared above it, offering an image of a sphere crackling with energy.

"What is it?" Jackson asked. "Other than what you came here looking for." The man motioned to the sphere and then pointed at Jackson, who shook his head. "I don't know what it is."

The man seemed to understand the head shake. His expression soured, and he grabbed the cube and stood up straight. Then he said something to the other soldiers before beckoning Jackson to stand. He pointed to himself, then the cube, and then Jackson, repeating the process multiple times.

"I don't know what it is," Jackson said again.

The man pointed down. Then he pointed at the cube. Then Jackson. It was obvious he was insisting that the sphere was on the Deliverance.

Jackson's thought about the armory. Was the object of their attention hiding down there, and they just hadn't found it yet?

"Who are you?" Jackson asked. He was sure of one thing. These aliens weren't the same as the alien that had left with Sergeant Card. That one had wanted to get out, and they wanted to get in. How were the two related, if at all? Were they enemies? Was that something he could use?

The man pointed at Jackson again and then the cube. He activated the hologram again, giving the Governor another look at the sphere.

"This is called a Quantum Dimensional Modulator," the man said suddenly, in perfect Earth English. "It was created by a race called the Axon. It is a power plant. The highest density power plant in the universe. Our sensors have detected one of them somewhere on this vessel. You will turn it over to me. In exchange, I will allow your civilization to continue breathing my air."

Jackson stared at the man. He had spent the last two hours making hand gestures to communicate, and now, all of a sudden this man was speaking fluent English, a language he had probably never heard before today?

"How are you speaking my language?" Jackson asked.

The man smiled, his expression going from sour to dark and causing the Governor to shrink back slightly. "The Relyeh speak all languages. Yours is one of the simplest of them all. Welcome, Earther, to Arluthu's World."

Chapter 10

"Arluthu's World?" Jackson said. "You mean Essex?" He swallowed hard. Riley Valentine had brought them here to fight something. Was that something standing right in front of him?

The alien soldier's eyes twitched before he spoke again. "Arluthu needs a Quantum Dimensional Modulator. There is one on this ship. We're certain of it. Was this a matter of good fortune, or was its delivery planned?"

The only thing that was planned was a war that would never happen. For the second time in the last hour, Jackson wondered if they would have been better off had Valentine gotten what she wanted.

"If you could speak English this whole time, why didn't you say so earlier?"

"I didn't want to, but gestures will only get us so far."

Jackson was expecting a logical answer. Such a simple, emotionally driven response made him more uneasy.

"You've come from another planet," the man said. "You have interstellar travel. But you aren't Relyeh. You aren't Axon or Inahri or Gusht. You aren't an Intellect. Where did you come from?"

"Earth," Jackson replied.

"Earth. We are not familiar with that world."

"What do you mean? Didn't you send the trife to Earth?"

"Trife? Ah, you must mean uluth. Yes. Arluthu sent the trife to Earth. I remember it now. But you shouldn't be here. Your kind has no starships, and you couldn't have survived long enough to build them. The Inahri virus should have killed many of you, and the uluth the rest."

"Inahri virus?"

"Yes. Developed from our own blood. We aren't so different, you and I. We both had our genesis on Earth."

"So you're human," Jackson said.

"Taken from our home by the Axon many thousands of years ago as subjects under their rule. Manipulated and used to build an army to fight the Relyeh. To challenge the Might of the Universe. As if the Relyeh can be challenged."

"Who are the Relyeh?"

"They are what is, what was, and what forever will be. The Might of the Universe. The Spreading Darkness. The Hunger. The Call. Those are some of their names, given by those they have conquered, cried out in horror at their coming, or in begging for their mercy. The Axon believed they could stop the advance. But it cannot be stopped. The only way to survive is to serve. If you serve, if your people serve, then they will survive too."

"And we can start by finding this Quantum Dimensional Modulator?"

"Yes."

Jackson was silent for a moment. Then he stuck his hand out. "I'd rather serve and survive. I think my people would agree. My name is Jackson Stone. I'm the Governor of Metro."

"I am Za Harai, leader of Shing Harai." He didn't take Jackson's hand, instead motioning to the other soldiers. "This is my unit."

"You're soldiers."

"Yes. Arluthu ordered us here after the orbital defense was destroyed."

The orbital defense. The one that had killed Orla. Jackson tightened his jaw. "That was five days ago."

"We have been observing you, hidden from your machines."

"I still don't understand how we're speaking the same language."

"I told you, the Relyeh speak all languages. Their eyes are everywhere. Even places where none have heard of the Relyeh, or where the Relyeh are treated as myth or legend. Even among the Axon, though they believe they're too superior to be deceived. Their arrogance only makes them easier to fool. All of this knowledge is shared across the Hunger."

Za Harai lifted the arm of his tunic, revealing something dark and moist wrapped around his arm. It shifted slightly in response, gripping the arm tighter and revealing that it was alive.

Jackson felt nauseous. "What is that?"

"This is a Relyeh Advocate."

"Advocate?"

"It's a link between the Relyeh and me. A symbiote. It understands your language, and is tranlating for me even now."

"Do all the Relyeh look like that?"

"No. This is a minor creature made to serve its masters, like the uluth."

"And like you?"

Za Harai didn't like the comment. His face showed his anger, and Jackson shrank back from him. "That was the Axon plan for us, which Arluthu in his kindness revealed. We turned away from the Axon when we learned what they did and why. With Arluthu's aid, we overthrew the Axon. We gained our freedom. Except…"

"Except what?"

"The Axon made the Intellects. The Intellects exploited a weakness in our technology and forced us out of our homes. They would have destroyed us if we hadn't run. They held the only Quantum Dimensional Modulators, and have prevented us from leaving this planet."

"If this is Arluthu's World, why do you want to leave?"

"To continue the work we started. To destroy the Axon. Every one of them, in Arluthu's name."

"You have ships, then?"

"Yes. We had a fleet of ships, but only one survived the rebellion. An Intellect defends it. We can't go near it without losing our minds and having all of our equipment shut down."

Jackson's mind turned to the alien that had left with Card. An Intellect, then. Card had said it wanted to come to this planet. But why? He looked up at Za Harai, considering whether or not to tell him what had happened.

"We saw the Intellect examine your ship," Za Harai said before he could speak. "And we saw one group of your people leave with another Intellect, as though they were companions. Did you come to aid the Axon? Is that why you're here?"

"No," Jackson replied, maybe a little too forcefully. "Like I said, we'd rather serve and survive. To be honest, we didn't bring ourselves here. Like you, we were brought against our will. Like you, we were supposed to fight the Relyeh."

Za Harai laughed. "You? You couldn't even kill one of my Shing."

"My point exactly. We aren't warriors. The people who surrendered their weapons to you, they were the best of what we have."

Za Harai's expression shifted. He looked dismayed. "That is the best you have to offer? Arluthu accepts those who serve, but they must have something of value."

"We have the Quantum thing. I'm not sure where, but if you say it's here, then I believe you. The people that brought us here, Space Force Command and Riley Valentine, they kept a lot of secrets."

Za Harai pursed his lips and nodded. "That might be enough. What of the group that left with the Intellect? What of the group that followed after? Your actions don't match your explanation."

"They were Space Force Marines. Part of the group responsible for us being here. I don't know if they were working with the Intellect. I told you, they kept a lot of secrets. All I know is that the thing killed a dozen of my people and helped them escape. The second group, I sent them after the Marines. Their mission was to kill them."

Za Harai raised his eyebrow. "Not as spineless as I had guessed. Tell me, how many are on this vessel?"

"Twenty-six thousand."

"A good number. The Free Inahri have less than twenty-thousand."

"Free Inahri ?"

"There is a faction of Inahri that broke from Arluthu. They believe the Relyeh are no better than the Axon. They're hiding somewhere in the temperate zone. We engage them on occasion, but they are too small in number to be of any significance. Even so, I'm certain adding your group to ours would be of value to Arluthu. If we could more rapidly expand our population, that would be of great value indeed."

"Expand our population? You mean interbreeding?"

"We're the same, your people and mine. Divergent only because of our different planets. There should be no difficulties. But we'll need to fix your weaknesses. Arluthu demands all subjects are prepared for the days to come."

Jackson's breath escaped him again. He didn't like the sound of that. "What do you mean, days to come?"

"When the Quantum Dimensional Modulator is found, then our attack can begin. We'll need more soldiers than we can yet provide."

"You want us to become soldiers? Space Force Command brought us here to fight. But we don't want to fight."

"Governor Jackson Stone, one way or another, you will have no choice but to fight. The only decision you can make is who and what you will fight for."

Chapter 11

Caleb opened his eyes when he sensed the transport slowing again. He turned his head left to look past the pilot, recoiling in a momentary panic that shoved him against Za Tsi. She put her hand on his shoulder, steadying him with her calm as the craft prepared to crash into the side of a cliff and the waterfall pouring down from it.

"Pu lio," she said.

Whatever that meant. The transport hit the waterfall, sinking through it without the spray of water or the downward pressure of the volume falling on top of them. It bypassed the rock face as well, entering a large, open cavern.

"A hologram," Caleb said, feeling stupid for reacting the way he did. Of course the Inahri weren't going to throw themselves into a mountain right after they went through the trouble of shooting down an opposing craft. He had gotten a deeper rest than he had planned, proving his level of exhaustion.

He recovered, shifting his position so he could see out better, taking in the landscape of the Inahri settlement.

It was nowhere near as impressive as he expected. The ample space was occupied by an assortment of vehicles at the front, a series of small, metal structures randomly placed around the center, which was an open, generally circular space. A set of large machines rested against the back, including the holographic generator, which was casting light forward to create the illusion of the waterfall. Everything in the cavern was dirty and dusty. Everything was coated in a layer of green-purple moss. The dampness was evident, as was the coolness. Inahri were moving between the structures, each of them dressed in thicker robes, tunics, shirts or pants in an assortment of styles he would have expected to find in a mall on Earth. They paused to look up at the transport as it descended toward the surface.

They were almost on the ground when a squad of armored soldiers emerged, running toward the ship, from the structure nearest the landing area. Caleb glanced back at Za Tsi, making sure she wasn't concerned with the reaction. The satisfied smirk stuck to her face told him she wasn't.

Caleb heard a groan at the back of the transport. He leaned over to see past the Inahri soldier. Dante was waking up, shifting against the restraint of the dampener and rubbing at her head. Her eyes opened, taking in the transport full of Inahri , her fear evident.

"Dante," Caleb said, the word getting both Dante and Za Tsi's attention.

"Sergeant?" she replied. "What's going on?"

"I'm not sure yet. But Za Tsi brought us to an Inahri outpost of some kind."

"Za Tsi?"

"Za Tsi." The soldier pointed to herself. "Caleb." She pointed at him.

"Sam Dante," Caleb said, motioning to Dante.

"Sammante," Za Tsi said. She coughed a short laugh.

"Does that mean they aren't going to kill us and eat us?" Dante asked.

"No guarantees," Caleb said. "We're still learning to communicate."

"We're not dead. I guess that's good, right?"

"That's what I've been going with."

"Roger that." She tried to move, groaning. "I think I broke a rib."

"Washington got thrown into you during the flight," Caleb said.

"That explains it."

The transport shook slightly as it hit the ground. Za Tsi and the other Inahri soldiers got to their feet. A hatch opened on the back right side. Za Tsi put her hand out, palm up, signaling Caleb to stay where he was. She let the pilot move past her and then followed her soldiers out of the hatch, which closed behind her and left the Guardians alone in the vessel.

"Do you think you can fly it?" Dante asked. "Get us out of here?"

"Doubtful," Caleb replied.

"What happened?"

"They got us in the Axon city-ship. Some kind of stun weapon. I woke up here, just like you."

"Not just like us. How come you got a first-class seat?"

"I think I earned their respect. After they stunned you and Kiaan, I tried to charge them."

Dante laughed. "Are you kidding? You're lucky you aren't dead."

"I'm not sure I'm lucky about that just yet. We were attacked on the way here. Another Inahri ship. Our pilot was better."

"So the Inahri are at war with one another? Do you have any good news to share?"

Caleb opened his mouth, trying to think of something. He was saved when the hatch opened again.

"Caleb," Za Tsi said, barking his name as an order. He stood and crossed to the hatch. She reached out and took his wrist, gripping it tightly as though she was claiming him as property.

Maybe that's precisely what she was doing.

He dropped onto the stone floor, and she walked him a few steps to where another Inahri was waiting, flanked by a second group of soldiers in combat armor. This man was older, his head bald, his face wrinkled. He was wearing a heavy purple robe, cinched at the waist with some type of powered belt. He eyed Caleb disinterestedly.

Caleb stood in front of him, unsure of what to do next.

"Yifou," the man said.

Za Tsi moved in front of him, reaching her hand beneath the collar of his combat armor and pulling.

Caleb pulled back, ripping himself out of her grip. Immediately, two soldiers took his arms, holding them tight.

"Caleb," Za Tsi said. She pointed to his armor and made a motion like she was tearing it.

"You want me to take it off?" he said.

She repeated the motion.

"They need to let go." He eyed the soldiers holding him. Za Tsi said something, and they let him go.

He reached for the combat armor's clasps. It was a little more challenging with one hand, but he managed to disengage them and shimmy out of the armor. He heard the soldiers hiss around him when he did, and he saw one of them staring at his replacement arm. They had thought it was part of his suit.

The older man stepped forward and pushed up the sleeve of his underclothes, checking his arm for something. He repeated the process on the other arm, and then turned him around and checked his back, making an audible sound when he saw the scars from the trife claws. He turned Caleb back around and stepped away. He tapped the belt before crossing his arms behind him.

They all stood in place. Caleb heard footsteps a moment later, and he turned to see a dark humanoid form walking toward them. An Intellect.

Caleb's heart started to race. What the hell was this? The Inahri and Axon were enemies, weren't they?

The Intellect approached, coming to a stop beside the man, who tapped his belt again. Caleb noticed something flash on the side of the Intellect's neck, and he realized the man was controlling it.

"Caleb," Za Tsi said. He looked at her. She pointed to her mouth, and then to his. Then she let out a stream of words.

"Inahrai," the Intellect said.

"What are you supposed to be?" Caleb asked it. "Some kind of iron monkey?"

"Earth," the Intellect said. "English." It paused. "I am not a monkey. I am an Inahri Intellect." It spoke perfect Earth English.

The man spoke in Inahrai . The Intellect spoke, translating. "I am General Goi. You are prisoners under my command. You will do exactly as I say, or you will die. Do you understand?"

Chapter 12

"I understand," Caleb said in response to General Goi's statement. The Intellect translated the answer, making for an awkward exchange that was only going to continue.

"Sergeant Tsi will take you and your soldiers to your barracks," Goi said. "You will be given a short time to become acclimated. Then you will be brought before me for interrogation. Do you understand?"

Caleb didn't hesitate. He jumped to attention. "Yes, sir," he snapped back in perfect form. Inside, he was feeling the tension of the situation. He wasn't about to show it.

Goi seemed pleased with the reaction. He nodded slightly. "Sergeant, take them to their barracks." He started turning away, and then paused, looking back at Caleb. "I expect you will keep your soldiers in line?"

"Yes, sir," Caleb replied.

Goi continued back into the line of structures, together with his entourage. Tsi and her squad stayed with him, and she motioned to the transport doors. One of her squad members opened the hatch.

"Tell them to come out," she said to Caleb, through the Intellect's translation.

"Guardians," Caleb said. "A-TEHN-SHUN!"

They didn't come as quickly as he would have liked, but they had been through a lot, and only Washington was a real Marine. When they did show, Washington was in the lead, moving deliberately to show the others how it was done.

"Line up!" Caleb said.

They moved into a line in front of him, again guided by Washington. They looked tired and sore, their combat armor scuffed, scraped and streaked with blood. Kiaan pulled up the rear, surprising Caleb with his almost correct posture.

"This is Sergeant Tsi," Caleb said, concluding za was a title equivalent to sergeant and not part of her name. "She'll be taking us to our barracks to get situated before debriefing. As of this moment, it has been made clear to me that we are prisoners under General Goi, who I assume is the leader of this camp?"

"Chi," Tsi replied. Yes.

"Prisoners in a barracks?" Dante said. "Not a cell?"

"I'm sure we'll get to that," Caleb said. "For now, I expect you to follow my orders to the letter, and not cause any trouble. You will answer me with yes, Sergeant."

"Yes, Sergeant!" Dante, Paige, and Kiaan said. Washington nodded his head.

"This one did not respond," Tsi said, glaring at Washington.

"He can't talk," Caleb replied. "You can see the injuries to his face and throat. They go deeper, to his vocal cords."

"I understand," Tsi said. She said something to one of

her soldiers, who ran away from the area. "Private Gol will retrieve Doctor Amali. She will examine your soldier."

"His name is Private John Washington," Caleb said. "We call him Wash for short."

Washington gave them the thumbs-up in response.

"I do not need their names. They are your team. They fall under you. You are responsible for anything they do."

"Yes, Sergeant," Caleb said.

They remained at attention for nearly a minute, until an elderly woman returned with Private Gol. Tsi spoke to the woman, and then the woman walked over to Washington and spoke.

"Come with me," the Intellect translated.

Washington looked at Caleb. He seemed like he wanted to go. Why not? The Inahri were calling them prisoner but treating them with a measure of respect. Or at least, treating him with respect. Their technology was more advanced. Depending on how much the Axon had shared with them, it could be hundreds of thousands of years more advanced.

Caleb nodded. "Permission granted. Do whatever she tells you, and nothing else."

The Doctor started walking away. Washington followed behind her, flanked by Private Gol.

"The guard isn't necessary," Caleb said. "He's a good Marine."

"Perhaps in time," Tsi replied. "What is a Marine?" She had trouble pronouncing the word. The Inahri didn't have an equivalent.

"A warrior. Like a soldier, but different training."

"I understand. Is that why you did not run?"

"In part."

"Follow me."

She turned and walked across the cavern floor, past the

assembled craft to the left side of the makeshift village. The structures were all composed of what appeared to be seamless earth, rising from the floor like dozens of anthills of various heights and lengths. Other Inahri were moving among them, most of them in matching tunics and pants. Uniforms. Each of them had a small pin on the left shoulder that emitted a hologram containing different symbols, which Caleb took to be their name, rank, and hardware.

"Is everyone here a soldier?" Caleb asked. The Intellect walked beside him, translating the question.

"We are all of the Free Inahri ," she replied. "We are soldiers by need, not want."

"But you killed the Axon?"

"Long ago. They enslaved us. Used us."

"But you found us in the city-ship, and your reaction is to stun us and take us prisoner?"

It was too blunt, too soon. Tsi stopped and whirled on him, her eyes fierce. "It is not the same. You know nothing of us, Earther."

Caleb lowered his head. He was usually more tactful. "You're right. My apologies, Sergeant."

She turned around again, leading them past some of the buildings. Caleb tried to look into them, but all of their doors were closed, their windows opaque.

"We have to be sure you are not with the Relyeh. We have to be sure you will have value to us. We do not have resources to nurture those without value."

"We didn't come here alone. We came on a ship."

"We are aware of your ship."

"Why didn't you come to us there? Why didn't you make yourselves known?"

"Because Arluthu is also aware of your ship."

Chapter 13

"Who?" Caleb asked.

"Arluthu is the Relyeh who subverted the Inahri," Tsi replied. "He twisted their minds, and now they belong to him."

"But you don't?"

"We are immune to his lies."

Caleb had a thousand more questions, but he figured it would be better to ask them in the presence of General Goi. If this Inahri militia were anything like Earth military, there would be only so much Tsi could say.

Caleb reached over and tapped on his dead arm. "This needs to be recharged. Do you think you would be able to help me with that?"

"An interesting device. Your enemies don't always go for the kill?"

"Oh, they do. They just don't always succeed."

Tsi laughed softly. "Yes, Pai can help you replenish your battery."

They walked in silence for a short distance more, before Sergeant Tsi came to a stop in front of one of the anthills, pausing in front of the closed door. It opened a moment later, a small, somewhat humanoid robot moving out from it.

"Za Tsi," it said, speaking to her.

"Intellect," Tsi said. "You will transfer your Earth language data to the Pai."

"Assurance," the Intellect replied. It moved to the small robot, placing its hand on it. Tendrils snaked out from its fingers and into the machine.

"How do you control it?" Caleb asked. "The Intellect."

"The Axon enslaved us," Tsi said. "They underestimated our intelligence and our motivation. We turned the collars back on them. The Intellects have value, but they were difficult to capture. We have only three." She pointed to a small device on its neck—a control collar.

The Intellect removed its hand from the machine. "It is done."

"Try speaking to it," Tsi said.

"What is it?" Caleb asked.

"A service robot. It will assist you with basic tasks and control your barracks."

"And watch and listen to everything we say?"

"To listen, yes. But it is programmed to respond to keywords, none of which are listed in your language. It will not know how to process your conversations effectively." She faced Caleb, reaching up and putting her fingers lightly against his chest. "I believe you are brave and courageous, and that you will bring value. You made it through the uluth in the jungle, and you defeated the Intellects guarding the city. You also refused to leave your comrades behind. I am putting my trust in you, warrior to warrior. I believe you can bring honor to me, and yourself. You are a prisoner today, but it doesn't have to remain that way. Do you understand?"

Caleb nodded. "Roger that, Sergeant Tsi."

The Intellect didn't know how to translate "Roger." Tsi looked at him quizzically.

"It means, I hear you and will do as you say," he said.

"Roger," she repeated, removing her hand.

Caleb smiled. "Exactly."

"Pai will be your guide inside the barracks. Please try speaking to it."

"Pai, do you understand me?" Caleb asked.

"Yes," the robot responded in a flat, synthesized voice. "What do you require?"

"A quick tour of the facility, I guess," Caleb replied.

"Roger," Pai said. "Follow me."

The robot turned and walked back inside. Caleb looked at Tsi again, making eye contact. "Thank you," he said.

Her face darkened slightly. Was she blushing? "Do not disappoint me, Caleb."

"My job is to protect the people I came here with," he replied. "I'll do whatever it takes to keep them safe. Do you understand?"

"Yes. I will take my leave of you now. Private Anzi will stand guard. I will return when General Goi is ready to meet with you."

She bowed slightly to him, and then she walked back the way they had come with all of her unit except Private Anzi, who took a guard position beside the door.

"Come on, Guardians," Caleb said, leading them into the barracks.

The room wasn't much different than what Caleb expected. It was a small space, with the mattresses arranged in a rotating pattern around a central beam that split the center of it, offering a spiral step-like layout to get from bottom to top. There were three lockers on either side of the rack, a pair of flat metal surfaces against the wall beside those, and two other devices at the back which looked like a shower and a toilet of some kind.

There was also an open space at the front of the barracks, with a small table that looked to have been cut from a single piece of stone in the center and carefully arranged hooks affixed to the walls on either side. Caleb spent a moment looking at the pattern of the hooks, trying to determine what they were for.

"Combat armor," Dante said, noticing his face. "I don't think we've earned it yet."

"We're lucky to be alive," Caleb replied.

"Thanks to you. You're so courageous and brave." She smiled and fluttered her eyes at him, drawing a laugh.

"I think something got lost in the translation," he said.

"I hope so. Otherwise, Sergeant Tsi might have a crush on you."

"I seriously doubt that. We're barely the same species. Completely different evolutionary paths."

"Pai, would it be possible to get a change of clothes?" Caleb asked.

The robot turned to face him. A blue beam launched from its forehead, quickly sliding up and down his body. It reminded Caleb of the beam back on the city-ship. The one that had locked them out of their escape.

"Requisition transmitted," Pai said. It turned to Dante and scanned her. "Requisition transmitted." Then it did the same to Kiaan and Paige.

"Sergeant, I have to admit, I'm terrified," Kiaan said.

"It'll be okay," Caleb replied. "They don't seem all that bad, overall. Let's try to get comfortable here. Once I get my sit-down with General Goi, we'll have a much better idea where we stand."

"What do you think they're doing to Washington?" Paige asked. "Do you think they can fix him?"

"I know we couldn't," Caleb said. "But the Inahri have better tech. They figured out how to control an Intellect."

"What happened to him?"

"After the trife came to Earth, society started to break down. There was this group of assholes that took his wife. They did things to her before they killed her. He went after them, followed them right into a trife infested building. Killed all four of the assholes, and about forty trife. He came out covered in blood, his face and neck torn up, right about the time the Vultures got to the scene. I never thought he would make it, but we brought him back to HQ with us. They patched him back together, and he joined the Marines the same day."

"Wow," Kiaan said.

"Your many-times great-grandmother was there when we found him. They were pretty close. And really, it's only been about two months of real-time for Wash and I since she died. It's still pretty raw. I've lost too many these last few weeks."

"I'm sorry, Sergeant," Dante said, putting a hand on his shoulder.

"Thanks. You always think it'll get easier. It doesn't." He sighed heavily and regrouped, turning to Pai. "Sergeant Tsi said you could recharge my arm."

The blue beam scanned his prosthetic again. "I will need to take your arm in my hand."

"Go ahead."

Pai reached up, barely tall enough to get to Caleb's shoulder. It wrapped its three-fingered hand around the control ring. "Delivering."

Caleb didn't feel anything, but when Pai removed its

hand the LED on the ring was green, and his arm was functional again.

"Perfect," Caleb said. "One more request."

"I am here to serve."

"Can you show us how to use the head?"

"I do not understand."

"The latrine? The toilet?"

"Yes." The robot walked across the barracks to the cube at the back of the room. "If you are wearing standard issue apparel, you only have to sit. The vaporizer will function through the material. Otherwise, you must first remove your apparel."

Caleb still wasn't sure how it worked. He looked back at the others.

"You're in charge, Sarge," Paige said. "You should be the one to try it out."

"Isn't there a partition or something that's supposed to come up?" Kiaan asked.

"I do not understand."

"For privacy?"

"You are all human. Why does your natural organic function embarrass you?"

"Are you familiar with Adam and Eve?"

"No. There is no partition."

"What about getting clean?" Caleb asked.

"Again, you must remove your clothing. Then simply stand there until the cleanser turns off. Step out, and you will be free of all contaminants. No. There is no partition."

Someone knocked on the door.

"That will be your uniforms," Pai said. "I will retrieve them."

Caleb grabbed his shirt, pulling it off. He reached for his pants. "Space Force Marine barracks have communal showers," he explained. He wasn't embarrassed about his natural organic functions.

"Men and women?" Dante asked.

"Yes. When you're spending your days trying not to be killed by trife, you tend to forget about gender. You just want to get the blood off your face." He pulled his pants off, and then his underwear. The rest of the Guardians were facing the other way by then.

"No offense, Sergeant," Dante said. "But I'm not a Space Force Marine."

"No offense, Sam," Caleb said. "But right now, you're more important than a Space Force Marine. You're one of the only people Metro can rely on to fight for them."

The statement caused Dante to turn back around. She kept her eyes locked on his face, but she didn't speak. Then she started taking off her combat armor.

Caleb walked over to the toilet. There was no opening. No water. Just a metal surface with a cradling slope. He sat down on it, finding the seat was already warm.

It got even warmer, and he felt that heat go up into him, his muscles relaxing uncontrollably. When the warmth faded, not only was his bladder empty, but his bowels felt completely cleared out too.

He stood and went over to the other device. A blue light turned on over his head when he stopped on it. He felt a tingling sensation along his body that faded within a few seconds. The light turned off, and he moved out, feeling as though he had just taken a long, hot shower.

Dante was taking her turn by then, while Pai was placing uniforms on each of the mattresses. Paige had already removed her SOS, following Dante's lead, while Kiaan was doing his best to both be part of the team, with everything that entailed at the moment, and avoid looking at the other naked humans.

Pai walked over to him and held his uniform up. Theirs were different from the others he had seen outside the barracks. Black instead of purple or green.

"What does the color signify?"

"It means you are in trial," Pai said. "You have not proven your value to the Free Inahri ."

"How do we prove our value?" Paige asked.

Caleb slid the loose-knit tunic over his head, finding it warmer than his discarded clothing despite the lightness of the material. He slid the pants on, noticing he had been given a simple leather-style cinch to wrap around his waist.

"There are many ways," Pai replied. "I'm certain you will find one."

Caleb finished dressing. "How do I look?" he asked.

Dante was finished with the cleanser and was walking to her rack. "It works for you, Sarge. Which one of these is mine?"

"Third from the top," Pai said.

Dante grabbed the underclothes and slid them on. "Perfect fit. And comfortable." She pulled on the black tunic and pants. "I feel like I'm wearing pajamas."

"They are comfortable," Caleb agreed.

"Which one is mine?" Paige asked.

"Third from the bottom," Pai replied.

Caleb found Kiaan standing closer to the head, still dressed. His clothes had been soaked through by the rain, stained with trife blood, and torn, but he was still uncomfortable getting out of them in front of the others.

Caleb went over to him. "Kiaan, it's not a big deal. We all did it."

"It's not right," Kiaan replied, eyes pleading. "I didn't ask to be a Marine or whatever. I don't want to shoot things. I just wanted to fly the transport."

"Things are going to get worse before they get better. I

respect how you feel about this. We'll face the other way. But you need to think about how something like this translates to being out there. The more comfortable you are with your team, the harder you fight for them. They become your family."

Kiaan nodded. "Yes, sir."

Caleb turned around, returning to Paige and Dante.

"Kiaan's a little shy. Just give him time."

"So am I," Paige said. "That wasn't exactly easy."

"That vaporizer thing is amazing," Dante said. "I wish I had one of those in my cube."

"Roger that," Paige said. "And—"

She stopped talking when the door to the barracks slid open. Caleb glanced over as Washington bent slightly to get through the too-low doorway. He had traded his SOS for a black tunic and pants that matched the rest of the team's, and he had a fabric band wrapped around his neck. The band glowed a soft blue at its base, and had other powered threads woven through it, creating an intricate pattern of gentle light.

"Wash," Caleb said. "Are you okay?"

Washington smiled and started to raise his thumb. He stopped. "I'm good, Sarge," he said, his voice a little raspy but otherwise functional. "Real good."

Chapter 14

The Guardians were sitting around the table when Sergeant Tsi returned. They had all calmed considerably by then, and having Washington among them with his voice restored had given all of them, Caleb especially, a fresh hope that maybe things would work out. The Free Inahri had treated them with unexpected kindness and hospitality, and a comfort Caleb hadn't felt since...he couldn't remember when. Probably since the trife had arrived on Earth.

Pai had revealed the two metal plates against the barracks wall as refrigeration and hydration units and had served them to a simple meal of some sort of soft whole grain like porridge and water infused with a native leaf that gave it a sweet taste. The meal was filling and had also helped to re-energize the group.

The Guardians all turned toward the barracks door when it slid open. Sergeant Tsi stepped in with Private Gol and the Intellect.

"Caleb," she said. "General Goi will see you now."

"Just me?" Caleb asked.

"Yes. You are the Sergeant of this squad and my charge."

Caleb nodded. He stood and faced his team. "Wash, hold down the fort for me?"

"Yes, Sergeant," Washington replied.

Caleb was still amazed that the Inahri had repaired his voice so quickly and easily. It was great to hear Washington respond, but it would take a while before he would stop looking for the familiar thumb instead.

He turned back to Sergeant Tsi. "I'm ready, Sergeant."

"First, you must learn basic protocol," Tsi said. "You will bow your head to your superiors when they address you. You will keep your head bowed determinate to the position of the superior who is addressing you, or to whom you are being addressed." She glanced past Caleb to the other Guardians. "This is true for all of you. When you are beyond the barracks and not in combat, and your Sergeant addresses you, bow your head. Before you address your Sergeant, bow your head. Understood?"

"Yes, Sergeant," the Guardians replied.

"In the case of General Goi, you will hold your head bowed for the count of three. One... Two... Three... Understood?"

"Yes, Sergeant," Caleb said, bowing his head slightly.

Tsi smiled. "Good. You are a fast learner. Private Gol will remain to stand guard over your squad."

"Is that necessary, Sergeant?" Caleb asked. "They aren't going anywhere."

"Yes," Tsi replied simply. "Follow me."

Caleb followed her out of the barracks with the Intellect. He noticed the air didn't seem as cool as before, his uniform keeping his body heat contained and helping him stay warm.

"You've been so kind to my team and me, I was

starting to forget we're prisoners," Caleb said as they walked.

"In all other cases, we have taken in defectors from Arluthu's Inahri ranks. When our sensors detected the energy field surrounding the city-ship had vanished, we were uncertain if it was a result of the actions of the newcomers, or our misguided brothers and sisters. It's not desirable for us to kill our own if it can be avoided. Even so, it's also not common for our opponents to exhibit such fearlessness and sacrifice. I have awarded you an honor, Caleb. Most who are put on trial are not treated poorly, but they are also not granted personal space and privacy. You are different."

"I didn't do anything special."

"That you believe those words so firmly is proof that you did."

"Pai said these uniforms mean we're on Trial, and that we have to prove our value. What does that entail, exactly?"

"I will leave it to General Goi to explain. Do not be concerned, Caleb. Your value is apparent to me. It will be obvious to the general as well."

Caleb glanced over at Tsi's face. Her expression was serious. She wasn't flirting with him or trying to butter him up. For whatever reason, she believed strongly in him, and the decision she had made to support him.

They crossed the village, passing through the center circle and turning left toward the back of the cavern.

"How does the hologram hide this place from sensors?" Caleb asked. "The Guardian Intellect didn't know you were here. I assume the Relyeh don't know you're here either."

She pointed to the sides of the cavern. "The rock is

infused with a heavy metal we call Datrium. Its primary value is in its ability to block even quantum waveforms."

"But you said you knew when the Guardian Intellect went offline. You must have units on the ground, outside the cavern."

"Yes. We call them Dancers."

Caleb imagined the real Inahri word sounded more impressive than the Intellect's translation. "And they've been watching the Deliverance too?"

"Your ship? Yes."

"How are things going over there?"

"I will leave it to General Goi to debrief you."

"He said interrogate earlier."

"Perhaps the Intellect chose an unsuitable word."

He preferred dancer.

They reached the edge of the center circle. A long building sat at the back, a pair of guards flanking the closed door. Caleb thought that would be the General's quarters or the CIC, but then Tsi led him around the building, to the structure behind it. It was half as wide and twice as tall, but otherwise as nondescript from the outside as any of the Inahri buildings. There were no guards here, but a man in dark blue robes emerged from the building as Tsi and Caleb neared the entrance.

"Bow your head," Tsi said, lowering hers. Caleb followed her lead, keeping his head down until the man had passed. He noticed the Intellect did the same.

"Who was that?" Caleb asked.

"Premier Atolate," Tsi replied. "General Goi is in charge of the compound. The Premier monitors the general for the civilian council."

"You aren't all warriors?"

Tsi smiled. "No. Many are, but we have others. They

live deeper inside. That way." She pointed to the back of the cavern.

It reminded Caleb of the story that had been passed down through Governor Stone's family. The people of Metro had spent their lives believing they were in an underground bunker instead of on a starship. These Inahri were living underground to evade notice by both the Intellect and the Relyeh. He hoped they didn't think they were on one of the city-ships.

Sergeant Tsi led him into the building. It was less open than the barracks, with a hallway leading to separate rooms and a set of stairs leading up to the second level. All of it appeared to be carved from a solid block of stone, as though they had made everything while excavating the cavern.

They probably had.

A female guard stood just inside the entrance. She bowed her head before saying something to Tsi, who responded with authority. The guard spoke again, only bowing the first time, and then motioned for them to ascend the stairs.

"General Goi has arranged all of the senior staff to attend," Tsi whispered. The Intellect matched her volume relaying the message.

"The more, the merrier," Caleb replied. Tsi gave him an odd look after the translation. "Some things don't translate well," he added. She nodded in response.

They reached the top of the steps. The entire upper floor was one open space and appeared to be the Inahri 's command center after all. The back of the room was lined with stations where a handful of Inahri in green uniforms sat, monitoring different flows of data on holographic terminals. Ahead of them, a surface that reminded Caleb of the holotable on the bridge of the Deliverance, and ahead of that a group of eight male and female Inahri , sitting cross-legged on small pillows, gathered around a flat, stark white mat.

Sergeant Tsi brought him to them and bowed her head. Caleb did the same.

"Esteemed," she said. "I present Sergeant Caleb of Earth, who I did capture aboard the Seeker soon after the fall of the waveform from that place, and who I have taken as my charge in advance of the Trial of both himself and his captured Earther companions."

She kept her head down as she spoke. She didn't raise it until General Goi responded from his place on the other side of the mat.

"Sergeant Tsi, you are welcomed to this meeting of the Esteemed, and offered a place at my side for the proceedings." Goi motioned to an empty pillow beside him. Caleb quickly noted there was only one empty pillow. "Sergeant Caleb of Earth, please take a place in the center of the proceedings." He motioned to the white mat.

Caleb bowed his head again. "Yes, General," he said, before moving past the other members of the Inahri military. He stood at attention there, facing Goi.

"You may sit," the General said. Goi looked pleased he had remained standing.

Caleb sat facing General Goi, matching his pose and posture. He didn't speak, waiting for the general to address him.

"Sergeant Caleb," Goi said. "Tell us how your ship arrived on New Inahri ."

"Yes, sir," Caleb said. "We launched from our planet, Earth, seeking to escape the trife. The uluth. They destroyed our society. Our civilization. Billions of us died. We were looking for a new home."

"And how did you come to choose this planet?"

"Sir, we didn't. We were supposed to rendezvous with the larger group of fleeing ships in the Proxima system. A star system only four light years from Earth. We had…complications."

"What manner of complications?"

"Sir, I'm not at liberty to discuss that."

Caleb knew Goi wasn't going to like that answer. The general's expression hardened, and he glared at Tsi.

"Sergeant, answer the question," she said. He could tell from her expression that stubbornness would get her punished as equally as him.

That normally wouldn't have been enough to make him talk, but they were already in a bad spot, and Space Force protocols hardly applied.

"One of our scientists brought a Watcher Intellect onto the ship. It was inert at the time, but events during the course of the journey led to its activation." He paused when he heard a couple of whispered comments behind him. "It wanted to come here so it could warn the Axon that the Relyeh were getting close."

Now he heard a few sardonic laughs around him.

"The Relyeh are closer than it knew," Goi said. "Arluthu circumvented your system to lay claim to ours before any others had the chance. They are growing more competitive."

"Sir, you mean the Relyeh?"

"Yes. How much do you know of the Hunger?"

"Sir, I didn't know anything about them until the Watcher decided me and my team could be of value to it. That was after we tried to get rid of it by ejecting it from our ship."

"If only it were that easy," someone said on his left, the Intellect translating the statement.

"So you were allied with the Intellect?" Goi asked.

"Yes, sir. At the time, I believed we had a common goal."

"What was that goal?"

"Sir, to find the enemy."

"You had an enemy at your side the entire time."

"Sir, ever since I left Earth, I've felt like I'm constantly surrounded by enemies. I don't know who to trust. What I can tell you is that the Deliverance is a colony ship. It is home to over twenty-thousand civilians. Not an army. For all I know, we're the last twenty-thousand Earthers in the universe. My job is to keep them safe. I allied with the Watcher because I knew it would help me reach the bigger threat."

General Goi was silent for a moment, considering his next question. "You defeated both the Guardian Intellect and the Watcher Intellect. How?"

"Sir, that's a complicated answer."

"In what sense?"

"Sir, my team didn't destroy the Intellect."

"Then who did?"

"Sir, that's where it gets complicated."

"I am a patient man, Sergeant."

Caleb spent the next ten minutes explaining everything he knew about Riley and David, and how they fit in with the creation of the Watcher and the death of the Guardian Intellect. He omitted anything that had to do with the QDM or Governor Stone.

General Goi was silent for nearly five minutes after he had finished, absorbing the information with his claimed patience.

"Your scientists were not wrong about the source of the attack against your world," he said at last. "Arluthu brought the uluth to your planet. Arluthu is responsible for the destruction of Earth."

Chapter 15

Caleb's breath caught in his throat. "Sir, Arluthu sent the trife to Earth?"

"I can not prove it definitively, but it fits with your story," General Goi replied.

"And he's here on Essex, sir?"

"Essex? He calls it Arluthu's World. We call it New Inahri . Yes, his city is here, and he is in it."

So Riley had been right. The alien responsible for the end of the world was here. If her plans had come to fruition, if she had made her hybrid army, maybe they could have gotten their revenge?

But what good would that do? Earth was already lost. It would have been better to settle the real Essex. It would have been better to stay far away from this place.

It was too late for that, too.

"Where is Riley Valentine now?" General Goi asked.

"Sir, I don't know. She ran from the Seeker's bridge. I didn't see her again after that."

"Sergeant Tsi, did you track another inside the Seeker?" Goi asked.

"No, General," Tsi replied. "But we did pick up an energy spike from the hangar as we were preparing to leave."

Caleb clenched his jaw. Had Riley found the hangar and a ship? Had she taken it from the city-ship? Why didn't she seek out Sergeant Tsi and try to talk to her? It didn't make sense. Then again, she was in the process of mutating into a Reaper. It was obvious during their interaction she wasn't stable.

Had she ever been stable?

"Why didn't you report this to me sooner, Sergeant?" Goi snapped.

Tsi lowered her head. "My apologies, sir. My intent was on Sergeant Caleb and his team."

"Can you be sure you weren't followed here?"

"Sir, we were attacked by the Relyeh on the way back. But there was no sign of any other craft in the area."

"Let us hope you didn't miss the sign," Goi said. "It seems to me this Riley Valentine is unpredictable."

"Yes, sir," Caleb said.

Goi returned his attention to Caleb. "Sergeant Caleb, you are wearing the black uniform of a warrior who has yet to pass a Trial. Do you understand what that means?"

"Not exactly, sir."

"As you can see, the Free Inahri have limited resources. We are dependent on this cavern and its adjoining network of tunnels as a place to hide from our enemies. Predominantly, the Relyeh. Every mouth we add to our settlement means a little bit less for everyone else. We can't allow anyone who doesn't add value to the community to become a member. In the past, that has always meant Relyeh defectors. Until today."

"I understand, sir," Caleb said. "What happens to the people who don't pass their Trial?"

"They know about our community. It is unfortunate, but we have no other option save execution."

Caleb had figured as much. He nodded. "To be honest, General, I would prefer to return to my people. To the Deliverance. I understand me and my team are some kind of prisoners of war. Except Earth isn't at war with the Inahri , and we have no intention of starting one."

Goi's expression turned more somber. Caleb's heart jumped slightly. It was the look of bad news. "You didn't mention it during your report, but I imagine that if your ship had a Watcher Intellect on board, it also had a quantum dimensional modulator on board?"

"Yes, General," Caleb replied.

"With the Guardian Intellect destroyed, the Seeker is unprotected. This is both a problem and an opportunity. The Relyeh Inahri will want to claim the ship in Arluthu's name and use it to begin an assault. Arluthu would be very grateful to claim more worlds for himself before the rest of the Hunger arrives."

"Sir, you mean the Axon?" Caleb asked.

General Goi considered. "The Axon, sooner or later. But right now? I wonder if Earth might be a more appealing target."

"You think that if Arluthu gets his hands on the QDM, he's going to send the Inahri to Earth to finish what the uluth started?"

"I do."

Caleb's whole body turned cold, sending a shiver tingling across every limb. "We can't let that happen." Caleb stood up. "I need to get back to my ship."

"Sit down!" General Goi snapped. "You were given no permission to stand!"

Caleb opened his mouth to argue. He had to stay calm.

He had to remember where he was. He forced himself back down.

"My apologies, General," he said, bowing his head again.

"I understand this is upsetting to you, Sergeant Caleb," Goi said. "It is upsetting to us as well. There has been balance for the last few ens—an equilibrium. But such things can't last forever. Life continues, and often in ways we don't desire or expect. I knew there was a reason Arluthu took such an interest in your vessel. I was afraid it was because you have a modulator. I'm thankful to Sergeant Tsi for bringing you here alive, and I appreciate your candor with us. Sergeant Tsi, we are finished for now. The Esteemed will discuss what we have learned. Return Sergeant Caleb to his barracks and await further orders."

"Yes, General," Sergeant Tsi said, getting to her feet. "Sergeant Caleb, you may stand."

Caleb stood up again. "General, did something happen to the Deliverance? Is there something you haven't told me?"

"Sergeant—" Tsi started to say, to admonish him for his lack of protocol.

General Goi put his hand up, silencing her. He came to his feet, looking up into Caleb's eyes. "The Relyeh Inahri attacked your ship. Our Dancers saw them enter the vessel and slaughter a number of your people. As of a short time ago, they are still inside."

"Looking for the energy unit," Caleb said.

"That is the most likely explanation."

"Damn it," Caleb cursed under his breath. If the Inahri found a way into the city, Governor Stone would fold like a cheap suit. "General, I need to go back to the Deliverance. We have to get the energy unit before they do."

"Sergeant Caleb, we will discuss our findings. Return to your barracks."

"General—"

"Return to your barracks!" Goi snapped. Caleb didn't need the Intellect to translate the man's meaning.

"Sir, if you want us to prove our value, this would be the perfect way to do it," Caleb said.

Sergeant Tsi grabbed Caleb's arm, pulling him off the mat. He didn't resist, lowering his head and falling into line behind her, with the Intellect behind him. He heard the Esteemed begin speaking almost on top of one another the moment they started descending the stairs.

"You're going to disgrace both of us if you refuse to show respect," Tsi hissed at him.

"I'm sorry, Tsi. I am. But if the Relyeh are already on the Deliverance, it's only a matter of time before they get into the city. It's only a matter of time before they get their hands on the QDM."

She looked into his eyes, calming suddenly. "Caleb, there is something more you aren't telling me."

How did she know? He nodded. "I told you, the people on the ship aren't warriors. If the Inahri threaten them they'll give up anything the Inahri want to avoid a fight."

"This is important information. I will inform General Goi as soon as I have returned you to your barracks."

"I can help you keep the energy unit from them. I can help you recover it. I know the ship and the people in it, and I'm happy to be your slave or whatever as long as it keeps those people safe."

"I understand, Caleb," Tsi said. "I will speak to the general. But you must follow our ways or you will do more harm than good."

"I know," Caleb said, taking a deep breath. "Please

thank Doctor Amali for me when you get a chance. For what she did for Washington."

"I will."

Sergeant Tsi led Caleb back through the compound in silence. Caleb sank into his thoughts, and by the time they reached the barracks he had made a decision:

He was going back to the Deliverance whether the Free Inahri helped him or not.

Chapter 16

Chief Engineer Joe King rubbed his forehead and eyes, trying to give himself just one more second wind before calling it a day. Parts of a small machine were laid out on the table in front of him, in a state of disarray that might have concerned anyone who didn't know Joe. He was comfortable with the mess. The inverter was halfway along in its repair, slowed only by the requisite hunt for a part that wasn't in worse shape than the one it was replacing.

It was still hard for Joe to believe how drastically every-thing had changed over the last week. He could still remember the day before the Marines had come when he had spent hours in the scrapyard looking for anything he could alter to match a part they had run entirely out of, even if it wasn't intended for the use. Two hundred plus years had worn out a lot of equipment which had been quickly and poorly made in the first place. It was one thing when he thought they were in an underground bunker on Earth. On another planet? It was something else.

"Joe, are you going to take a break any time today?" his wife, Carol, asked, standing in the doorway.

"I'm almost done," he replied.

"You said that the last three times I stopped by."

"Do you want to go for four?"

She entered the room, leaning over him and curling her arms around his neck to get a better look at what he was doing . "Did you find the piece you were looking for?"

"Yeah." He pointed to it. "Right there. I know how it goes back together. I'm just a little beat."

"You've barely slept all week. Governor Stone has you running on fumes."

"You should talk," Joe said. "You've been just as busy."

"Somebody has to fix this place up so we can break it down again."

"Did you see Jackson and Beth leave the mansion earlier?"

"I saw them from the window. The conquering heroes." She shook her head. "He threw those poor Marines under the bus."

"And then he stomped on their corpses," Joe said. "And now he's going to live outside, right next to the river. I hope something sneaks up on him and bites him in the ass."

"Joe!"

"What? He deserves a lot worse than that. I heard from Sweeting that he sent Sheriff Dante out to find Sergeant Card and the other Guardians. He couldn't just leave it alone."

"We should think about moving outside," Carol said. "We'd certainly have enough work to do, and I'd love to feel a real breeze on my face."

"It isn't safe out there," Joe said.

"The Governor thinks it is."

"The Governor is an idiot. I think we've already proven that."

Joe had known Governor Stone since Jackson was a

boy. A spoiled brat then, and a spoiled brat now. His father was a great Governor. A kind man. How had things turned out so wrong?

"He has the best intentions. I believe that. Even if his methods are horrible sometimes."

"That's an understatement. He was going to execute Private Flores publicly. That's sick, Carol."

"It wouldn't be the first time."

"And that makes it okay?"

"I didn't say that. Never mind. I think the exhaustion is making us both a little testy."

"Yeah, that's probably it. Sorry, love."

Carol kissed his cheek. "I forgive you. I'm sorry too." She stood up straight, squeezing his shoulder. "But you should get some rest. That inverter isn't going anywhere."

"Yes, ma'am," Joe said. He stood up and turned off his work light. He was supposed to be sleeping. He had snuck the inverter home to work on it without any of the other engineers knowing.

They moved out of the spare bedroom of their cube. The room was usually reserved for any children they might have had, but Joe and Carol were never able to conceive. It was painful for a time, but acceptance had followed, and then it had become a shared workspace.

It was right next to the master bedroom, which Carol pulled Joe into. Joe glanced outside through the window beside the bed. It looked out at South Park to the south and the Governor's Mansion to the east, offering a high-end view reserved for the most important people in the city. As a pair of engineers, Joe and Carol were overqualified for that status.

There was little action from the strands below. In fact, as he stared down at them, he realized they were empty.

"Carol, where is everybody?" he asked.

"What do you mean?"

"Look."

She joined him at the window. "Oh. That's strange. It's only four o'clock."

"Well, everything's been a little strange since we landed. I hope Stone's having a good time skinny-dipping with his wife while we're slaving away in here."

Carol punched him in the arm. "Joe, I doubt Governor Stone even knows what that is. I'm surprised you do."

"You never went to Block Thirty-two when you were a kid?" Joe asked. "You never went to the Watering Hole?"

One of the residents had managed to build a basin on the rooftop that caught the water from the atmospherics. It took about a month for the pool to fill, but when it did he had invited all the neighborhood kids to come swim. The only problem was he wasn't supposed to have a pool on the roof, so they couldn't get their clothes wet. It had seemed innocent to Joe as a ten-year-old boy, and nothing had ever happened to any of the kids as far as he knew.

"No. I think that was before my time."

"It's probably better that way."

"Take off your shirt and lie down. I want you asleep in the next five minutes."

"Okay, Boss," Joe said, grabbing his shirt and pulling it over his head. "Are you going to cuddle up?"

"Maybe."

Joe smiled. "Do I need to convince you?"

"Maybe."

He reached out for Carol, but she danced away.

"You need to be quicker than that, old man."

He laughed and rushed toward her, getting his hand on her arm. He pulled her close without resistance.

Someone knocked on the door.

"That's strange," Carol said. People didn't usually

knock on their door. If they needed either one of them, they used the comms.

"Could be a neighbor tired of us making so much noise," Joe said, laughing. They were hardly ever in their cube, and even then they spent most of their time either working or sleeping.

"I'll get it," Carol said. "You lie down."

"Okay, okay. I'll wait for you."

Carol left the room, making the short trip to the door and pulling it open.

"Sheriff Zane?" Joe heard her say. "What brings you here?"

Chapter 17

"Is Joe here?" Zane asked. His voice was tense. "It's very important."

"I'm here," Joe said, coming out of the bedroom. "Come on in, Sheriff."

Carol moved aside to let Zane in.

"I'm sorry to bother you, Joe. I know you've been working like a dog. I just got off the comm with the Governor."

"How's he doing on the other side?" Joe asked.

"To be honest, things aren't going well." Zane waved his hand as if to dismiss all of the problems. "I'll keep it simple, Joe. I know Sergeant Card asked you to safeguard the energy unit. It turns out the Governor needs it."

"Huh?" Joe said. "Needs it for what?"

"I'm not at liberty to say," Zane replied. "He asked me to come get you so you can get me the unit. I don't suppose you have it here?"

"No," Joe lied without missing a beat. "It isn't here. I left it in the secured storage area in Engineering."

Zane's expression changed. The sheriff bit his lower

lip. "Are you sure, Joe? I know you haven't been sleeping much. You may have forgotten you brought it home?"

Sheriff Zane knew he was lying. Joe swallowed hard. "What's going on, Sheriff? And I mean, what's really going on? There's nothing Jackson can do with the unit out there. It would just be a big paperweight for him."

"He needs it, Joe. That's all."

Joe looked at Carol. She shook her head slightly. Something was up and neither of them liked it.

"I can't give it to you," Joe said. "Not without knowing. It's dangerous in the wrong hands. You have to know that."

"I do." Sheriff Zane's hand drifted toward his sidearm. It wasn't a standard issue Law revolver. It was a VP-5 from the armory. "But that's what the Governor wants. Don't make this hard, Joe. You're a valuable part of the community."

"Are you threatening my husband?" Carol snarled. "How dare you."

Sheriff Zane's eyes passed back and forth between the two of them. A bead of sweat ran down his brow. He was too nervous.

"What the hell is going on, Sheriff?" Joe asked.

"Fine," Zane replied. "The city is under siege."

"What?" Joe said. He pointed to the window. "Nothing is going on out there."

"I know. We've got everybody back to their cubes. The Governor was attacked outside the city. We lost fifty DDF soldiers already."

"Geez," Carol said.

"What about the seals?"

"The Governor closed the seals. It held them back for about ten seconds. They cracked the programming and opened them right back up."

"Who?"

"The Governor called them the Inahri . I don't know. They're keeping a low profile in engineering. The Governor says if we do what they say and give them the unit, they'll leave us alone and nobody else gets hurt."

Joe laughed. "Are you kidding? What assurance do we have of that?"

"They gave their word."

"They speak English?"

"Apparently."

Joe shook his head. "This is ridiculous. You do realize the energy unit is a near limitless power source? What do you think an alien race that's already threatening our lives might do with something like that?"

"It isn't my call, Joe. It isn't yours either. The Governor needs it. He made the deal. We give up the unit, or they come into the city and find it themselves."

Joe stared at the sheriff. Their eyes met, facing off in silence. Joe wasn't a young man. He was five years away from retirement or would have been before the Deliverance landed. It would be easy to turn over the unit and hope for the best. It would be easy to go back to bed and maybe wake up in the morning. Or maybe not.

He blew out a stream of air, trying to release some of the tension. "If Stone hadn't framed the Guardians for something they never did, we might not be in this mess."

"I keep hearing that allegation. I haven't seen any proof."

"I was there, Kevin. I know what I heard."

"It doesn't change anything."

"It changes everything."

Zane finally looked away. "Look, are you going to give me the energy unit, or do I have to do something I don't want to do? They didn't give us all day to meet their demands."

"And what would that something be?" Carol asked. "Are you going to shoot us, Kevin? Are you going to kill the next two most valuable people in the city after Sergeant Card and his team? Do you really aim to screw things up even more than you already have?"

"I don't want to die, Carol," the sheriff said. "That's a pretty strong motivation."

"They're going to kill you anyway. Or take you away for something else. I guarantee it. Don't be an idiot."

Sheriff Zane's hand slid to his sidearm. He wrapped it around the handle, beginning to pull it up. "Please don't make me do this."

"Go to Hell, Kevin," Joe said. "You're going to have to shoot us to get the unit. If you can find it."

"I guess I will," Zane said, drawing the weapon and pointing it at Joe.

Carol grabbed a pan from the counter, moving quickly. Sheriff Zane pivoted toward her as she swung it, the metal smashing him in the face at the same time the VP-5 discharged.

Joe's entire world collapsed.

The round hit Carol in the chest, powerful enough to go right through, expanding the damage on the way out. She stumbled back as blood hit the back of the cube behind her, along with the slug. Zane fell back too, nose broken, face bloody. He collapsed onto the floor at the same time Carol did.

"No," Joe said, rushing to his wife's side. "No, no, no, no, no. Carol!" He fell to his knees beside her, leaning over. "Carol!"

There was no time for a loving goodbye.

She was already gone.

"Nooooo!" Joe shouted, tears streaming from his eyes. "Damn you, Kevin. Damn you, Jackson." He looked down at his beautiful wife. He couldn't believe it. Everything had happened so fast.

He looked back at Zane, and then to the VP-5 on the ground beside him. The man was unconscious. That would be easy too.

The LED on his badge turned green.

"Sheriff, are you there?" Governor Stone said. "Sheriff Zane? Report. Did you get it?"

Joe stood up. He didn't have time to mourn his wife. She hadn't died so that asshole could get the energy unit anyway.

He stepped over Zane and rushed to his workshop, pushing the false back away from his desk and revealing a small storage space. He opened it and grabbed the containment box the active unit was resting in. Then he went back to where the sheriff was prone on his floor. He picked up the VP-5 and took the badge from the sheriff's collar, sparing one more look for his wife.

"I'm sorry," he said. He could barely manage the pain, except through his sudden and desperate need to get the energy unit as far away from Metro as he could.

The Deliverance was a big ship, and he had been through a lot of it over the past week. He wasn't sure what was going to happen next. Maybe the aliens would kill everyone in Metro. It wouldn't get them what they wanted. Maybe Sergeant Card would find his way back. Sheriff Dante at least.

It didn't matter. They had just killed Carol. They had murdered his precious bride. Screw them. They were never getting their power source, no matter what. Not as long as he was still drawing breath.

He spit on Sheriff Zane and then headed out of his cube into the hallway.

He knew exactly where he was going to hide.

Chapter 18

"Sheriff Zane," Jackson said for the fourth time, trying to get the sheriff to reply.

"Is there a problem?" Sergeant Harai asked.

Jackson looked at the Inahri leader, his throat tight. "My man isn't responding."

"That sounds like a problem."

"I'll handle it."

"You will."

Jackson swallowed hard. He was standing in the middle of Engineering Control. Sergeant Harai rested on one of the chairs in a confident, relaxed posture, his eyes lowered like he was half asleep. For all the urgency they had put on him to retrieve the QDM, the man hardly seemed to be in a hurry.

"I need to go to Metro," Jackson said. "I need to go to Law myself, round up some deputies and find out what happened."

The last thing Zane had said was that he was inside the Kings' block, headed up to their cube. Jackson knew Joe was the last one to handle the quantum dimensional modulator. He had been slightly worried the engineer wouldn't be too quick to hand it over. After all, Joe knew he had lied about the Guardians, and he was the kind of man who didn't take kindly to any manner of deceit.

He didn't expect that Joe might have actually hurt a sheriff.

"Corporal Nan will go with you," Harai said, pointing to one of his soldiers. The man stepped forward.

"No offense, but I thought you were trying to keep things calm? Sending one of your men into the city will not keep things calm."

"The streets should be clear, should they not?" Harai asked.

Those were the orders he had given to Law. To enforce a curfew and get everyone off the streets. He was sure the soldiers who had escaped earlier told their families what was happening. Word was going to get out sooner or later. But Harai wanted to remain away from the city. QDM first. New subjects for Arluthu after.

"Yes, but we still have windows," Jackson said.

"Watch your tone, Earther," Harai snapped. "I don't need you as much as you need me."

"My apologies," Jackson said, face flushing. "I didn't mean to offend."

"Besides, no one will think anything is out of the ordinary. Nan, remove your armor."

"Yes, Sergeant," Nan said. Two other soldiers moved in to help the corporal out of his battle armor.

Jackson saw the man was wearing a seamless black suit beneath it. He watched in amazement as Nan raised the bodysuit over his head, completely obscuring himself with it. Then he tapped a small device on his wrist and instantly became a perfect replica of Beth Stone.

"Uh," Jackson said. It was all he could manage to say.

"Axon technology. The suit is made from the outer shell of a Basic Intellect. We modified it for Inahri use. Impressive, no?"

"Y-yes," Jackson stammered.

"Nan has no Advocate and will be unable to speak to you. His role is only to make sure your loyalties remain with Arluthu. Do you understand?"

"Yes, Sergeant," Jackson said.

"Good. Now go and find my modulator. Dismissed."

Jackson swallowed again, unable to clear the lump in his throat. He turned to the exit, Nan coming to join him at his side. The Inahri soldier reached out for his hand like his wife would. He had no choice but to take it.

They made their way through the engineering corridors to the South Park entrance into Metro. The strands were empty, the city quiet despite the early hour. Jackson looked over to the block across from his mansion, finding Joe King's window. The light was on, but he didn't see any hint of movement inside.

He walked briskly, his legs shaking beneath him. This was all too much to take. Beyond his fear for his life and the lives of his people, he was worried about the real Beth. Had Doctor Rathbone gotten her out of her shock?

He went directly to the Law Office with Nan at his side, keeping a grip on his hand. All of the heads in the office lifted when he entered, and then the sheriffs and deputies each fell to a knee in respect.

"Stand up," Stone said. He made a quick visual of the room. There weren't that many officers here. Most were still out enforcing the curfew. "Bashir, Wilks, Chen, I need you."

The three deputies came right over. "Governor?"

"I sent Sheriff Zane to Joe King's cube. He isn't responding to his badge."

"Sir, you think Joe did something to him?" Bashir asked.

"That's crazy," Chen said.

"We need to find out," Jackson replied. "Follow me."

The deputies followed him out of the office. It was a short walk to Joe's block.

"Governor." A woman ran up to them when they entered. Jackson knew her as a nurse at the hospital. "You heard?" she asked, noticeably distraught.

"Heard what?" Jackson replied.

"I heard a gunshot and then a pair of hard thuds that shook my ceiling. Isn't that why you're here?" she asked, looking with concern from Jackson to Nan.

Nan nodded. "Yes, it is." He waved his deputies toward the lifts. "Come on, let's hurry."

They took the first one to open all the way up to the thirtieth floor. The Kings' floor. Zane stumbled out of Joe's apartment just as Jackson and the deputies ran down the corridor toward him..

"What the hell?" Jackson said, noticing all the blood on the sheriff's face, and the sad state of his nose.

"Carol knocked me with a pan," Zane replied, his voice muffled from the damage. "I shot her. Oh, Governor. I shot her. It was an accident. I didn't mean to."

Zane was almost crying he was so distraught.

"Where's Joe?" Jackson asked. "Where's the QDM?"

"Joe's gone. He probably took it with him."

"Why didn't he give it to you?"

"He doesn't trust you, sir. Not after what happened with the Guardians."

Jackson growled under his breath. "Did you tell him why I wanted it?"

Zane looked at the floor. "I did. He said the aliens are

going to kill us anyway as soon as they get what they want."

"They aren't."

"How do you know that for sure, sir?"

"They promised to take us in. To give us a home." Of course, that wasn't entirely true. They wanted a number of the male citizens for combat and the women for cross-breeding. It was still better than death.

"What kind of home?"

"With them. What does it matter? We get the damned QDM, or we die. Do you understand that?"

"Sir?" Bashir said behind him.

Jackson spun around. "Don't question me, Deputy. Do as I say, or you'll be the next person who gets shot."

Bashir paled in response. "Y-yes, Governor."

Jackson turned back to Zane. "We need to find Joe. How long ago did he leave?"

"I think I was out at least five minutes," Zane said.

"So he has a five to ten-minute head start. Sheriff, get everyone in Law looking for him, and then make your way to the hospital to get that face of yours looked at."

"Yes, sir," Zane said.

"The rest of you, let's go."

Chapter 19

"I don't know what's taking them so long," Caleb said.

He was lying on his rack at the top of the winding bunks, staring up at the smooth stone ceiling. Two hours had passed since Sergeant Tsi had brought him back to the barracks. He had quickly debriefed the others on his meeting with General Goi before grabbing a little sleep.

The mattress was comfortable, but not too comfortable. It let him relax, but didn't allow for deep sleep, and now he was starting to get restless.

"It shouldn't be a hard decision," he continued. "It's a problem for them if the Relyeh get the QDM. The QDM is on the Deliverance. We know the ship better than they do, and we want to keep the Hunger from it too. It's simple logic."

"Not so simple for them," Washington said. His voice was getting less raspy with each word he uttered, the fabric around his neck adjusting to him. "They're the rebels on this planet. Guerillas. They can't rush headlong into anything."

"True," Caleb agreed. "But they could let us rush

headlong into it. Give us some gear and set us loose. I'm more than willing to ally with them. Instead, they insist on keeping us prisoner here and forcing us to earn our keep."

"But they won't let us do it the best way we can," Dante said.

"Frustrating," Paige said.

"Agreed," Caleb replied, letting out a soft sigh. "It would be nice if Tsi would at least come back and tell us what the hell is going on."

"I don't think they think they owe us anything, Sergeant," Kiaan said.

"Also true," Caleb agreed. "But they say they respect me for standing up against impossible odds instead of running, but they don't think we can run this mission. Is that it?"

"We don't know they think that," Washington said. "Not until they come back."

"If they come back," Paige said. "I feel like we're going to rot in here. The gruel isn't bad, but I don't want to live on it."

"Roger that," Washington said.

Caleb closed his eyes again. He would have thought after the last couple of weeks he would appreciate a little downtime. Instead, it was leaving him antsy. He knew now that Metro was in trouble. As long as he was here, he wasn't there to help. He wasn't doing his job.

He sat up, dangling his legs over the side and hopping down. "Huddle up," he said, calling the Guardians to him. Pai walked over too.

"Pai, how about you go stand over there?" Caleb suggested, pointing to the corner near the door.

"How can I hear your requests from over there?" the robot replied.

"Go." Pai did as it was ordered. It didn't have a choice.

The Guardians gathered close to Caleb. He spoke softly. "We may need to break out of here."

"Do you think we can?" Kiaan asked. "There's a lot of Inahri here, and they're all soldiers."

"I know. I'm not saying it will be easy. But we need to start coming up with a plan. What do we have, and what do we know?"

"What we don't have is any weapons," Washington said.

"And nothing we could use as a weapon," Paige said. "Unless you want to try to beat through battle armor with a spoon."

"Okay, but what do we have?" Caleb asked.

The Guardians were silent. It wasn't an easy question. They didn't have much.

"We have your arm," Washington said. "How's the charge?"

Caleb reached over with his left hand, tapping the control ring. Two bars lit up. "Twenty percent."

Washington shook his head. "Not great."

"No. If I could touch a QDM, I'd be back to full strength in an instant." He paused. "But that is one thing we have."

"You have Sergeant Tsi's respect," Kiaan offered.

Washington laughed. "What's he going to do with that?"

Kiaan's face turned red and he shrugged. "I don't know."

"We know the Inahri value bravery," Dante said. "We also know they treat prisoners well. And I don't think they want to *not* trust us. I think they're open to bringing new people into the fold, or we wouldn't be here, cleaned and fed, and Washington wouldn't have his voice back."

"Good points," Caleb said. "Anything else?"

"We're on trial," Dante continued. "Only it isn't really us. It's you, Sarge. We're your underlings. Like extra appendages."

"You know," Washington said. "That makes me think."

"What's cooking, Wash?" Caleb asked.

"Maybe Kiian's onto something."

"*I am?*"

"The Inahri are in hiding here, right? Which means they don't go out all that much, and if they do they probably try to keep a low profile. But they can't spare the resources to wait weeks for someone on trial to prove themselves. In which case they'd have to organize something."

Caleb smiled. "I think I know what you're getting at. The center of the compound is empty, and roughly in the shape of a circle. When you've got limited space, does it make sense to waste it like that?"

"Unless they aren't wasting it," Dante said.

"Exactly. I think they use it for trials."

"What kind of trials?" Kiaan asked.

"Hand-to-hand combat, maybe? I guess it would depend on the value a prisoner is trying to bring to the community."

"What does that have to do with Sergeant Tsi?"

"I'm going to challenge her to a fight," Caleb said. "To prove we're worthy."

"That might work," Paige said. "There's only one problem."

Caleb looked back to the door. "Pai, come here."

The robot walked back to them. "How can I help you, Sergeant?"

"Can you go out to Private Gol, and tell him I want to challenge Sergeant Tsi to combat? Tell him to tell her I want to prove myself and my team right now because if there's any question about us going back to our ship, I want to take it out of the equation."

"As you ask, I will do," Pai said. "One moment."

The robot walked back to the door and opened it. Caleb could hear it speaking quietly to Gol in Inahrai . Gol turned to look into the barracks, and Caleb could swear he saw a smirk on the guard's face.

Pai returned, closing the door behind him. "He is telling her."

"Now what?" Kiian asked.

"Now we wait," Caleb replied.

Chapter 20

The Guardians didn't wait long.

Sergeant Tsi entered the barracks in a hurry, her face taut with tension and simmering anger. The Guardians were sitting at the table near the front of the space, and she moved to the empty space opposite Caleb and slammed her fist down on it.

"What do you think you're doing?" she hissed, the Intellect struggling to catch up to her and translating on the move.

"I told you, Sergeant," Caleb replied. "I need to get back to my ship. I'm not letting the race that destroyed Earth get off this planet. Not if there's anything I can do to stop it. I'm also not going to let them decimate my people."

"I asked you to be patient."

"I gave you two hours. The Relyeh Inahri may have destroyed Metro in that time."

"They haven't. We have Dancers in the area. The Inahri have entered the ship, but there is no indication of continued violence."

"Are they in the ship, Sergeant?"

"No. They have sensors that will register discharge from our energy weapons."

"What if they aren't using energy weapons?"

Sergeant Tsi didn't respond to that question because she didn't know.

"Regardless, Caleb," she said. "The Relyeh are moving on the Seeker. They know the Intellects are dead, and they're aiming to take the ship, to be ready when the modulator is recovered."

Caleb stared at her without responding right away. He let go of the defensiveness. "What are you going to do about it?"

"We were discussing it when I was interrupted to come and deal with you," Tsi said. "We can't allow the Relyeh access to the Seeker. We have to send units there." She shook her head. "I don't know if they will be enough. The R'leyh badly outnumber us."

"We can help."

"I know you can. And if you had remained patient, I might have gotten you what you wanted. Now?"

"I don't understand. All I did was challenge you to a fight. To prove our worth."

Tsi shook her head. "Ah, Caleb. You know nothing of our ways, yet you try to use them to your benefit? You have no idea."

"Why don't you tell us, Sergeant?" Washington said.

"I'm your sponsor, Caleb. I'm not permitted to fight you. I'm too invested."

"Okay. So if I can't fight, we don't have a problem."

"I didn't say you can't fight."

"Another soldier, then? I'm not a greenie."

"I don't know what that is, but your cocky attitude is

going to get you into even more trouble if you aren't careful."

"I think it's already too late for that," Dante said.

"You might have gotten what you wanted if you had simply waited another hour," Tsi said. "Now you have to fight. None of us have a choice in the matter."

Caleb sat back in his chair. "Okay. If I have to fight, then I'll fight. When?"

"Right now."

"Now?"

"Yes. We're on the verge of a direct confrontation like we haven't seen since we overthrew the Axon. A confrontation your arrival caused."

"You can't blame us for that," Paige said. "We didn't know."

"No, you didn't. And I don't blame you. It was bound to come to this sooner or later. In a sense, we're fortunate to have Earthers instead of more Relyeh or Axon. But your weakness leaves us in a difficult spot."

"Weakness?" Dante said. "I think we're holding up pretty well, all things considered."

"Dante," Caleb said in warning. She closed her mouth, sitting back and crossing her arms. "Look, we have the same enemy. We should be on the same side."

"I agree," Tsi said. "As does General Goi. Some of the other Esteemed aren't as sure, but they don't have final say."

"Thank goodness for that," Washington said.

"So we can skip the challenge," Caleb said. "Forget I mentioned it. We have work to do."

"I wish it were that simple," Tsi replied. "That isn't possible now."

There was a knock on the door.

"I'll get it," Pai said, hurrying to open it.

Two of Tsi's soldiers entered the barracks. One was carrying a suit of combat armor. The other was holding a bodysuit made of too-familiar dark fabric and a pair of objects that looked like metal rods.

"Corporal Kizi and Private Awak will help you prepare," Tsi said.

Caleb stood up, still eying the equipment the two Inahri soldiers had brought in. "What is this stuff?"

"That is the skin of an Intellect," Tsi said, pointing to the smaller bodysuit. "Modified for our needs. The other is our standard battle armor. Very strong and durable. The two rods are what we call xix. Private Awak, please demonstrate."

Awak put the Intellect skin onto one of the hooks on the wall. Then he turned and held out the two rods, pressing on something to activate them.

The length of the rods started to glow blue. When Awak tapped them together, sparks flew away from them, and as he spread them out, lines of blue energy like lightning arced between them.

"In open combat, you can throw the energy toward your opponent. You can also use it as a defensive shield, depending on how you weave the energy along the rod surfaces."

"Cool," Paige said.

"The benefit of the xix for trial is that it can be set to non-lethal levels."

Caleb nodded. It was an impressive weapon, but he had a feeling it took a lot of practice to use it effectively. "The Intellect skin. What do you mean, modified?"

"It was designed for interface with the Intellect's nodes. We introduced an underlying web of thin wires connected to engineered nodules. It shares many of the properties of the Basic Intellect, only much less durable. Having the wires severed in the wrong place can disable the entire skin."

"But they work together? The armor and the skin?"

"No. You must choose which of these you prefer. The battle armor is more powerful and durable, but less agile and dynamic. The Skin has some other advantages, but we've found they often balance one another out, depending on the skill of the wearer with each."

"It would help to know who I'm fighting before I decide," Caleb said. "If it's someone fast, I'll go fast. If they're brute, I'll go brute."

"I'm sorry, Caleb. That is not possible. You do not know who your opponent will be. Your opponent does not know who you will be."

"Do you have other prisoners on trial here?" Caleb asked.

"We have one," Tsi said.

"Are they small and fast or big and strong?" Washington asked.

"I can't tell you anything else. You will choose your armor. Then you will have a short time to acquaint yourself to the xix. Then you will fight." She smiled. "I know you will do us both great honor, Caleb."

Something was unsettling about Tsi's expression. There was something she wouldn't or couldn't say that she knew he wasn't going to like.

Who was this opponent anyway?

Chapter 21

There was no privacy in the Inahri barracks, which meant there was no big reveal when Caleb decided on an approach for his trial. He spent a couple of minutes considering the two options before settling on the Intellect Skin.

The battle armor was tempting because he had seen how it could absorb damage. But ultimately he decided that between what he had seen of the Basic Intellect's capabilities and his unique possession of an Axon alloy arm, it gave him the best balance of strength and speed to handle pretty much any opponent.

The Skin was exactly as advertised, especially in the sense that it was a second skin. All of his clothes had to come off to get into it, and when he pulled it on, he could feel it shrink against him. He had never been into Speedos, but the Skin hugged him similarly. It might have been embarrassing if the stakes weren't so high.

Otherwise, it was much, much more comfortable than he expected. It kept him warm, it breathed well, and it allowed him a full range of motion without any resistance.

He ran through a quick series of punches and kicks in it, satisfied that he could move as well as anyone. His ankle was still a bit tender from the damage it had taken during the landing of the ship, but Doc Brom's work had healed it well, and the Skin seemed to support it even better.

"What else can it do?" he asked Sergeant Tsi.

All of the Inahri present had watched him change into the Skin with a heavy dose of curiosity. They were both human, but their evolutionary branches had diverged thousands of years ago. The Inahri were smaller framed, lithe and nimble. He was lean but muscled, and years of fighting trife had left him in better shape than when he had been a Marine Raider. It left him with more tone than he could identify on any of the Inahri. While he hadn't seen any of them unclothed, the way the robes and tunics sat on them suggested they were built more like long-distance runners.

"Pull the mantle over your head," Tsi replied.

It was resting on the back of his neck. He lifted it, stretching the material over the top of his head, drawing a laugh from the Inahri.

"All the way over," Tsi said. "Down to your chest."

"Over my face?" Caleb asked.

"Yes."

He grabbed the edge and pulled it over and down toward his chest. He was surprised that it was able to stretch that far. He was equally surprised when it connected to the opening for his head and stuck, pulling tight across his nose and covering his mouth. He was grateful to discover he could still breath as though it wasn't there at all, and he gasped when the Skin's HUD activated in front of him.

It wasn't like the Marine combat armor HUD, showing flat marks that followed targets on a transparent screen, keeping a clear separation between the HUD and the world beyond. It was augmented reality, casting data out to where it was needed, positioning it perfectly to keep his vision clear and still provide information about both his surroundings and the Skin itself.

"Wow," he said. The Skin marked Tsi with a green outline, showing small, alien symbols over her head that moved with her. "Does it know English?"

The symbols changed as he said it, as though the Skin was reading his mind. Tsi laughed, already aware of how the technology would adjust.

"Yes, it is reading your mind," she said. "Think of a shield, a disc on your arm."

He imagined he had a shield against his forearm. He didn't feel a change, but when he glanced down at his arm, there was a blue disc of energy filling out part of it as a shield.

"This is crazy," he said.

"I don't see anything," Dante said.

"Me neither," Paige added.

"It's visible through the mantle," Caleb said. "It's composed of energy." He turned to Washington. "Try to hit me."

"Are you sure, Sarge?" Washington replied.

"Yeah. Come on, big guy. Try to hit me."

Washington threw a hard punch. Caleb barely got the shield up in time, catching the blow. He barely even felt the impact, but he did notice the energy intensify along it.

"The Skin's shields will absorb kinetic energy to help power the system," Tsi said. "By attacking an Intellect, we help keep it charged. We were never able to defeat them until we created the disruptors."

"The anti-Intellect gun?" Paige said.

"Yes. A disruptor will render the Skin non-functional.

It is not a worry for the trial. The opponent will only have xix."

"They developed the disabling waveform in response?" Caleb asked.

"Yes. The disruptors would shut down before we could get near them. We were working on the algorithm, but it is an order of magnitude more complex than the original neural disruption waveform."

"Does the Suit have any weapons?"

"It can normally activate a few focused energy weapons, like blades. A Basic Intellect will expand itself to create a physical edge to go with it, as it is more effective against the battle armor. The weapon systems are disabled for the trial. Only xix are permitted."

"And I'm guessing the shields won't help much against them?"

"You are a quick learner, Caleb. The shields will help you against secondary attacks. The Skin itself will absorb some of the damage from the xix and convert it to stored energy."

"Fair enough. Is there anything else I should know about the suit?"

"It's advanced sensors will, in many cases, give you warning of incoming attacks before they occur, though it is not always able to detect them in time. That is where the agility of the Skin becomes valuable. While a strike will hurt, you will be more difficult to strike in the first place."

"I like the sound of that."

"There is one other property of the Skin, it probably won't help you in the trial, but it is worth learning. Look at one of your people and think about capturing their likeness. Not Washington, though. He's too big."

Caleb turned to Kiaan, imagining he was taking a

picture of him. A light came out of the top of the mantle, quickly scanning over the pilot.

"Now think about your appearance matching his," Tsi said.

Caleb did as Tsi said. A red light flashed on his HUD, but that was the only indication anything was happening.

"What the heck?" Kiaan said.

"Whoa," Paige said.

"What is it?" Caleb asked. His words drew a new reaction.

"That's incredible," Dante said.

"And messed up," Washington added.

"What is it?" Caleb repeated.

"You look just like me," Kiaan said. "You sound just like me too."

"It's a three-dimensional projection," Tsi said. "Placed millimeters from the Skin. The scan takes into account bone structure, palate, vocal chord length, and thousands of other factors to produce an identical change to your voice through the membrane over your mouth."

Caleb reminded himself the Axon were hundreds of thousands of years ahead of humans in terms of technology. They had already been through the artificial intelligence singularity and had come out the other side. What he thought was unbelievable, they had called basic.

"How do I turn it off?" he asked.

"You just did," Washington replied.

"Corporal Kizi," Tsi said. "The xix."

The corporal came forward with the two rods, handing them out to Caleb. He took them, holding one in each hand and getting a feel for their weight.

"Put pressure on the handles to activate them," Tsi said.

Caleb gripped the rods a little tighter. The energy formed along the length of them.

"Tap them together and pull them away to create a web."

He did as she said, marveling at the arcs of energy that passed from one to the next.

"To weave, turn the rods around one another. Don't be concerned if you struggle with it. The xix are unique to our camp, and your opponent's experience with them will be equally limited."

Caleb turned the rods around one another, watching how the lines of energy seemed to take on a spider-web like quality as he did. It didn't take long for him to get them tangled such that the arcs held the two rods only inches away from one another.

"Tap them together to deactivate the web," Tsi suggested.

He did and started over again.

"My grandma used to knit all the time," Washington said. "She taught me when I was a kid."

"You know how to crochet?" Caleb said.

"What? You think that isn't masculine?"

"No judgment intended."

"Gimme the sticks."

Caleb handed them to Washington. He tapped them together, and quickly made a net with the energy, offering Caleb a smile of superiority.

"Show off," Caleb said.

"I always knew learning to knit would come in handy someday. I can also make beanies and sweaters. I can teach you, Sarge."

"There isn't enough time," Tsi said. "We only have a few more minutes."

Washington handed the xix back to Caleb, who spent a

couple more minutes toying with the weapon. He managed to make a simple web, thick enough that it could probably block an attack.

"Don't do it in here, but if you flick one of the xix toward your opponent, it will send the energy out at them like a whip."

Caleb could sense how that would happen based on the feel of the weapon. "Roger that, Sergeant."

Corporal Kizi spoke to her in Inahrai. She nodded.

"It's time."

Chapter 22

Tsi and her squad led Caleb and the Guardians out of the barracks. Caleb lowered the mantle as they left the building, feeling slightly self-conscious as they moved across the compound. It seemed all of the Inahri in the community had heard about the challenge already, and they had all dropped whatever they were doing to come and watch.

There were dozens of them in the street, and they stopped and moved aside to let their group through, staring at Caleb on the way past. He wasn't only interesting because he was on trial. He was an Earther. An alien to them. A visitor many of the Inahri had yet to learn were on their world. They gawked at him as he passed, pointing and commenting.

He felt a little less self-conscious when he realized more of the attention was going to Washington. Not only was the other Marine bigger and broader than Caleb, his skin was also darker than any of the Inahri they had seen so far, and the Inahri fabric around his neck only served to make him more interesting. A few of the Inahri tried to touch him on the way past, drawing angry barks from Tsi and her soldiers and forcing them to step back.

Washington smiled at the attention, seeming to enjoy it.

It took a few minutes for the entourage to cross to the center of the compound. There were already hundreds of Inahri there, in a sea of green uniforms and blue and purple robes. They gathered in organized chaos, calm and polite to one another, finding a position to see the proceedings and giving way to allow others a spot. A set of rafters had appeared on top of the guarded building in front of the CIC, and Caleb noticed General Goi and the other Esteemed perched on it, awaiting the trial.

"Is there always a crowd like this?" Caleb asked.

"No," Tsi replied. "But you are special."

"Because I'm from another planet?"

"Yes."

"But you already knew about Earth, even though we didn't know about you?"

"Yes. But none of us had seen a live Earther before today. With your level of technology, we never expected you would come to us."

"How come you never came to Earth?"

"It is illegal to interfere with any species before they have developed the technology to discover their place in the universe on their own."

"Didn't the Axon interfere by taking your ancestors from Earth?"

"If that is how we came to be, then that would be a violation of the laws. But the Axon wrote the laws."

"Meaning they're allowed to break them?" Caleb laughed. It seemed some things were true no matter the species or the planet. "I can relate."

Tsi brought them to a stop on the east side of the rough circle, where a small area was reserved for them. A similar space was reserved on the west side, though Caleb's opponent had yet to arrive.

"What are the rules for this?" Caleb asked.

"No fighting outside the circle," Tsi replied. "If you get pushed out, the trial is reset. No deaths. If you kill your opponent, you will also be executed."

"What about injuring them?"

"As long as it is not immediately fatal, we can treat most injuries."

"Any other rules?"

"No."

"So in terms of the fight itself, anything goes?"

"Yes."

"Roger that."

They reached the side of the circle. There were no lines to mark the area, leaving Caleb to assume as long as they weren't in the crowd they were in play. It was a large space, close to a quarter-kilometer around, maybe a little more. Plenty of room to maneuver and fight.

"Also, be careful not to hit a bystander with the xix," Tsi said. "That will also lead to failure of the trial."

Caleb nodded. "Understood."

He heard a controlled commotion on the other side of the open ring, turning his attention to the opposite area. His opponent was moving into their space. They were wearing Inahri battle armor, marked with a black cross to show they were in trial. Their helmet was on, face concealed behind an opaque plate.

"Why is their faceplate opaque?" he asked.

"We have had trials where Inahri have battled their sibling. This prevents them from knowing who their opponent is."

"They can see me."

"Only because you removed your mantle."

Caleb grabbed it and pulled it back on. Not that who he was probably meant anything to the Relyeh defector.

"Does the loser of the trial lose their place in the community?" Caleb asked.

"No. The outcome isn't as important as the challenge."

Caleb didn't expect to lose, but it was good to know how he looked out there was more important.

He looked across the circle again. His opponent was holding their xix, ready for the trial. He realized now how much he had given away by choosing the Intellect Skin. His size and gender and the fact that he wasn't Inahri. But maybe that last one would make his adversary nervous. He was confident they had never fought an Earther before.

There was no fanfare leading to the trial. No announcement from General Goi. Tsi squeezed his shoulder and leaned in toward him. "Go ahead."

He glanced at her and then back at his opponent, who was moving into the ring.

"Good luck, Sarge," Dante said.

"Kick his ass, Sarge," Washington said.

"You can do it," Paige said.

"Good hunting," Kiaan said.

Caleb stepped into the circle. The crowd of Inahri fell silent, quickly leaving the echo of his opponent's heavier feet as the only sound in the compound.

They walked toward one another, closing the gap. Caleb tapped his xix together, activating them. His challenger did the same.

Showtime.

Chapter 23

Caleb intended to take measure of his opponent. To circle them in a battle-ready crouch and take quick shots to see how they reacted.

His rival never gave him a chance. They charged forward, taking three quick steps and launching into the air, quickly creating a web of energy between the xix and flicking it out toward him. Caleb's Intellect Skin flashed a warning a split-second ahead of the attack by placing a white outline around the xix, to which Caleb reacted too slowly. The energy lash snapped into his xix, sending a shower of sparks up from it and knocking one of them out of his hand.

"Shit," Caleb cursed, rolling away as his opponent's battle armored feet came down in front of where he had been standing. He got to his feet, surprised to find his opponent had already pivoted to follow him and was in the middle of a hard punch. Caleb barely got his weight shifted to take the blow off his shoulder before he was hit hard enough to go reeling backward.

He let himself fall again, tumbling onto his back and

somersaulting back to his feet, his momentum still taking him in the wrong direction. The challenger threw another lash of energy from their xix. Caleb heeded the warning of the Skin more quickly this time, still moving backward and bouncing to his left to get his footing and digging in. He found his other xix a few meters behind the oncoming battle armor and shifted his remaining rod from his right hand to his left.

"Come on," he said softly, crouching into a defensive stance and closing his replacement hand into a fist.

His rival didn't slow, continuing the hard charge. He moved at the last second, breaking to the left and driving his replacement hand hard into his opponent's abdomen. Metal crashed into metal, and he felt the strain of the battle armor resisting the punch, the impact throwing the armor to the side and taking him off-balance with it. He rolled in the air, twirling like an acrobat and somehow landing on his feet. The battle armor turned and hit the ground hard, sliding to a stop.

Caleb heard small murmurs through the crowd, impressed with the outcome but so much more contained than any Earth spectators would ever be. He eyed his opponent, already getting back to their feet. He had a half-second to choose between pressing the attack and going for his lost xix.

He went for the xix, sprinting across the field and bending to grab it before spinning back the other way. His battle armored challenger was up and walking toward him unhurriedly.

Caleb tapped the rods together, reactivating them. He made a quick web and threw it at his opponent. They didn't even try to evade it, letting the energy hit the armor. It left a mark on the alloy but didn't cut through.

"I chose wrong," Caleb said. His challenger was

creating a web of their own, their motions smooth, as though they had been using the weapon for years. Hadn't Tsi said his opposition had no experience with it?

He followed the Skin's warning more astutely this time, already moving by the time the lash came out at him. He dodged it easily, charging the battle armor as his challenger took two more quick strikes at him, missing both times. Caleb closed the distance, getting a feel for the Skin and becoming more confident.

Their xix met one another, moving together in a quick cadence of strikes that showered sparks all around them. They clapped together again and again, a furious dance of strikes, blocks, counterstrikes, and moves that sent them angling across the circle. The crowd seemed to sense there was something about the fight, and their excited pitch started to increase.

The melee lasted almost a minute before whomever was in the battle armor broke it off, taking a few steps back to reset. Caleb could hear the buzz among the onlookers, and he spared a glance to the Esteemed, noticing that General Goi was leaning forward with intense interest.

He put his attention back on his opponent. He didn't need to win to pass the Trial. They had already put on a good show. Probably good enough for both to get in. His challenger was skilled. Very skilled, and able to match his moves as though they knew what was coming even without an Intellect Skin. Not that it couldn't be worn beneath the armor, but wouldn't it be cheating to let his rival have both?

They faced off again, circling one another toward the center of the field. Was this former Relyeh representative of all the Relyeh soldiers? If they were, both the Deliverance and the Free Inahri were in deeper trouble than he had thought.

"Come on, Sarge!" Washington bellowed from the sidelines. "Finish him!"

Caleb smiled, turning his head toward his Vulture but keeping his attention on his opponent. They took the bait, rushing toward him to take advantage of the distraction.

Caleb let them come, dropping at the last second and thrusting forward with the xix, certain he was going to get a substantial hit on his rival.

He didn't.

Instead, the person in the battle armor slowed and shifted, a heavy foot swinging toward Caleb's head. He had only an instant to call for a shield in front of his face, fortunate that it came up in time to catch the attack. It absorbed most of the kinetic energy, but not all, the force pushing him down onto his back.

Another foot came down toward him. He got a shield up in front of it to absorb the pounding force of the blow, but it didn't do anything for the weight of the armor. It pressed down on him, pinning him to the ground while his opponent swung a xix toward his head.

Caleb threw his replacement arm at the leg, putting enough force behind it to push his assailent off him. He rolled away just in time to avoid the xix. Bouncing to his feet, he swung his xix in one smooth motion, the rod slamming hard into the faceplate of the battle armor. Energy coursed through it, and it cracked beneath the force, a pair of shards dropping away.

Caleb froze in place.

"Valentine?" he said.

Her eyes were narrowed in anger, and she hissed as she used his surprise against him, smashing his chest with an unpowered xix. The blow threw him into the air, cracking his ribs and sending him across the field. He hit the solid ground hard, coming to a stop on his stomach.

Waves of pain ran through him. What the hell was going on? Where had Riley come from? And why were the Free Inahri about to take her in?

He pushed himself up. Riley was charging him again. Rushing his position.

She had taken a ship to search for the Inahri. How had she found them here? What did she want with the Free Inahri? Had she learned they weren't the dominant race on this planet? Did she know the Relyeh were in charge?

It didn't matter right now. She was coming at him, eager to win the fight.

Over his dead body.

He pulled himself up, ignoring the pain. He stood in front of her, tapping his xix together to energize them. She was inhumanly angry. Out of control. Her transformation to a human-trife hybrid had continued, turning her into a monster.

Caleb stood strong ahead of it. He thought about a picture of Harry, Riley's dead teammate. He didn't have the exact measurements, but he was hoping just thinking of him would project some kind of likeness.

It must have, because Riley's eyes went wide in surprise, and she slowed a step or two. It was enough. Caleb drove toward her, using one xix to smack her arm out of the way, and shoving the other up beneath her arm. He shouted as he used his replacement arm to lift her off the ground with the xix, turning her and throwing her to the ground. He didn't slow from there, jumping at her and coming down on her chest, putting the end of the xix only centimeters from her face.

"Surrender!" he shouted.

She smiled in response. A primal grin that took him off-guard.

"Screw you, Card," she said.

Then something hit him in the side, hard enough that he was thrown away from her again. He hit the floor, his shoulder breaking at the impact as he came to a stop a second time. He laid there, turning his head to see Riley back on her feet and coming toward him.

"Enough!" he heard Sergeant Tsi shout nearby. Then she was standing over him, her squad with her.

For a moment, it looked like Riley wasn't going to stop. She continued marching toward him, tapping the xix together.

"I said enough," Tsi repeated. "Stand down, now!"

Caleb watched Riley's face through the broken plate. One second, it seemed wild. The next, it was almost normal. She finally came to a stop. She dropped the xix to the ground.

"Caleb. Caleb, are you okay?" Tsi asked.

Caleb tried to affirm that he was.

He passed out before he could answer.

Chapter 24

Caleb woke up in the Guardians' barracks, in his bed at the top of the rack. He remained still for a moment, nervous about trying to breathe in. He remembered the pain in his chest at the end of his fight.

Valentine.

The violence of the thought forced him to take a breath. He winced in anticipation only to find there was no pain. He exhaled, breathed in again, and shook his head.

Inahri medicine put Earther patches to shame.

"Sarge, you okay?" Washington asked.

Caleb turned his head. He couldn't help but grin when he saw Washington. The big Marine had traded his black tunic for a green one.

Then he remembered Valentine again.

He sat up. "Physically, sure," he replied, quickly scanning the room. The other Guardians were nearby, all of them rising to go to him. "Where's Tsi?"

"Not here," Dante said. "How are you feeling?"

"Pissed off and confused. How long was I out?"

"From the time they carried you out of the circle? About an hour."

"They healed my broken shoulder and ribs in less than an hour?"

"They aren't completely healed," Dante explained. "Tsi told me they're bound by a calcium nano-scaffolding that'll be absorbed into the bones over time. Whatever that means."

"It means it doesn't hurt," Caleb said. "You all saw Riley?"

"Yeah," Washington said. "She keeps popping up, doesn't she?"

"She does," Dante said. "And I'll take bets as to whether or not she's up to something."

"I don't think any of us will bet against that," Caleb said. "Pai, where are you?"

The robot came out from behind Washington. "Yes, Sergeant?"

"I need to talk to Sergeant Tsi."

"You're no longer in Trial, Sergeant. You're free to move around the compound as you see fit."

Caleb looked down, realizing he was dressed in a green tunic too. A small badge on his shoulder projected his name and rank, the former written in English with the symbol for 'za' ahead of it.

"It's a good thing we didn't get executed because you lost," Kiaan said.

"I didn't lose," Caleb snapped back. "Valentine sucker-punched me after I had her."

"Technically, you lost, Sarge," Washington said. "Sergeant Tsi said no rules, remember? It wasn't over until she said she surrendered."

"Whose side are you on, Wash?"

Washington smiled. "I'm just saying."

Caleb jumped down from his bed. "Pai, where can I find Sergeant Tsi?"

"She's been called to meeting with General Goi," Pai replied. "Along with the other new recruit."

"Valentine is in a meeting with Goi?" Caleb said.

"Yes, Sergeant."

"Son of a bitch. Could this get any worse?"

"I'm sure it could," Washington said.

"Wash, Dante, with me. Kiaan, Paige, wait here."

"Roger," Paige said.

Caleb stormed out of the barracks with Washington and Dante right behind him. The Inahri nearby stopped to stare when they emerged, offering smiles and waves when Caleb looked at them. It drained enough of his fury for him to return the gesture, but not enough to remove any of the urgency. There was no way to know what Valentine had told Tsi and the general. Whatever it was, he doubted any of it could be good.

They crossed the compound, returning to the central circle and navigating to the command center. They entered the building, brought to a stop by the guard inside. She smiled at Caleb when he entered, making a comment he couldn't understand.

"I need to go up," he said, pointing to the stairs.

She shook her head and said something else in Inahrai.

"Up," Caleb repeated.

The soldier blocked his path, putting her hand firmly on his chest.

"Goi?" Caleb said.

"Goi," she replied, pointing to the stairs.

"I have to go up there," Caleb insisted.

The soldier didn't move.

"Sorry about this," Caleb said. He put his replacement hand on her shoulder and shoved her out of the way, sweeping past her. She recovered and tried to grab him from behind, but Washington got a grip on her, slowing her just long enough for Caleb to run up the stairs. He turned the corner to find Riley in the same position he had been in a few hours earlier. The proceedings came to an abrupt stop as all eyes turned to Caleb.

"Caleb," Tsi said, eyes furious at his intrusion. He knew the Inahri would find his actions dishonorable, but that was less important than letting Valentine spew her lies to them.

"I'm sorry," Caleb said. General, you can't trust her." He pointed at Riley. "She's dangerous. Very dangerous."

Riley glared at him. "That's where you're wrong, Caleb. Believe it or not, I came to help." She smirked. "I'm sorry about your ribs. I guess I underestimated the strength of the exosuit."

Caleb ignored the remark. He opened his mouth to speak again.

"Sergeant Caleb!" Goi shouted. "You are way out of line. Again. If you can't behave with some level of decorum, I may be forced to change my decision on your position in this community."

Caleb clamped his mouth shut to keep from saying anything. He straightened up, bowing his head like he was supposed to. He kept it bowed, remaining fixed in front of the Esteemed.

"I intended to involve you with our situation as soon as you completed your recovery," General Goi said, speaking calmly. "Sergeant Tsi is here for that very reason. Take a place behind me."

"Yes, General," Caleb said, raising his head and moving to stand behind the general.

"General, do you mind if I present Caleb with a quick update?" Sergeant Tsi asked. Her face softened when she looked at him. Now that the anger had passed, she seemed relieved he was upright again.

"Go ahead, Sergeant," Goi said.

"We were discussing how to resolve the situation with the Relyeh," Tsi said. "Not only have they apparently gained a foothold inside your ship, but they've also taken a foothold inside the Seeker."

"We're playing catch-up," Riley said.

"General, permission to speak plainly?" Caleb asked.

"Granted," Goi said.

"Riley, what do you mean, we? You don't know the meaning of 'we.'"

"You hurt me, Sergeant," Riley replied. "I'm trying to atone for my sins. To make up for my mistakes."

"I already told them how we wound up here," Caleb said. "They know what you did."

"I'm aware. I told them the same thing. I admitted to all of it. What's done is done, isn't it? Water under the bridge?"

"What's your game, Valentine?" Caleb asked. "If you remember, you told me yesterday you don't give a shit about Metro. So why are you here?"

"I also told you I was interested in allying with the Inahri," she replied. "So here I am."

"And you know these Inahri aren't running the show on this planet?"

"I'm aware. General Goi explained Arluthu to me. You really don't expect me to go looking for help from the monster who destroyed Earth in the first place, do you?" She had a point. Caleb couldn't argue it. She kept talking anyway. "I didn't mean for all this to happen, Card. Everything I planned has gone horribly wrong. I can't deny it. I also can't change the past. But I can help now."

"What's in it for you?"

"Is that what you think of me? That I only care how I can benefit?"

"Yes. You've never given me a reason not to think that. You murdered David because he knew what you did."

"Murder is a strong word. He was a stowaway. He wasn't even supposed to be there. I was within my rights to kill him based on the protocols."

"And that justifies it?"

"Yes."

"Whatever helps you sleep at night, I guess. If you even need to sleep anymore. Do Reapers sleep?"

Riley scowled at the statement. Caleb could see the skin on her forehead was hardening and beginning to change color. How long would it take for the transformation to make her more demon than human?

"All the more reason not to waste time arguing," she replied.

"Fine," Caleb agreed. He looked at Tsi. "So we're losing on two fronts. General, have you considered my request to return to the Deliverance to deal with the Relyeh Inahri there?"

"Yes," General Goi replied. "Doctor Valentine has spoken on behalf of your value in preventing Arluthu from recovering the modulator. We, the Esteemed agree with her assessment and were only awaiting your recovery. Do you feel you are combat ready, Sergeant?"

"Yes, sir," Caleb replied.

"Good. Sergeant Tsi, take them both to the armory and get them prepared. You'll leave immediately."

"Yes, General," Tsi replied.

"General, one more word, please," Caleb said.

"What is it, Sergeant?"

"I strongly recommend not allowing Doctor Valentine to return to the Deliverance. She can't be trusted."

"She has been nothing but honest and upfront with us, Sergeant," Goi replied.

"With all due respect, sir. I used to believe that about Riley too. She doesn't know the meaning of honest and upfront."

"Do not forget she defeated you in the Trial," Goi said. "She has proven her worth just as you have. The decision of the Esteemed is final."

Caleb clenched his teeth, looking at Riley again. She smirked slightly. "I want the modulator away from Arluthu as much as you do, Card."

Caleb believed that part was true. She didn't want Arluthu to get the energy unit. She probably wanted it for herself.

"Come," Sergeant Tsi said. "We don't have any time to waste."

Chapter 25

Caleb followed Sergeant Tsi and the Translator Intellect from the room, down the stairs to where Washington and Dante were waiting. Washington's face fell when he saw Riley come down the steps, while Dante looked like she wanted to stab the doctor in the eye.

"Your squadmates will return to the barracks," Tsi said upon seeing them.

"I want them with me on the mission," Caleb replied.

"That isn't an option."

Caleb came to a stop. "What do you mean? How are we going to get the Relyeh out of the Deliverance with only three of us?"

"We aren't," Riley said. "The plan isn't to save Metro. Not yet, anyway. We recover the energy unit and we get out."

"And leave our people in the hands of the enemy? Won't they try to ransom them for the unit?"

"No. They'll know the Free Inahri have the unit and won't negotiate for the lives of Earthers. Metro will become worthless to them."

"So they might as well kill everyone in it."

"Come on, Card. Now you're transferring Earther thinking onto more advanced humans."

"So you think the Relyeh won't slaughter the people of Metro because they're more advanced?" Washington said. "They did a number on Earth."

Riley glanced at the big Marine. "Well, look who got their voice back. I'd theorize that the people of Earth did worse by one another when the trife came than the trife ever did. Do you remember the streams, Private? Looting. Vandalism. And worse."

"I don't need to remember seeing it online," Washington replied. "I lived it."

"Then you know what I mean. The trife were designed for a purpose. What was the purpose in humans killing other humans as though the enemy needed the help?"

"The Inahri have allied with Arluthu," Tsi said. "They won't kill in cold blood regardless. Once the modulator is out of your people's hands, they will be more safe, not less. I swear my life on it."

None of this was sitting well with Caleb, especially with Riley involved. He was sure she had an ulterior motive. Her entire life was an ulterior motive. Why did she want to go back to the Deliverance? Was it only for the modulator?

What if she could launch the Seeker on her own? Would she bring it back to Earth?

"How big is our team?" he asked.

"You, me, her, Corporal Kizi and Private Awak," Tsi said. "They will meet us in the armory."

"What about my Guardians?"

"They'll be put to use. We're planning an assault on the Seeker in conjunction with our attack on your ship."

"Get the energy unit, get the ship, bring the energy unit to the ship and power it up. Is that right?"

"The Seeker has weapons systems that will help us defend against a Relyeh counter-attack."

"What if we don't get the unit?"

"A lot of Free Inahri are going to die."

"You're sure this is a good plan?" Dante asked. "Why don't we get the energy unit first, and then worry about the ship?"

"We can't delay that long," Tsi replied. "Arluthu's forces will harden their position on the Seeker and we'll never be able to dig them out."

"Do we have to worry about trife?" Caleb asked. "Uluth, I mean?"

"No. They have proven less effective against us than our own kind." Tsi shook her head. "We made a bargain with a monster a long time ago, thinking that we would earn our freedom. For many, we simply traded one master for another, only they don't see how Arluthu controls them. They worship him like a god. The Relyeh aren't gods. Their power comes from fear, but I believe they can be challenged and defeated."

Caleb watched Tsi's eyes as she spoke. There was something in them and in the force of her words, even if he couldn't understand them directly from her lips.

"You're a deserter, aren't you?" he said. "A convert to the Free Inahri."

"I escaped Arluthu when I was twelve years old," she replied. "My mother brought me out of Sverg Althu. She stole a transport. It was taken down a hundred kilometers from here. She died in the crash. The last thing she said to me was that the day we stop fighting for freedom, even if only within our hearts, is the day we lose our souls." She closed her eyes, recalling the memory. "I spent a week alone in the jungle before the Free Inahri found me. I never served Arluthu, but my mother did. She said the Relyeh are evil, and Arluthu is the worst kind."

"What kind is that?" Washington asked.

"He has ways of entering your mind. Of taking root and growing until you believe his way is the right way in your heart. He suffocates your free will from the inside out through deceit and manipulation."

"That sounds familiar," Dante said, looking at Riley.

Riley didn't respond.

"I've already said too much," Tsi said, breaking out of her thoughts. "Our time is short. Your squadmates will return to the barracks and await further orders. Your second-in-command will take charge of organizing for the assault on the Seeker."

"Wash, that's you," Caleb said.

"Not the sheriff?" Washington asked.

"No offense to Sheriff Dante, but she's not a Marine."

"None taken," Dante said. "I have to admit, I'm not eager to become a foot soldier in an alien race's civil war."

"This isn't about their war," Caleb replied. "This is about protecting Metro. If this is the best way to do it, then this is how we do it."

"Do you really think it's the best way?"

"No. But right now, it may be the only way."

"Roger that, Sergeant."

"Washington, Dante, you're dismissed," Caleb said. "Return to the barracks and wait for your next orders."

"Yes, Sergeant," they replied and headed out of the building.

"Tsi," Caleb said, turning to her. "If possible, can you keep Kiaan out of this? He isn't any kind of fighter. He's a pilot. A civilian pilot."

"I will have someone inform General Goi. We can

instruct him on the use of our craft, and he can continue in that capacity. I can't promise he won't be hurt."

"I'll take what I can get."

"Follow me."

Chapter 26

Caleb and Riley followed Tsi and the Intellect out of the CIC and around to the front of the long building. Tsi spoke to the two guards stationed there and they opened the heavy stone door to allow them to enter.

Corporal Kizi and Private Awak were already inside, standing in a small atrium at the front of the armory. A third person was with them, an older woman with the largest eyes Caleb had seen on any of the Inahri. She wore a light purple robe that matched the color of her eyes, giving her an almost ethereal appearance.

"Weapons-master Lito," Tsi said. "This is Sergeant Caleb and Doctor Riley, two of the newest members of our community."

She regarded them both. "Has this one seen a healer?" she asked, pointing at Riley.

"They said there was nothing they could do," Riley said. "The mutation is too far along."

Caleb caught the sadness in Riley's voice. The hint of despair. At that moment, he almost felt sorry for her.

Almost.

"A shame," Lito replied. "I saw the way you both fought during the Trial. You are valuable new assets to our cause." She looked at Tsi. "I've already been debriefed on the mission parameters and have selected the appropriate armament. Follow me."

She led the group out of the small atrium, through a door in the back. It fed into another small room where Lito had already laid out five sets of equipment on five of the twenty or so racks in the room, which were designed for that purpose.

Windows on both sides of the room revealed the full extent of the armory. Through them, Caleb could see six long rows of equipment—everything from battle armor to xix, to anti-Intellect guns, energy weapons, and the stunners that had taken he and his Guardians out. There were also plenty of weapons he didn't recognize. A variety of guns along with an assortment of tools whose purpose he couldn't discern.

"This doesn't look like enough for an entire army," Caleb said, eying all of it. The collection was impressive but small, especially compared to what he had uncovered beneath Metro.

"All of the barracks are already equipped," Lito replied. "There are nearly a thousand barracks in the compound, composed of close to four thousand Free Inahri troops. Also, the armory continues twenty levels deep."

"I stand corrected."

"We don't use most of the weapons," Tsi said. "But we're stockpiling them for when the Axon return."

"Don't you mean if the Axon return?" Caleb asked.

"No. We believe they will."

"Why? If Arluthu is here and more Relyeh are coming, isn't it better to consolidate further back?"

"They will look to test their readiness here."

"Against the Inahri?"

"Against both Relyeh and Inahri. It is only a question of when."

"Sergeant Caleb, that is your dock," Lito said, pointing to one of the stations. "And that is yours, Doctor Riley."

Caleb walked over to his station. An Intellect Skin was clipped to the wall. Beside it, a small shelf where a small handgun rested beside a belt made of the same material as the Skin. The belt had a short, dark blade snapped horizontally across the back.

"This is it?" Caleb said.

"Anything more and the Skin won't be able to hide you," Lito said. "This is a stealth mission, Sergeant Caleb."

"I've been on stealth missions before," Caleb replied. "I was expecting your tech would offer more options for equipment."

"Everything you need is part of the Skin. Be careful not to destroy it. They're irreplaceable."

Caleb looked at Tsi. "You gave me one for the Trial."

"I told you that you're special, Caleb," Tsi replied. "It was my Skin to give."

"I'm really not special."

"Is it a coincidence that you're here now? Is it a coincidence that your ship came at this time in the history of the Inahri ? Our stalemate has continued for ens, but in one moment, in one ship, in one warrior, everything has changed."

"You make that sound like a good thing. You could lose everything."

"Or gain everything, The opportunity is worth the cost, and it's better than living in wait for a day that might never come. Only it has come. And today we'll take the first step to free the Inahri people from the Hunger."

"Shi-shi," Awak and Kizi said sharply in reply. The Intellect didn't try to translate it, but Caleb understood the intention.

For the second time in a few hours, Caleb stripped out of his clothes to don the Intellect Skin. He couldn't help but spare a glance at the Inahri as they undressed, as curious to get a look at the build beneath their uniforms as they had been to examine him. Despite their petite frames and lack of body fat, they also didn't have much by way of visible muscle. There was no definition on their stomachs, arms, or legs. No bulges, no hard tissue, no rippling. Their bodies were smooth and unblemished, and nearly free of hair. While Tsi's face was distinctly feminine in structure and feature, her chest was hardly different than Kizi or Awak's, save for the larger protrusion of her nipples from their base. Conversely, the male Inahri's genitals were much smaller and nearly vanished completely once they were in their Skins. It was as if the Inahri were deep in the process of losing their gender differentiation and becoming more homogenous across the board.

Caleb also managed to get a quick look at Riley as she changed. The marks on her face were kind compared to the rest of her body. The skin of her arms and legs was flaky and hard, reforming in dark brown, leathery splotches. Her entire back was nearly converted to thicker skin, and the muscles across her stomach were larger and bulkier, suggesting her strength was increasing as her humanness decreased.

The sight of it sickened him, but it also brought back a measure of compassion for her situation. He didn't agree with most of the decisions she had made or who she was as a person. He also didn't think anyone deserved to turn into a literal monster, knowing they were changing and having no way to stop it. He wasn't sure what he would have done in her shoes. Probably handled it as long as he could while making sure Washington was ready to end it when it became more than he could control.

The team was outfitted and ready within twenty minutes. Sergeant Tsi took command, lining them up in a single row and quickly examining their equipment.

"Sergeant, I think Riley and I could use a quick primer on the sidearm," Caleb said.

"Of course," Tsi replied. "The weapon is a standard ion blaster. It's a balanced weapon, useful against both machine and organic targets. It can pierce battle armor at close range, and also temporarily scramble Intellect nodes."

"Downsides?"

"You will have only fifty shots. The weapon cannot be reloaded, but is discarded after completed use."

"Sergeant, it sounds great, but aren't we missing something?"

"What do you mean?"

"This is lethal," Caleb said, tapping on the sidearm. He motioned to the blade. "So is this. What if we have to disable instead of kill?"

"I don't recommend disabling the Relyeh."

"I'm not referring to the Relyeh. What about the people of Metro? They might try to stop us. I didn't mention it earlier, but I'm a wanted man there."

"I don't understand."

"The Governor set us up to take the blame for the lies his family told the population," Riley said. "Card is right. We might have to defend ourselves from our own people."

Tsi looked confused. "This is out of the ordinary. I will need to consult with General Goi."

"There's no time for that," Caleb said. He didn't want the General to change his mind about sending them. But he didn't want to risk hurting anyone in Metro either. "I know you have stun weapons."

Tsi turned to Lito. They exchanged a few sentences, and then the Weapons-master left the room through a door into the armory proper. Caleb watched her walk down one of the aisles, stopping at a rack and withdrawing a pair of alternate guns.

"She will retrieve stunners for you and Doctor Riley," Tsi said.

"What about you?" Caleb asked.

"If your people attack us, we will defend ourselves."

"You don't need to kill them."

"We might. I'm not risking the safety of my team."

Caleb couldn't bring himself to argue. He probably would have done the same thing.

Lito returned with the two guns already holstered. She handed one to Caleb and one to Riley. "You must travel light, so no recharge. If you need to use more than twenty rounds, you've done something very wrong."

Caleb nodded as he took the offered gun. "Agreed." He moved it to his side, where the holster grabbed onto the belt. He adjusted the positioning slightly. "I'm ready."

"What about the blade?" Riley asked, taking her stunner.

"Made of Skrilline," Tsi said. "A crystalline alloy that is lighter and stronger than the standard Axetiron, the alloy your arm is made from, as well as our city-ships. It is very rare and difficult to work, but it will pierce nearly anything. Also, be aware that the offensive systems of the Skin are enabled for this mission. Also be aware that all of the equipment we have, our opposition possesses too."

"Speaking of opposition, do we know what we're walking into?" Caleb asked.

"Our Dancers report a single platoon is responsible for

the attack on your ship. Nine to fifteen Inahri soldiers in full battle armor. Our goal is to circumvent them, not get into a drawn-out firefight that would put others at risk."

"Agreed," Caleb said.

"What about that thing?" Riley asked, pointing to the Intellect. "Is it coming with us?"

"No," Tsi replied. "The Skins will translate between us in near-real time."

"Nice trick."

"A reminder to all of you. I am in charge of this mission. You will follow my orders. Do not dishonor yourselves or me with non-compliance. Sergeant Caleb, Doctor Riley, I am relying on you to help us navigate the interior of the craft without being seen."

"Yes, Sergeant," Caleb said.

"The quantum dimensional modulator is the only objective. Once we have control of it, we will leave immediately and bring it back here for safekeeping until we have word that the Seeker is ours. Do you understand?"

"Yes, Sergeant," Caleb and Riley said.

"Chi Za," Kizi and Awak said in unison.

"Very good. We will meet Captain Ulia on the Bochun for immediate departure. A moment of prayer for safe returns."

The Inahri bowed their heads, so Caleb did the same. Riley remained fixed, an expression of amusement crossing her face. Caleb glanced over at her when the Inahri raised their heads again, questioning the reaction.

She sidled up to him as they exited the armory, crossing the open circle toward the lines of vehicles closer to the mouth of the cavern. "They were given access to technology we can only dream of. They understand the vastness of the universe and the multitudes of intelligent life in it. And they still believe in prayer."

"Maybe to them, a deeper understanding of the universe is a deeper understanding of God," Caleb offered.

"Oh please, Card. Don't tell me you buy that bullshit."

"What do you believe in, Riley?"

"Myself."

"Maybe that's your whole problem."

"Or maybe that's why I'm going to come out of this alive."

"How can you be so sure? Have you looked in a mirror lately?"

"Funny, Card."

"What's your motive here, Riley? And don't tell me it's anything benevolent because I wouldn't believe you. Maybe you have the Inahri snowed, but I've got your number."

"That may or may not be true, but it won't help you either way. I'm going to do what's best for me. Maybe that will coincide with what's best for you and these Inahri. Maybe it won't. It should be fun to find out."

Her smile was raw and almost feral and sent a shiver down Caleb's spine. Riley sped up, moving ahead of him to join the others, angling toward a transport where a gloved and goggled Inahri pilot was waiting.

Caleb had a feeling this was going to get ugly.

Very ugly.

Chapter 27

Joe slumped against the back of the control box, his knees drawn up and head bowed into the crook of his arm. His tears flowed freely, soaking his shirt. He didn't dare make a sound, sobbing in silence to overcome the mass of grief frozen in his chest and clogging his throat.

He had met Carol in engineering school when they were both eighteen. She was the prettiest girl he'd ever seen, and apparently she was just as enamored with him as he was with her. Their relationship gathered momentum in a hurry. Engineers marrying one another was a dream for the Governor, as it typically meant raising the next generation of mechanically inclined citizens to keep the city from falling apart. They had the blessing of Governor Jason Stone before they had the blessing of their parents, which had come quickly enough.

Six weeks after their first date, they were married and assigned to a cube in Block Two. It was on the third floor, a similar cube to the one they had shared on the thirtieth floor, only it wasn't a corner unit like their latest place. Just as they'd had to earn their way up the ladder to their positions as lead engineers, they'd had to work their way up the building too. It was a challenge Joe had been happy to take on with his new bride.

They had been married for forty years. A long time, especially where Metro was concerned. They had never succeeded in having children. Sometimes, things like that just didn't work out. Sometimes there was another plan for some couples.

This wasn't supposed to be part of theirs.

He wiped his eyes on his sleeve, trying to calm himself. He knew he couldn't continue to linger here. The governor and Law would know to check the control boxes sprinkled throughout the splits, and it wouldn't do to still be sitting in it when they did. He couldn't afford to get caught, not with the energy unit still in his possession. He knew where he wanted to hide it, but his grief had slowed him down, left him here, overcome with grief.

With Sheriff Zane's badge in his possession, he could hear all the communications between the governor and Law officials Governor Stone had sent most of Law after him. They would find him soon if he didn't move.

He struggled to his feet, wiping his eyes and nose again. He picked up the energy unit, holding it under his arm. He held the VP-5 in his hand, hoping beyond hope they wouldn't force him to use it. He didn't want to hurt anyone, but he couldn't let the power source fall into the enemy's possession. That would lead to everyone's death. He was sure of it.

He moved to the door to the control box and tapped in the control pad code. The door slid open, revealing the split beyond. It was dim in the alley between the blocks, the lighting above only partially functional. It offered him some protection from being seen, but not nearly enough. It would take a bit of luck for him to make it to his destination. His final hiding place.

HE MOVED out of the control box, turning left and jogging to the end of the split. He peered out into the strand, scanning for Law. He saw an officer further away, heading in the other direction. Otherwise, the coast was clear.

He ran across the strand to the opposite split, stopping there and turning around, heart racing as he waited for someone to call in an alarm. The call never came. He heaved a sigh of relief and crossed the split, coming out almost back where he started. He crouched in shadow near the end of the split, staring across it at the back of the Law Office.

It was dark and deserted. There was no access to the Office from the rear. At least, there hadn't been for years. The transports and drones Law used to have at their disposal were gone now, broken down for parts to fix more critical components. The motor yard was abandoned, emptied out and left to history.

Joe wasn't interested in the motor yard. What he was after was inside the office, accessible from the rear through a locked and rusted roll-up metal door. He was taking a huge gamble that he could open the door to get inside without being seen or heard. The door wasn't exactly smooth as silk on its runners.

If he got caught in the open, Law would kill him sooner than later. He had no doubt about that. Even if Stone didn't want to execute him, the enemy wouldn't give him a choice.

He scanned the area again and then ran across the split to

the back of the office, planting his hands on the low wall and vaulting over it into the motor yard. He landed awkwardly, thinking himself more agile than he was. His ankle turned and he collapsed, stifling a cry as he hit the floor. He sat there for a few seconds, rubbing his ankle and staring at the camera in the corner, wondering if it was still active.

He didn't think so. The cameras were as much a victim of their years in space as anything else in Metro, and they didn't hold enough value to bother repairing.

Joe crossed the yard to the door, crouching low in front of it. He dug his fingers under it and tried to lift it.

Locked.

He expected it would be. Reaching into a pocket in his overalls, he withdrew his laser cutter and positioned it against the door. Judging the position of the lock inside the mechanism, he activated the device. A tight beam of light began digging into the door, making quick work of the lock behind it. Joe knew he was through when he heard the metallic clank on the other side. He reached under the door again, pulling it up. It gave way this time, and he slowly lifted it until it was high enough for him to slide beneath.

Hopefully, he wouldn't crawl right into the waiting feet of a sheriff.

He pulled himself through, rolling onto his back when he cleared the entrance, allowing the rolling door to fall back into place. He scrambled to his feet, aiming the VP-5 toward the inner door. The door was closed, the room empty save for a few small stacks of debris strewn across the cold metal floor.

The armory laid below. He had only been in it once. He knew where it was supposed to be but it was hidden at the moment, the floor sealed.

That was about to change.

He moved the debris away from the access panel, unscrewed the metal from the wall and quickly joined the two detached wires. Then he put everything back in place before heading over to the control panel.

Joe froze when he heard a voice in the hallway outside. He glanced through the small window and saw a Law Officer coming toward the room. Damn it. He found a taller stack of garbage in the corner and ducked behind it, holding the VP-5 close to his chest. He had never fired a weapon before. He didn't want to start now.

The officer came to the door and pushed it open. Joe ducked further down behind the junk as the deputy surveyed the room. His heart thumped hard in his chest, which was already tight with grief. He held his breath as if he could wish the officer away.

A moment later, she left, closing the door and heading back the way she had come.

Joe exhaled sharply before rushing to the control panel. He activated the lift, crouching on it as it dropped into the darkness. It took almost two minutes for it to descend.

Two minutes that left him completely vulnerable and utterly terrified.

He made it down without incident, jumping off the lift and heading to the terminal that would send it back up. He tapped on the controls, backing away while the platform began to return to its resting position. Then he ran to one of the vehicles still in the massive room, ducking behind it and counting.

Two minutes. Then he would be safe.

Joe counted one hundred twenty seconds. He heard the platform lock into place. Then he smiled. He had made it.

He turned and slumped against the back of the APC. His legs gave way again, his exhaustion returning. He wasn't going to cry again. He couldn't cry for the rest of his life.

Or maybe he could.

Forty years was a long time. It was seventy percent of his life. And now she was gone, just like that. They had always dreamed about escaping the confines of Metro. Of going outside and enjoying the real sun, fresh air, and all the open space they could ever want.

Carol would never see that dream brought to reality. He had to survive. He had to make it outside, even if only for a minute.

For her.

The decision helped him calm himself. His pulse began to slow, his head began to clear. He was safe down here.

For now.

How long would it take for Governor Stone to decide to look here? Probably a while. The Governor didn't want the enemy to know the armory existed.

He lifted the energy unit and carefully opened the containment box. The sphere of energy pulsed within the box, arcing out into the metal as though it were desperate for a connection.

He snapped the box closed. He could imagine a million reasons why the enemy wanted the power source, and none of them were good.

He put it down beside him and leaned his head back against the APC's large, studded wheel. Closing his eyes, he brought up a vision of Carol from his memory. Their wedding was simple. Vows in front of the Governor. A small cake. His parents. Her parents. It had been more than enough.

He started to doze, his head lolling to the side as he drifted off...

A soft hiss caught his attention, and his eyes snapped

open. He sat up. Where had the sound come from? No one was supposed to be down here.

Joe picked up the energy unit in one hand and the VP-5 in the other. He scanned the area ahead of him.

A soft tick to his right drew his attention. He swung the gun toward it. Nothing. He heard another on his right. He spun around. Again nothing. But was that a shadow he had caught from the corner of his eye?

He swallowed hard, his breathing becoming short and ragged. He heard more small clicks nearby, but again, when he turned to face them there was nothing there.

But something...someone...*was* there. Something was making those sounds. He began to slide along the side of the APC, trying to get to the back, to the hatch there. He could hide inside the vehicle. Nothing could get to him in there.

How could something get to him in here?

He came to the corner of the vehicle, leaning to look around it.

A dark face greeted him, mouth opening to reveal rows of razor-sharp teeth. A soft hiss escaped the thing's mouth.

And everything went dark.

Chapter 28

On its way from the Free Inahri base, the Bochun carrying Caleb, Riley, Tsi and the others swept low over the mountains and around the west side of the Deliverance. They stuck to the river then, streaking along it at such low altitude Caleb was amazed Captain Ulia could maintain such calm control of the craft, with its short wings passing less than a meter above branches and other obstacles. At the same time, it was amusing to watch how the creatures along the river reacted to their passing. Fishers leaped in front of them and disappeared deep into the water. Birds retreated deeper inland, and the larger predators stared at them, displeased with the disturbance.

Caleb looked away from the viewport to Sergeant Tsi. Her face was hidden by the mantle of the Skin, her features smoothed out to the small protrusion of her nose. Everyone on the craft had their mantles raised, using the Skin's comm systems to translate between their languages.

"So many life forms here," Caleb said. "Were they here when you arrived?"

"Yes," Tsi replied. "We believed when we came that

this was an undiscovered world, inhabited only by lesser intelligences. We never knew the Axon had already scouted the world and chosen it as our prison and testing grounds."

"They pitted you against the uluth."

"Yes. In increasingly difficult scenarios. This was many ens ago. Long before I was born. Long before any of us were born. The history is oral now, the true data lost during the rebellion when the Intellects chased us from the Seeker. Despite what is happening now, I am personally grateful to you for destroying the Guardian and giving us a chance to reclaim our birthright."

"You're welcome," Riley said.

Caleb glared at her.

"Well, I was the one who shot the Guardian. It never saw it coming." She laughed harshly.

"Sergeant, we're approaching the ingress point," Captain Ulia said.

They were still ten klicks short of the Deliverance. The ship wasn't even close to visible from their position, still hidden behind plenty of twists and turns in the river. According to Tsi, they were risking the edge of what Ulia considered the safe zone to come this close. They would take a boat for half of the remaining distance and then run the remainder.

"Kizi, prepare the skiff," Tsi said.

"Yes, Sergeant," Kizi replied, moving to the rear of the transport. He removed a long tube from its latch on the cargo space wall and took it forward to wait at the sealed hatch.

"Corporal Kizi will go first," Tsi explained. "He will expand the skiff so we can jump into it while he holds it in position. Remember, stay low and silent."

"Yes, Sergeant," Riley said.

"Chi Za," Caleb said, using the Inahri response. Tsi glanced at him and nodded in appreciation.

"Kiss ass," Riley charged.

"It's called respect," Caleb replied.

The transport slowed quickly, forcing Caleb to brace until it was hovering static over the river. The hatch opened and Kizi jumped out, jumping feet first into the water with barely a splash. He activated the tube, and it quickly began to change shape, expanding and stretching into a long, narrow boat that reminded Caleb of an oversized canoe.

"Go," Tsi said, motioning for them. Awak went first, then Riley. Caleb moved to the edge of the hatch, found an open spot in the canoe, and jumped down to it, ducking low when he landed.

The Bochun was already on the move by the time Tsi landed in the skiff, spinning around and rising slightly as its thrusters gained power and flared over their heads. The transport shot away across the river, vanishing in seconds.

They remained silent as Kizi climbed into the boat and handed Tsi one rod from a pair of xix. They sat next to one another, each of them placing their xix in the water and activating it. The energy glowed a light blue beneath the surface and then began propelling them forward.

Caleb had to bite his tongue to keep from asking if he had actually gone into combat with a pair of oars.

The ride didn't take long, but it afforded Caleb with an opportunity to take in the jungle at twilight from an entirely new perspective. The colors of the flora were breathtaking, the planet growing more beautiful to him with each passing minute. It was a shame the planet was already a place of war and strife.. It could have made a good home for the colony.

Maybe it still could be. He wasn't ready to give up on it

just yet. It wasn't as though they had a choice, anyway. They had no way off the planet. At least not alone.

He glanced over at Awak. What would the Free Inahri do with the Seeker once they restored it to full power? Leave the planet behind? Leave them behind? He respected the Free Inahri. He wanted to believe in them and trust them as ongoing allies, but people like Valentine were making it hard for him to trust in anyone like that.

The skiff made its way to the five-kilometer mark, at which point Kizi and Tsi used the xix to maneuver the vessel to the southern shore. Caleb would have preferred to take it all the way in, but Tsi insisted the Inahri would be keeping a watch on the river. It was too obvious as a passage in.

They all climbed out of the boat, remaining silent as they climbed up the shore and into the woods. The sun was already beginning to set, and the canopy blocked most of the remaining light, casting them into darkness. At least for a moment. Caleb found the Skin adjusted automatically, providing almost the same level of detail as he'd had in broad daylight.

They continued close to the river, with Tsi setting the pace at a fast jog. Caleb had no trouble keeping up with her, maneuvering over roots, fallen branches and loose river stones, all of it covered in moss and hard to spot.

The potential to come across a group of wayward trife was always present in Caleb's mind. The demons, not the Inahri, were the reason for their silence. While Hal had destroyed any of the trife who were directly under the Guardian Intellect's control, there was a high probability others were either out of range or not under the Intellect's thrall.

It took fifteen minutes to cover four and a half of the last five kilometers, bringing the group to a stop at the edge of the clearing created when the Deliverance landed. They dropped behind the trunk of one of the many fallen trees, scanning the area.

Caleb's eyes immediately landed on the beginning of Metro's migration, surprised that Governor Stone was already moving the city outside. There were no guarantees of safety. The planet was mostly unknown to them. But he had decided to leave the safety of the ship's hold? It didn't make sense.

Then he saw the bodies. The soldiers were splayed across the ground, some intact, some less so. He felt their deaths in the pit of his stomach, and he glanced at Riley without turning his head. This was her fault as much as Stone's. Knowing she was here now for herself and nothing else made it that much worse. He had to figure out what she was planning before she followed through with it.

As if they had nothing else to worry about.

His eyes rose to the large, open space of the main hangar. He could see the damage to the lift even from a distance, the metal bent and mangled, the lift dangling awkwardly off the edge. He thought about zooming in and the Skin responded, offering him a better view of the area.

An Inahri soldier stood at the edge of the hangar in full battle armor, a rifle cradled across his chest. He was facing southwest, away from them. Caleb pointed to his face. Tsi waved her pinkie. They had gone through the hand gestures on the ride over. Hers had the same meaning as thumbs-up. She had seen him too.

Tsi pointed toward the few large containers already on the ground and then held up her hand, shifting her position to get ready to spring into a sprint. The others did the same.

They watched the Inahri soldier for a few more minutes, waiting for him to turn away. The moment he did, Tsi dropped her hand and the entire squad came out of hiding, charging the quarter-kilometer toward the containers with Caleb in the rear. The Inahri soldier remained outlined the whole time, his position clear in Caleb's peripheral vision. The soldiers turned as Caleb neared the container.

He wasn't going to make it.

He dove to the ground, keeping his entire body flat and static.

"Hold," Tsi whispered through the comm.

They waited like that, counting heartbeats. Caleb was up to five hundred when Tsi told him to move. He scrambled to the others, making it to safety. Kizi patted him on the shoulder. That had been too close for comfort.

They moved to the other side of the container, getting their eyes back on the guard. He remained fixed for another thirty minutes as the sun continued to set, forcing them to remain where they were. Finally, the man walked along the edge of the hangar, to the east and away from their position.

Tsi pointed to Caleb, motioning him to take the lead. He moved to the front and then urged the group forward.

Sprinting again, they crossed the open space and past the hangar, making it beneath the ship and angling for the massive front left landing sled. While the lifts hadn't been installed inside the landers, the center was still hollow and would allow the squad to climb inside.

Caleb led them across to the lander. The massive foot had sunk nearly four meters into the soft ground, leaving only the very top of it exposed. They climbed up onto the thick leg, where Riley quickly opened the access panel.Entering her security clearance, the lower door opened, revealing the empty tube inside.

They were in.

Chapter 29

Caleb, Riley, Tsi and the rest of the team scaled the lander tube, using the Intellect Skins to climb up the smooth metal face of the cylinder. A slight charge to the hands and feet caused the skin to pucker, creating millions of tiny fibers on the surfaces that resembled a gecko's toes.

It only took a minute for them to scale fifteen meters into the lowest deck of the starship, with Riley taking the lead to open the secured hatch at the other end. Caleb was the first one out into the corridors. He held the ion pistol in a ready position, swinging it down both ends of the passage and waiting for the Skin to offer a target.

There were none.

"Clear," he said into the comm, bringing the rest of the group out into the corridor.

"Caleb, you have the lead," Tsi said. "Take us to Metro."

"Chi Za," he replied, getting them moving in the right direction. He was going to bring them the long way around the main hangar, not wanting to risk trouble by passing through. It would triple the time to reach the city, but they didn't have to hurry. Now that they were on board, all they had to do was not be seen.

They wound their way to the passage behind the hangar, connecting to a stairwell there that rose from deck eight to twenty-two. They moved cautiously and purpose-fully, the potential of having someone stumble on them unlikely but ever-present. The ship was huge, but there were only a dozen or so of the Relyeh Inahri inside.

A half-hour passed during the course of their move-ments up to Deck Twenty-two and then back down. They approached the large blast doors that would allow the loaders into the city, interested to see if the Governor had time to lock Metro down. From the sealed state of the massive doors, it appeared they had.

"How many entrances are there to your colony?" Tsi asked.

"Six that I know about," Caleb said. "This one is closest to the hangar, but it only has control access from the inside. There's another up on Deck Sixteen. We blew that one open to get into the city. I don't know if Stone had it repaired. I hope so."

It was the biggest unknown of the whole mission. Had the Relyeh managed to storm the city before it could be locked down? If it had been locked down, did the enemy have the tools and tech to open it?

"It's likely the opposition will have entered this way," Tsi said.

"Which means we probably shouldn't," Caleb replied. "We can swing around to the opposite end of the city. It'll take more time, but if we come in from the north, we can probably get in unseen by Inahri or Earther."

"We need to make a stop first," Riley said.

"What do you mean?" Caleb asked. "We didn't come here to sight-see."

"At the Research Module."

"Why?"

"I need something there."

"Famous last words. What kind of something?"

"Damn it, Card. Look at me." She grabbed the mantle and lowered it from her head. The flaking, thick skin was spreading, and it had only been a few hours. "I might be able to stop this. I might be able to reverse it. There's a sample in the module. I don't know if it will work, but I need to try."

"Always looking out for everyone else, aren't you?"

Tsi put her hand on Riley's shoulder, beckoning her to put her mantle back on. "We're going to the north end of your colony," she said. "No extra stops."

"Sergeant," Riley said.

"No extra stops."

"I see. Well, good luck getting into the city then. You don't have access. I do."

She leaned against the bulkhead with no intention of moving. Caleb wished he was surprised, but he had expected her bullshit from the moment they left the Inahri compound.

"You're going to get us all killed," he hissed at her.

"I'm going to have a fate worse than that."

Caleb looked back at Tsi.

"I could simply kill you, Doctor Riley," Tsi said.

Riley moved faster than Caleb could believe. One moment she was against the wall, the next she had Tsi's head under her left arm, Tsi's ion gun in her right hand, holding it against the sergeant's temple. Kizi and Awak pointed their weapons at Riley. Caleb shook his head in disbelief.

"I could kill you, Sergeant Tsi," Riley said. She let go of her, holding out her gun. "I have nothing to lose. Do you understand? But you do have something to lose. All of you."

Tsi's face was invisible behind the mantle, but Caleb could nearly feel the heat of her anger coming out through it. "Where is this Research Module."

Riley motioned down an adjacent passage. "That way. Not far. I can go alone and meet you at the north entrance. I won't be long."

Caleb opened his mouth to argue. Leaving Riley alone was the worst idea he could think of.

"No. Corporal Kizi will go with you."

"Sergeant," Caleb said. "That's not—"

"Corporal Kizi will go with you," Tsi repeated, cutting him off.

"Yes, Sergeant," Kizi said.

"We'll cross to the north entrance to ensure the way is clear. Doctor Riley, I have eyes on you through the Skin. Do not think to double-cross us."

"I could have killed you already if that was my intent," Riley replied. "I want a possible cure. A chance to keep my humanity. That's all. We'll meet you back at the north entrance. Kizi, let's go."

Riley vanished down the corridor with the Inahri in tow. Caleb turned to Tsi. "That's a mistake."

"What would you have me do, Caleb?" she replied. "We didn't come all this way to be stymied by a door. She's right. If she wanted to harm us, she could have already." She put her hand on her neck and rubbed at it for emphasis.

"Maybe what she wants to do would be worse than killing us," Caleb suggested. "I don't trust her, and you shouldn't either."

"I'm in charge of this mission. It's my decision, and it's final. If you want to be of service, stop arguing every other point with me."

"Chi Za," he replied tensely.

Things were going downhill fast.

Chapter 30

It took nearly an hour to wind around Metro from the outside. Not only was the route anything but direct, but the area to the north of the city wasn't as abandoned as Caleb had hoped.

They had nearly stumbled directly into a group of soldiers moving through the area, likely in the direction of the smaller secondary hangar where the starfighters and atmospheric transports were housed. Evading them had been more luck than intention, with the slightly better range of the Skin's embedded sensors giving them early warning of the enemy. They had come to an immediate halt and waited, the targets continuing to travel perpendicular before vanishing from their extended sight.

They had continued even more cautiously from there, finally arriving at the north seal without any other interruptions. They grouped together in the small alcove ahead of the blast door to wait for Riley and Kizi.

Caleb was surprised when she and the Inahri corporal rejoined them only a few minutes after they arrived. He couldn't see Riley's face, but her body language and a new bulge beneath the belt on her hip suggested she had gotten whatever it was she wanted from the area.

She turned her head toward him as she walked past to the seal's access panel, putting her wrist up to it so it could scan her identification chip. "I'm not always up to no good, Card," she said, smirking at him.

"That remains to be seen," he replied.

He could see her face widen into a smile beneath the mantle. She tapped her wrist against the control panel and the seal unlocked, the heavy door beginning to slide up.

"Stay alert," Tsi said. "We don't want to be seen."

The north seal fed into a short secondary corridor similar to the passage opposite the south seal, only much shorter. It afforded the group time to get deeper into Metro from outside the city, bringing them around to a second hatch that led into the city itself. That hatch was the smallest leading into Metro, a heavy blast door barely large enough for someone to step through. It fed out into an alley between Block Forty-two and Forty-three, the oldest and most run-down buildings in the city.

The blocks were also deserted, abandoned after Metro's civil war had cut over ten-thousand from the population. They were being used only for scrap now, the functional parts already stripped out of the structures, leaving them in a dilapidated state. Caleb had never been to this end of Metro before. He knew from the protocols the citizens were organized by value from most to least, with the artists, creatives, and other least-valuable workers typically relegated to the Blocks numbered above the mid-thirties.

A pair of forms in ragged hoodies crossed the split almost at the same time he stepped through the raised hatch, turning their heads in nervous surprise.

"What the hell?" one of them said, raising an arm to point at them.

"Take them out," Tsi said without hesitation.

"What? Wait," Caleb protested, jumping into the line of fire and reaching for his stunner.

The two men's eyes dropped to their guns.

"Let's get out of here," one of them said.

Caleb whipped the stunner from his hip, firing two quick shots at the men before they could take their first step. The rounds hit them in the side, and both targets convulsed and dropped to the ground.

"Sergeant Caleb!" Tsi hissed.

His head snapped back toward Tsi. "You don't need to kill them."

"No witnesses, Sergeant," she replied. "They saw us."

"It may not mean much to you to kill my people, Sergeant," Caleb hissed back. "It means a hell of a lot to me. I took care of them."

"Until they wake up."

"We'll be long gone by then."

Tsi didn't look happy, but she also didn't protest again. Caleb approached the downed citizens, leaning over them to push their hoods back. They couldn't have been more than sixteen years old. Just kids.

"We can use them," Caleb said. "We can't walk around here like this anyway."

He looked down at one of the boys, thinking about taking a picture of him. The Skin quickly scanned the unconscious teen and then projected his image around Caleb.

"Awak and I will project that one," Tsi said. "Riley, Caleb, and Kizi will project the other."

They quickly scanned the pair. Afterward, Kizi helped Caleb drag them deeper into the alley, closer to the seal.

"Is all of your Metro like this?" Tsi asked when they were done, observing the run-down surroundings.

"No," Caleb replied. "But the ship wasn't designed for us to be in space for so long. A lot of components began breaking down. This is the result."

"I see. Well, we're inside. Do you know where the modulator is being kept?"

"I don't know where," Caleb replied. "But I know who has it. I left it with the ship's Chief Engineer, Joe King."

"His name is Joking?" Awak said.

Caleb was confused until he realized the translator must have combined his first and last names and converted it to a different word in Inahrai. "No. First name Joe. Last name King. Dante told me where he lives, but it's all the way on the other side of the city. If he isn't there, he might be in Engineering, which is adjacent to the south seal."

"If the Inahri got through the seal…" Tsi said.

"If he was in Engineering at the time, he's probably dead," Caleb finished for her. There was no sound save for the soft hum of the atmospherics above them. " But I get the feeling the two we dropped weren't supposed to be out of their cubes. The city sounds like it's on lockdown."

"Which would mean the Inahri are inside," Tsi said. "We must be more cautious."

"Agreed. We can't be caught walking around looking like this," Caleb said, motioning to the two pairs of identical projections. "We should split up. Keep heading south until you reach the end of the blocks. The buildings. Watch out for anyone wearing a uniform. If the city's locked down, they'll detain you and try to scan your wrist to see where you belong. Since you don't have identification chips, it won't end well, and I'd strongly prefer to do this without you killing any of Metro's citizens."

"I'm sorry, Caleb. I don't want to seem cruel. But this is more important than two of your people."

"Caleb and I will form one group. Kizi, Awak, and Riley, you will form the other. We will stay connected through the comm."

"We'll need a third scan," Riley said, looking at Kizi. They were identical twins. Same clothes sitting the same way on the same frame. Same tired face. Same everything.

"You can scan the next individual you come across from cover, even from behind," Tsi replied, "and the system will interpolate."

"Roger that."

"If you can scan an officer, you can convince them you're taking two stragglers home," Caleb suggested.

"My thought exactly, Card." Riley sneered at him, "I'm not an idiot."

Caleb bit his tongue. This wasn't the time or place.

"Riley, you three head down the left split. Caleb and I will go the other way. Contact us immediately if you spot any Inahri. And remember, they may also be projecting their appearance."

"Roger," Riley replied.

As she headed off with Kizi and Awak in tow, Tsi turned back to Caleb. "Lead the way."

Chapter 31

Caleb and Tsi chose the starboard side of the city to make their way south, navigating the splits and strands a few blocks from the direction of the south seal. On first impression, the city seemed deserted. There was nobody on the strands. Businesses were all closed. Even the cubes rising off the deck were mostly dark. It was as though the colonists knew something bad was happening and they were doing their best to hide from it.

And maybe that's precisely what it was. Maybe the colonists knew the Inahri were in the city, and they wanted to stay clear of them. But if that were true, where were the battle-armored soldiers? Where were the signs of fighting?

Or had Governor Stone simply handed the entire colony over to the Relyeh? Had he surrendered the city without a fight?

Caleb hated the thought. What he hated more was that it wouldn't surprise him if it were true.

"Is this how Earthers live?" Tsi asked, taking in the sight of the city. "In tall boxes with small windows?"

"You live underground, in small boxes with no windows," Caleb replied.

"Not always. You only saw a little of the Seeker. When it is fully operational, it is a beautiful place. You never made it to the gardens." Her voice lowered, becoming sad. "I've heard they were amazing. They're surely all dead now."

"Gardens in the ship? You have a jungle right outside."

"My ancestors were prisoners, Caleb. Not allowed to leave the ship. Barely allowed to leave our cells. We only experienced the world outside as testing grounds before Arluthu came."

"Why did you turn against Arluthu if he helped set you free?"

"Free? No, Caleb. From one master to another, but not free."

"Then why do the other Inahri still support him?"

"Some Inahri love power more than they love one another. Don't tell me Earth is any different."

"I can't tell you that. We were the same way."

They stopped talking when the Skin's sensors captured a pair of bodies coming around the corner up ahead. They quickly ducked into one of the splits, just before the law officers emerged, walking in their direction.

"I don't think they saw us," Caleb said. Their AR overlays appeared through the solid wall of the block, the Skin tracking their movement toward them. Just because the officers hadn't seen them didn't mean they weren't coming to check the split. "This way."

They headed deeper into the split, following the dark alley for twenty meters before turning right at the first intersection. They stopped again, watching the marks as they paused at the entrance to the alley.

"What are they doing?" Tsi asked.

"I don't know. We'll keep heading this way."

They followed the split, turning south again at the next intersection. Two more marks appeared ahead.

"Somebody must have seen us out of a window and called Law," Caleb said. "They're trying to round us up."

"We could disable them," Tsi suggested.

"We could, but they'll be scheduled to check-in every few minutes. They won't be missed for long, and then all of Law and the Relyeh will know something's up."

The marks were moving again, closing in on them in the split.

"Other ideas?" Tsi asked.

Caleb found an intersection twenty meters down. "Make it there before they do."

They ran, sprinting for the intersection. The law officers were getting closer, taking a more steady pace in their general direction. They would never guess the two kids from the upper-blocks had tracking sensors.

They broke into the junction and turned right, continuing to run toward the port side of the ship only a few seconds ahead of the officers. Another mark appeared down a split ahead and to the right.

"Keep going," Caleb said.

He glanced at the officer as they passed the alley.

"Stop!" the officer ordered, breaking into a run of his own. Caleb and Tsi didn't slow, the officer coming out onto the split behind them. "Stop, or I'll stop you!"

Caleb glanced back. The officer was pulling his revolver. He also didn't know these two kids already knew their guns had no bullets, stunning or otherwise.

They reached the next intersection. Another officer was marked by the Skin as the net continued to tighten around them. The end of the split was up ahead, spilling them out into a strand on Block Fifteen. An officer was approaching that exit, ready to block them in completely.

"Don't slow down," Caleb said.

Tsi did as he said. They reached the end of the split as the officer came around the corner, weapon already out. Caleb threw his shoulder into the woman, spinning her to the ground as they continued sprinting across the street.

"Where now?" Tsi asked.

"Straight." He pointed toward a pair of open doors on the building ahead.

"Straight?"

Caleb and Tsi burst through the open doors, into the lobby of the hospital. There was nobody in the waiting area, but there was an admin behind the help counter. She opened her mouth to yell at them for running, but they were already gone by then, turning right toward the lifts and the emergency stairs.

Two of the law officers were behind them, still a few seconds out from the hospital and quickly losing ground. Caleb and Tsi reached the door to the stairwell, and Caleb shoved it open, leading her up into the hospital.

"Where are we going?" she asked.

"We'll go up, across, and out on the other side. If we hurry, we can make it before they surround the place."

"How do you know where to go?"

"I've been here before. A couple of times."

They made it to the third floor at the same time the door at the bottom of the steps opened. Caleb led them out into the hospital proper, still running as he bypassed a pair of nurses chatting in the corner.

"Wait," Caleb said, stopping and turning. "Say cheese!" he said, as his Skin scanned the one on the left. Tsi followed his example, quickly scanning the other one. He changed the projection as he ran, noticing she did too.

They reached the corner and slowed to a walk, taking on the role of the two nurses. Caleb continued across the floor at a more leisurely pace. Even if Law surrounded the building, they were looking for two male hoodlums, not two female nurses.

He was starting to like the Intellect Skin.

"We can take the lift back out now," he said, cutting left at the next corridor. There were rooms on either side of the hallway. Caleb glanced in each of the windows, noting they were all empty.

Wait. Not all of them. He froze after nearly passing one, stopping and taking a step back. He peered through the window.

"What is it?" Tsi asked.

"Give me a minute," he replied.

"Caleb, we don't have time."

"This might be worth it."

He pushed the door open, entering the room. Doctor Rathbone's head turned as he entered, and she gave him an angry glare.

"Celia, what are you doing here? Didn't I tell you to go home and be with your family?" Her head shifted slightly as Tsi entered behind Caleb. "Donna, you too. Why are you still here?"

Caleb shifted his attention from the doctor to her patient, lying flat on the bed, eyes open, spittle slipping from her open mouth. She made a soft gurgling moan every couple of seconds like she was terrified of something.

Caleb turned off the projection. Doctor Rathbone took a step back as if to defend the patient.

"Rathbone," he said, grabbing the mantle and pulling it away from his face. "It's me. Caleb Card."

Rathbone's frightened expression turned into a shocked, joyful one. Her mouth spread into a smile, and she rose up and clasped her hands together. "Sergeant Card. Thank God."

"I don't have a lot of time," Caleb said. "I need you to tell me what's been happening here. Quickly. I need you to tell me what happened to her." He pointed at the patient.

Beth Stone.

"Oh, Caleb," Rathbone replied. "It's all a mess. The Governor wanted to move outside the city, to show the people there was nothing to be afraid of. Only there is something to be afraid of. We have enemies here."

"I know. We have allies too." Caleb motioned to Tsi, who dropped the projection and pulled back her mantle.

"What the?" Rathbone said. "Who…uh…what are you?"

"Tsi," she said, pointing to herself. "Hello."

Caleb glanced at her. Where had she learned that?

"They're here for the energy unit," Caleb said. "We're here to stop them from getting it. Where's Joe King?"

"Oh no," Rathbone said. "The enemy, they attacked the Governor. They killed dozens of our people. Poor Beth is in shock and I can't seem to get her stabilized. Between this and losing Orla? It was just too much for her. Too much for the Governor too. The enemy wants something. I guess they want the energy unit, whatever that is. They told him to get it or else they're going to start killing colonists."

"Are they in the city?"

"No. According to Sheriff Zane, they're staying in engineering, waiting on Stone to do the hard work. I don't know, Caleb. I don't know what's going to happen if they get it. Are they really going to leave us alone?"

Tsi said something in Inahrai , forgetting it wouldn't be translated.

"I wouldn't count on it," Caleb said. "These enemies,

they're the same race as Tsi. Inahri. But they're allied with another race. The Relyeh. It was the Relyeh that sent the trife to Earth. They're not a benevolent race. Do you know where Joe is?"

"No. Nobody does. That's probably a good thing. His wife. Caleb, Sheriff Zane killed Carol. He shot her. It was an accident. She knocked him a good one too, and when he came to Joe was gone. All of Law has been looking for him for hours. They pulled all but a skeleton crew out of here, and they won't let anyone leave their cubes. Last I heard they were starting to search door to door. One cube at a time."

"Damn it. We can all guess what's going to happen if they don't find him."

"I don't want to guess," Rathbone said. "We..." she trailed off, her eyes shifting past them again.

"Doc Rathbone, I just got word from HQ," Sheriff Zane said, coming around the corner and entering the open room. "We chased two kids in here and who the hell are you?"

Caleb looked back at Zane, who recognized him immediately. The sheriff started reaching for a sidearm that wasn't there, mouth opening to shout.

Tsi spun on her toes, hand whipping around and grabbing his neck, momentum carrying him into the door. He hit hard, and she followed it with a quick strike to his temple from her other hand, letting him go as he tumbled to the floor.

"Ouch," Caleb said in response to the violent outburst,

"Caleb," Tsi said. It was the only word he understood. She pulled her mantle back on, and he did the same. "We're out of time," she repeated.

"Chi za."

Caleb turned back to Doctor Rathbone, quickly scanning her. Then he moved to Sheriff Zane and scanned him too.

"What are you doing?" Rathbone asked.

"Disguises," Caleb said, projecting the sheriff. "Tsi, get Beth Stone."

Tsi moved to Beth's bedside and quickly scanned her while Caleb waited at the door.

"Whatever you're planning, I hope it works," Rathbone said.

"Sit tight," Caleb replied. "We'll get this mess cleaned up one way or another."

"We're counting on you, Sergeant."

Tsi rejoined Caleb at the door. They switched their projections at the same time, back to the pair of nurses. Then they left the room.

"The good news is that if Law can't find Joe, there's only one place I can think to look," Caleb said as they walked to the lift. "It's also the last place Governor Stone wants the Relyeh to know about." He hit the controls. The lift door opened and he entered the cab, still projecting Beth Stone.

"What is the bad news?" Tsi asked, changing her projection to Sheriff Zane.

The lift doors closed.

"We have to walk right through Law to get there."

Chapter 32

"Sheriff Ortega, report," Jackson Stone said, glancing nervously at the Relyeh Inahri projecting his silent wife.

"Governor, we've finished sweeps of the splits from Block Thirty to Thirty-five. Sheriffs Johnson and Anali are checking every cube across the city. There's still no sign of Joe."

Jackson's chest tightened at the news. The Inahri barely reacted, but he could tell the soldier was displeased by the tiny twitch at the corner of the projection's eye. It was almost spot-on to the same twitch his real wife exhibited when she was upset. Was their technology really that precise?

"Governor, at this rate it could be days before we find him. It takes at least an hour to search an entire block full of cubes."

"I know how long it takes," Jackson snapped back. His nerves were completely frayed. His confidence shattered. Every minute that passed, every report was leading the colony closer and closer to disaster. "Focus on the upper blocks. He couldn't have gone that far."

"Yes, Governor," Ortega said.

"Stone out." Jackson tapped his badge, still looking at Nan. "I'm doing the best I can. I'm sure you can see that."

The Inahri stared back at him. He didn't speak English. What the hell was the point in talking to him at all? He didn't need to speak English to know things weren't going well. They didn't have Joe King or the modulator. That was easy enough for the soldier to figure out on his own.

"Governor?" Deputy Bashir said. "Are you okay? No offense to your wife, but I don't think whether or not we're trying hard enough is her decision. "

Jackson spun on the deputy. The Law with him didn't know Nan wasn't Beth. He and his entourage had been searching for Joe for nearly four hours, going through every cube in the man's block. Bashir and the others had to think it was strange Beth hadn't said a word or showed little expression the entire time. It was hardly the Beth any of them knew, yet they seemed to accept his explanation that this whole situation was putting a lot of stress on her. It was enough conciliation to keep Jackson from taking out his frustration on the deputy.

The lies didn't matter now anyway.

Deputy Bashir and the other deputies with him shared an expression of surprise as the Inahri soldier dropped the projection. Nan raised his right arm and tapped on his wrist with his left hand. A new projection appeared. Sergeant Harai.

"Governor?" Bashir said, his voice shaky. "What in the hell—?"

"Not now," Jackson hissed back when Harai's voice came over the comm.

"Governor Stone, it has been half a cycle since you entered your city in search of my quantum dimensional modulator. Why are you still in there, instead of out here with my device?"

"Sergeant. We're doing our best. All of us. Joe is the ship's Chief Engineer. He's highly intelligent. He's evaded us so far, but he won't evade us forever."

"That's good because you don't have forever. Arluthu is regaining control of our ship as we speak. He expects that I will deliver the modulator to it the moment it is prepared to receive it. Do you understand?"

"Y-yes Sergeant. We're trying. I have all of my people on it."

"Maybe you and your people need a little more motivation. Nan..." Harai spoke in Inahri after that.

"Chi Za," Nan snapped back. In one smooth motion, he grabbed something from his belt and whipped his arm forward. Deputy Shane gurgled and fell backward, a dark blade sprouting from his throat.

"I can kill them all, if I need to," Harai said. "I can enter your city and find the modulator myself. Your engineer will be quite easy to find on our sensors once all of the other life forms are removed. Do you understand?"

Jackson could hardly breathe. He looked back at the other deputies. Their faces were pale. They were terrified. He was, too.

"Nan," Harai said.

Nan stepped forward, grabbing one of the frightened deputies. His neck broke with a sharp crack, and the Inahri let him drop to the ground.

"I expect fast responses," Harai said. "I expect results. My patience is running thin, Governor."

Jackson felt the tears welling in his eyes. This was a disaster. A total disaster. And it was all his fault. If Sergeant Card and the Guardians were here, he knew they would have been able to stand up to these assholes.

But Sergeant Card wasn't here. Jackson was on his own, and it was his own damn fault. All because of his pride. His arrogance. His stupidity.

"Governor, I'm waiting for an answer," Harai said. "Should I kill another?"

"No," Jackson said. "Wait. No, damn it. Stop. Please. Just give me a moment to think."

"You've had half a cycle to think."

"Wait. I. I think I may know where he is. There is one place we haven't looked."

"Why not?"

"It's." He lowered his head, shaking it. He had tried to keep the armory a secret. They would need the weapons if they got out of this. But if they didn't get out of this. All of those years. All of this way. And they were all going to die in the blink of an eye if he didn't make the right decision now. "There's a deck beneath the city. S-supplies and storage. He shouldn't have access, but maybe—"

A flash came from the split to his left, his eyes drawn to the brightness. He turned his head toward it, eyes widening in shock as the bolt rushed toward him.

Nan hit him in the side, knocking him out of the way just in time to avoid the full force of the blast. Even so, it scraped across the side of his chest, burning its way past. Jackson fell to the ground, rolling onto his stomach and clutching at the wound.

"Ahhh," he moaned, raising his head as Nan ripped the handgun off what appeared to be a nonexistent belt and began firing back. Raising his other hand, he blocked further assaults against the governor with an invisible shield.

Jackson looked toward the split, finding a pair of figures crouched at the corner. They were wearing ragged clothes and hoodies. Nothing more than a couple of kids from the upper blocks. Where the hell had they gotten guns like that?

He watched as one of them held up a hand, and a matching shield blocked Nan's return fire. A third person appeared from behind the first two, grabbing one by the shoulder and pulling him back. All three fled back down the split.

What the hell was going on?

The shooting stopped, the exchange of fire over in the space of a few pained breaths. Jackson rolled onto his back, lifting his head to look down at his side.

Nan holstered his weapon and kneeled beside him, withdrawing something from the belt around his armor and placing it against the wound. The pain subsided instantly.

"Governor," Harai said.

Jackson looked at Nan's wrist. Harai's projection was still there, moving with the motion of the soldier. He had witnessed the attack "Say again," Jackson asked.

"That deck beneath the city," Harai said. "Where is the entrance?"

"Law," Jackson replied. "The entrance is in Law."

"Good. Get up and take Nan to it. I will meet you there."

"What? No. Please let me take care of it."

"You had your time to take care of it," Harai said. "The enemy is upon us. No doubt they're searching for the modulator too. You're lucky you're still alive. You don't need to be."

"Enemy? What enemy?"

"It's not your concern. Your concern is getting to Law before they do. If they capture the modulator ahead of us, I will make my previous threats seem like sweet promises."

Chapter 33

Joe didn't expect to wake up.

When the demon found him, he'd been sure it was the end of him. That he was going to join his beloved Carol in the next place, his responsibility for the energy unit and the Deliverance, along with its citizens, finished.

He was wrong.

He came to almost as quickly as he had passed out, a lapse of time missing from his memories. He didn't even recall passing out. He only remembered the scraping noises and the shadows, the sounds of something approaching in the dim light of the armory. The fear and exhaustion.

He didn't remember the faces of the demons. The sound of their hissing or the stink of their breath. Not until he opened his eyes. Not until he wiped them free of debris and blinked away the dryness to bring them back into focus.

It was almost enough to send him out again.

They were directly in front of him—a wall of black, leathery flesh pressed together and covered in some kind of ichor that connected them to one another like adhesive snot. They hissed softly in a rhythmic pattern his engineer mind picked up on almost immediately—a rise-fall-fall-rise cadence that joined the humming of surrounding machinery.

Joe didn't move. He was too scared to move. He shifted his eyes left and right, trying to figure out where he was. He looked down. To his arms and legs and his lap, which was empty. Where was the energy unit?

The room was glowing with the unit's blue light. The light was spilling out from among the demons. They had it.

His left side was resting on a tall black column. It was warm. He leaned over a little more, putting his ear to it. He could hear the soft hum of energy coursing through it. He could feel the warmth. He glanced up at the blinking green light. Another column rested ahead of it, between him and the monsters. Its light was blinking red.

Servers. They were servers. This had to be the ship's mainframe. Its primary datastores. He had always wondered where they were hiding. The Engineering mainframe was networked into them and had limited access, but only the bridge would have complete control over these dozens of machines and petabytes of information. Maybe not even the bridge.

He turned his head, looking at the columns, forgetting the demons in his curiosity. More of the servers had flashing red lights. Damaged. His instinct was to get up and see if he could fix them.

Then he remembered Carol.

He squeezed his eyes shut as they instantly teared up again. Damn it. What the hell was happening here? Everything was falling apart so fast.

Focus. He had to focus. He was still alive. Governor Stone was still after the energy unit. There were more than enough guns in the armory to get through the creatures that had taken him, whatever they were. The unit wasn't safe. He wasn't safe. Neither were these things. He didn't want Stone to kill them. They clearly weren't dangerous. They could have killed him, but they didn't. They just wanted the energy unit. It seemed everyone wanted the energy unit.

But what for?

He gathered himself, forcing himself to concentrate. He had to try to talk to them, to tell them they were in trouble. To see if they would help him.

He almost laughed out loud. How was he going to communicate with these things? How was he going to express that he needed help? It seemed useless.

Too damn bad. He had to do it anyway. Trying and failing was better than not trying at all.

He cleared his throat as loudly as he could.

The demons didn't react.

"Uh, hello?" he shouted.

Nothing.

"Hello?"

Again, nothing.

He approached the back of the group. He froze as they began to split apart, hissing more loudly, the pattern of the noise shifting. He moved back to where he had started, suddenly afraid again.

A ridged back appeared at the center of the group. It was larger than the others, nearly twice the size at least. A body rose and unfolded itself. Thicker, larger, more muscled. It spread massive claws and unfurled a large head, its face pointed directly on Joe.

"Don't pass out," he said to himself, his lips barely moving, his heart racing. He clutched the edge of the server, holding himself steady. He could see the energy unit now, its power crackling from the floor into the demons. They seemed energized by it.

The central demon continued to straighten, forced to crouch beneath the ten-foot ceiling of the deck. It was massive and terrifying. Had the other demons saved him so it could eat him?

It stared at him with small black eyes. There was no hint of aggression in them. It was more of a curiosity. It regarded him from a distance at first, and then slowly began to lean toward him. The other demons moved out of its way, pulling themselves apart, the sticky goop spreading in thin tendrils across them before snapping and trailing to the floor.

Joe put his hands up. "I come in peace." He winced. What the hell did he just say?

The demon's head neared him. It was as large as his torso, its dozens of teeth the length of one of his hands. It took all of Joe's will to stand there as it drew near. To stay calm, to keep his bowels from emptying.

It kept coming, closing within inches. One quick snap and it could remove his head. At least it would be over quickly.

Instead, it ducked its head slightly, pressing the top of its skull gently into his chest. Then it backed up slightly…and *bowed*?

At least, that's what it seemed like. It kept lowering its head to the floor before raising it again and looking at him. Joe looked past it to the other demons. They were all facing him now, and all of them were copying the same movement.

What the hell? Were they pledging their allegiance to him?

What were these things?

Joe reached out tentatively. The largest demon watched

him but didn't move. He put his hand on its head, pressing down slightly in a similar show of… what? Affection? The demon hissed softly as he pulled his hand away.

"I guess that makes us…*friends*?" Joe said.

The demon stepped back. The rest of the group turned away. Joe stared at them, noticing the large one was expelling something from between its legs. Were those larvae? His eyes shifted back to the energy unit, resting in the open on the floor. The containment box was beside it. That was why these creatures had paid homage to him; they were thankful to him for bringing it.

Did they know he wasn't actually delivering it to them? Did they care? It didn't seem like it. They hovered around it protectively. Especially the large one.

She was their queen.

Like an ant queen, or a queen bee. It was creating new demons and using the energy unit as fuel. His engineering mind did some basic math. How many could it produce using the unlimited power of the unit?

These things could take over the whole planet.

He couldn't let that happen. No matter what these things were. No matter where they came from. No matter if they were peaceful or not. This was humankind's world. Metro's world. They hadn't come all this way to give it to these things, just like he wasn't about to let Governor Stone turn it over to some invading enemy. They had to fight for what was theirs.

He moved forward, into the group of demons. They watched him, their hisses changing slightly, but they didn't stop him. He positioned himself beneath the queen. She looked down on him with curiosity. He picked up the containment box beside the energy unit. It was intact enough to put the power source back in. He didn't want to touch it. He held it up to the queen.

"I need it back in the box," he said. Then he motioned to the unit and to the box. He put the box beside the unit, pointing to one and then the other. "Inside."

Would the creature listen? Did it have enough intelligence to begin to comprehend what he was asking? Would it kill him for even suggesting it? He had no idea. He knew nothing about these things except they weren't human. They weren't from Earth. Had they gotten into the ship somehow? But how was that possible? There was only one way to get down here.

Which meant they had been on the Deliverance the entire time.

Which meant...

He froze again, the realization hitting him hard. He looked up at the queen with new fear, though she continued to look down on him with common interest, not violent intent.

These were xenotrife. The aliens that had destroyed Earth. The creatures that had killed billions.

Joe's engineer mind stopped everything. His fear, his panic, his output of emotion. None of this added up. None of this computed. These things weren't killers. They had shown him reverence instead of tearing him to pieces. Either these weren't xenotrife, or something had happened to them. Something had changed them.

Was that why they were down here?

He shook his head slightly to clear it. It didn't matter. He had to focus on the now, not on all the questions that were suddenly darting through his mind. He returned to the task at hand, pointing at the energy unit and then the containment box.

The queen turned her head slightly, looking from one to the other and maybe beginning to understand. She looked at him again, hissing tersely, as if to say she didn't want to put the unit away.

He pointed more forcefully. Would she comply? Or would she kill him?

She hissed back woefully.

"Do it," he snapped like he would snap at one of his junior engineers when they balked at a unique solution to a critical problem.

The demons around him hissed in response, the sound an obvious warning. The queen lifted her head and hissed back at them in admonition. Then she lowered her head to Joe and slowly reached down to the energy unit. Blue arcs of power snapped against her flesh without harm as she picked the glowing sphere up and dropped it into the waiting box.

"Thank you," Joe said, smiling. "You're a good girl." he reached up and pressed his hand against the queen's head. He couldn't believe any of this.

The queen's head turned suddenly, whipping away from him toward the door. She hissed sharply, and four of the trife broke from the group, the hatch opening ahead of them. They moved out into the corridor and disappeared.

Joe looked at the queen, and then at the box. "I hope you'll help me keep this safe."

Someone was coming.

Chapter 34

Private John Washington looked up from the table when the door to the barracks opened. He smiled as Kiaan entered, matching the smile on the kid's face.

"How was it?" he asked, not that he needed Kiaan to answer. The Inahri had taken him out to teach him how to fly one of their transports. His joy was obvious.

"I thought the sims were fun, sir," Kiaan replied. "It was like that, only a thousand times better."

Paige and Dante both laughed at the response. They were sitting at the table with John, trying to pass the time as they nervously waited for Kiaan to come back and the real fun to begin.

John wasn't nervous. He had been through too much to ever be afraid of much of anything. Maybe there had been a time a long time ago. At least, it felt like a long time ago. Multiple lifetimes, though it had only been a little over two years.

Two years since Marla's death. Two years since the better part of him had died with her. The event had turned him into a killer. It had made him something he never wanted to be. And at the same time, becoming what he was today had saved so many lives. Had helped so many people. He didn't talk to others about God's plan, but time had taught him to believe in it.

"You don't have to call me *sir,*" John said. "I'm a Private." He smiled. "You don't have to call Sergeant Card 'sir' either. He isn't an officer."

He reached for the film around his throat. It still hadn't sunk in that he could speak again. The damage to his throat and face was so extensive, he never thought he would utter another word out loud. He had barely been able to believe it when he had woken in the Space Force field hospital and they had told him he was going to survive.

Only not all of him had survived. That was okay. He had become what he was supposed to become. He had done what he was supposed to do. As a Vulture. Search and rescue. Hundreds of saved civilians, thousands of dead trife. He would see Marla again one day. Until then, he would fight.

"Yes, sir," Kiaan replied.

"You just can't help yourself, can you?" Paige asked, with a grin.

"Sergeant, Private, whatever," Kiaan replied. "You're still a Marine, sir. That's more than any of us are."

"You're doing your part," John said. He looked at Paige and Dante. "That goes for both of you too. The only difference between you three and me is training. We all have courage. We all have heart."

"Yes, sir," Kiaan said.

The door opened and a Translator Intellect walked into the barracks, along with an Inahri soldier John had never seen before. He was wearing the blue robe of an officer, his projected rank and hardware visibly impressive. He was taller and more sturdy in appearance than most of the Inahri John had seen. If it weren't for the larger eyes and exaggerated facial bones, he could have passed as an ordinary Earther.

"I'm Colonel Jax," the Inahri said. "You will stand."

John hurried to his feet, eyeing the others to ensure they did the same. He stood at attention. Paige, Dante, and Kiaan mimicked his posture.

"Better," Colonel Jax said. "I will forgive your lack of haste this one time since you are new to our ranks." Jax looked at John. "You are the one Sergeant Caleb calls Wash?"

"Yes, sir," John replied.

"Congratulations. You are being promoted to squad leader, with the rank of Sergeant."

"What?" John said. He couldn't help but smile. It wasn't a lack of skills or intelligence that had kept him from earning any kind of advancement in Space Force. They hadn't even wanted to let him stay in because of his inability to speak, but between the desperation of the times and Caleb's insistence that he needed a man like John on his team, the brass had been forced to acquiesce.

"Sergeant Caleb is currently on assignment, and the Earthers need an Earther to lead them. Squad leaders require a rank of Sergeant or higher."

"Yes, sir," Washington said.

Colonel Jax let slip a small smile. John could see the others smiling too.

"Not that we have that out of the way," Jax continued. "We're preparing an assault on the Seeker, our city-ship which has been grounded for the last five ens, and which up until you arrived was protected by an Intellect we could not overcome. Your defeat of the ship's defenses has forced our hand, as the Relyeh are also moving quickly on the target. In fact, according to our Dancers they have already arrived, and are in the process of fortifying the position. Time is of the essence, which is why we need to keep this brief. Private Kiaan has spent the last quarter cycle with the rest of our secondary pilots, taking a crash course in Yun flight maneuvers."

"Yun?" Paige asked.

"The transport-slash-fighter," Kiaan said.

"Private Paige, you will address me as Colonel or sir," Jax said. "Private Kiaan, you will refrain from speaking out of turn."

"Yes, sir," Paige and Kiaan said.

"Private Kiaan's scores were at the top of the group," Jax continued. "It is a benefit to your squad, and brings honor to both Sergeant Tsi and Sergeant Caleb."

"Thank you, sir," John said.

Two more Inahri soldiers entered the barracks behind Colonel Jax. They were pulling a floating cart which had three suits of battle armor hanging from a rack, along with three crates of what John assumed were firearms.

"Corporals Gunsh and Hori," Jax said, introducing them. "They will help you get outfitted with your gear and provide basic instruction in its use. We are leaving in one-tenth cycle."

"How long is that, sir?" Dante asked. "In Earther terms?"

"A cycle is approximately ten Earth hours," the Translator Intellect answered. "One-tenth cycle would be one hour."

"Got it," Dante said.

"Your Yun is called the Mengin. It will transport your squad, including Gunsh and Hori, as well as Battle Command."

"Battle Command, sir?" John said. "I assume that means you?"

"Yes, along with my squad."

"Sir, is that a good idea?" Kiaan asked. "I'm not very experienced."

"Our more experienced pilots are needed to run interference against the Relyeh. Private Kiaan is the best of our reserves." Jax looked at Kiaan. "I'm sure you'll do perfectly well, Private."

Kiaan's face paled. "Thank you, sir."

"Private, I wanted you here for the basic squad briefing. You're dismissed. Go out to the launch area. Captain Shri will find you and point you to the Mengin. Prep the yun and wait for our arrival. We will have a more detailed company-wide debriefing before launch."

"Yes, sir," Kiaan said. He bowed slightly, glancing at John before leaving the barracks again.

"Sergeant Wash, I leave your squad in your hands. Gunsh, Hori, and the Intellect are yours." Jax removed the Intellect's control belt from his waist and handed it toward John. He took it, almost laughing because there was no way it would fit around his much larger waist. He wasn't even sure he would fit into the Inahri battle armor.

"Sir, how do I use this?" he asked.

"Preface your thought with 'Intellect.' It will interpret the next command."

"Yes, sir."

"I recognize it won't fit on your waist. You can wear it around your neck, as long as some part of it touches flesh."

"Yes, sir."

"You are being given a great honor in the control of an Intellect. It is normally reserved for officers of Major and above. We have only three, and they are irreplaceable."

"Yes, sir."

"Of course, these are not normal times, are they Sergeant Wash?"

"No, sir."

Colonel Jax sighed. "In many ways, I am glad for it, Sergeant. The hour arrives when we least expect it, but at least it has arrived. At least we can settle this once and for all."

"Yes, sir. Even if we lose, sir?"

"Losing is not an option, Sergeant."

John appreciated the Colonel's conviction. It was the kind of attitude that was needed to fight against the steep odds they faced. The type of mentality that made good Marines better Marines. It was one of the things he respected most about Caleb, and now he admired it in Colonel Jax.

"Yes, sir," John replied with equal conviction.

"One hour, Sergeant. I trust you'll be ready."

"We'll be ready, sir."

John bowed his head the way Tsi had taught them. Jax returned a curt bow and left the barracks.

"I just wanted to be a sheriff," Dante said. "Not get mixed up in an alien civil war."

"Look at it this way," John replied. "What we're about to do might actually be easier than what Caleb's trying to do."

"That doesn't help," Dante said. "I'd rather be in Metro."

"Me too," Paige said.

"Metro is depending on us," John said. "Nothing has changed there. Only the venue has changed. We watch each other's backs, we take care of one another, we stay alive. Understood?"

"Yes, Sergeant," Dante and Paige replied.

"Gunsh, Hori. Show us the goods."

Chapter 35

"Earther squad," Colonel Jax said over the comm. "It's time."

John turned his head to look at Dante, Paige, and the two Inahri soldiers assigned to his unit. Like him, they were all wearing Inahri battle armor. Unlike him, theirs was standard issue.

He had always been big. Even as a kid, his family and friends had always told him he would be a football player one day. A linebacker, maybe. He had played in college too and might have gone pro if life hadn't intervened. Another blessing in disguise. A torn ACL led to meeting Marla, which led to love, which led to realizing that living with chronic traumatic encephalopathy wasn't something he was particularly interested in, regardless of how much money he might make.

That had led to a career in marketing, which he'd liked well enough, and between his job and Marla's job as a nurse, they were comfortable.

Then the trife had come, and everything had changed.

"Sergeant Wash, respond," Colonel Jax said sharply, ripping John out of the memory.

"Earther Squad online and ready," Washington replied. There was a two-second delay while the Intellect translated the statement over the comm.

"Depart for the Mengin immediately."

"Yes, sir. Earthers, move out."

John took a step forward, his battle armor a bulky extension of himself. The armor was similar to Marine advanced tactical combat armor, in that it held a self-contained suite of smart sensors, comm equipment, augmented weapons targeting systems, and the like. It was different in that it was much larger and bulkier, owing to the enhanced exoskeleton that rested inside the suit itself, which provided the wearer a nearly three hundred percent increase in strength.

The wearer needed it too. The armor was twice as heavy as a suit of ATCA, but also much better armored. It was made of the same alloy as the Cerebus armor, but it was close to three times thicker. The thickness and composition made it impervious to most Earther weapons save for maybe a direct hit from a railgun or a hard strike from a missile and almost as impenetrable from Inahri weapons too. According to Gunsh, it could take a few hits from an ion rifle before it would buckle, and even the advanced mass drivers of the Inahri Yun had a hard time cutting an armored soldier down with one hit.

The real challenge was in learning the interface. It was all written in Inahrai, which meant memorizing the symbols more than understanding what they were. He knew how to activate the comms, how to mark targets on the tactical, which was head and shoulders better than the Marine version, and how to lock his ordnance and his squad's on a mark. Hori claimed there were fifty more subsystems they hadn't touched on, but the small set of ten would be more than enough for a basic assault.

John went to the door, where Pai was waiting. The small robot bowed to him as he neared.

"Good hunting, Sergeant," it said.

John found the external comm. "Thank you," he replied. He ducked and turned his body to angle it through the opening, the size of the door his first challenge in the suit. He bumped the frame on the way through, emerging into the cavern.

The entire compound was a flurry of activity, especially around the two dozen transports that would carry the Inahri assault team to the city-ship. Each transport could hold up to four squads, twenty soldiers, as long as they squeezed in tight. Almost five hundred battle-armored Inahri were heading to the Seeker to reclaim it from the Relyeh. How many Relyeh were waiting to stop them?

He was going to find out soon enough.

"Sergeant, I'm about ready to wet myself," Paige said through the squad comm, walking single-file behind him.

"Seconded," Dante said. "Is it too late to play sick?"

"I understand you're nervous," John replied. "I can't say I was ever scared because I lost that when I lost Marla. But I can tell you I spent two years fighting trife with Caleb in some of the worst conditions and situations you can imagine. Heck, you probably can't even begin to imagine them. We survived by working together then, and we'll do it today too."

"Yes, Sergeant," Paige said.

John hefted his ion rifle in his arms, glancing down at the weapon. Two connectors ran from the gun to his armor. One was for the targeting computer, the other for the energy supply. The rifle had nearly unlimited ammunition as long as it remained linked to the battle armor. Even if it did run out, his kit had included a ion pistol and pair of xix, just in case he needed to fight hand-to-hand. Knitting jokes aside, the xix were serious weapons, and at full-charge powerful enough to to tear the helmet from a suit of battle armor and land a secondary killing blow.

John wasn't thrilled with the idea. He had never killed another human. He had only killed trife. Lots of trife. He understood this was war and the fate of the Deliverance depended on it. It still didn't sit all that well.

There were a few other Inahri along the squad's path, and they stopped and bowed to the soldiers on the way past, showing their respect for the mission. John waved back to them, appreciating the show of support.

The squad cleared the structures of the compound quickly and in better spirits than when they had left the barracks, reaching the edge of the launch area and navigating through the other assembled squads to where John's armor told him Colonel Jax was standing. He made visual contact with the Colonel a few seconds later, easily identifiable in battle armor painted a deep blue with gold accents. He guided the rest of the team to the side of their transport.

"Earthers, line up," he said into the comm when they reached the colonel. He came to attention at the front of the line, the rest of the unit joining him in a neat column, with the Intellect taking up the last position.

"Sergeant Wash," Jax said. "I trust you're accustomed to the armor?"

"Yes, sir," John replied. "We're ready, willing, and able, sir."

"Good." Jax pointed to the Mengin's hatch. " Your pilot and the rest of the assets are already inside. Join them."

"Yes, sir. Earthers, move out."

John led them to the Mengin's entry hatch, climbing into the transport. He stopped to bow to the members of Battle Command, officers all of them, easily identifiable by the blue marks provided by the battle armor's tactical systems and the blue lines painted on the shoulders of their armor.

The officers nodded back, and John found five empty places near the front of the craft. He also found Kiaan standing beside the pilot's seat. He had the metallic control-gloves on his hands and the AR goggles resting on his forehead.

"Sergeant," Kiaan said, bowing to John as he approached the front of the craft.

"Private. Don't crash." He smiled. Kiaan's face paled. "It was a joke."

"Yes, sir," Kiaan replied, laughing meekly.

John sat at the edge of the bench seat. Dante sat beside him, while Paige, Gunsh, and Hori perched on the opposite side. The Intellect moved to the cargo area in the back of the ship, tucking itself in as much as it could.

John closed his eyes, trying to calm his rapidly beating heart. It wasn't fear that raised his pulse. It was anticipation.

He turned his head to the right as Colonel Jax boarded the transport, his presence signaling everyone on board to come to attention and bow their heads.

"Heads loose," Jax said.

The soldiers relaxed slightly, lifting their heads.

"Opening a company-wide channel," Jax said. "Transferring briefing visuals now."

John's HUD flashed and showed a new set of alien symbols in the top left corner. The symbols changed color, and a schematic of the city-ship faded into view in front of his eyes.

"This is the latest report from our Dancers," Colonel Jax said, the city lighting up with red marks symbolizing Relyeh targets. "Three hundred enemy soldiers, four Abominations, and at least two automatons marked appropriately on the schematic."

"Abominations, sir?" John asked.

"Like battle armor, only larger and more powerful," Jax replied. "The Relyeh make them. Grotesque machines, piloted by the worst kind of slaves. The abominations are too complex to work like a yun or armor. They require a direct mind interface. When the pilot is selected, they are melded to the machine. Once they enter the Abomination's cockpit, they never come back out."

A shiver ran down John's spine at the statement. He couldn't begin to imagine being a slave to a machine like that.

"There are different kinds," Hori added. "Each as frightening as the next. When we encounter them, the best thing we can do is run."

"The Abominations are unique to the Relyeh Inahri like the xix are unique to us," Colonel Jax said.

"That doesn't seem like a fair trade," Paige said.

"There is a reason we are the ones in hiding. Regardless, we must persevere." A pair of spots lit up on the schematic. "The Dancers have also identified engineering teams that have been deployed here and here. Our engineering team's best guess is that one Relyeh team is focused on prepping power conduits and ensuring the modulator will deliver energy appropriately, while the other will be testing the ship's thrust, guidance, life-support, and anti-gravity systems. There may also be a Relyeh commander present in the city."

John noticed the sharp, nervous exhale from the officer sitting beside Dante in response to the news.

"Is that an added concern, sir?" John asked. "A Relyeh commander?"

"It isn't an immediate concern," Jax replied. "Our primary objective is to route the enemy forces and seize control of the Seeker. Our secondary objective is to disable one of the two engineering teams. This will serve to delay any potential launch while we regroup and reinforce. Our tertiary objective is to destroy the portal chamber." Jax looked at John after he said it, switching his comm to squad level in anticipation of the question. "I will explain if needed."

"Yes, sir," John replied.

"Each of your platoon commanders has been provided individual orders for the assault. We may have superior numbers at the outset, but don't get sloppy. The Relyeh have proven their ability to overcome perceived shortfalls many times in the past. Good hunting to you all."

"Chi Cox," hundreds of Inahri said over the comm.

Jax shifted, head swiveling to cover each of the soldiers on the Mengin. "Dojun squad, you will be responsible for covering a potential evacuation. You'll follow the bulk of the attack force to the position marked on your display and then dig in. It will also be your responsibility to defend the Mengin and Battle Command aboard it."

"Chi Cox," the members of Dojun squad said.

"Earther squad, I've prepared a route for you to follow into the city to the modulator housing. There is a high probability one of the engineering teams will be active there. You are to make contact with them and destroy them. Once that objective is complete, you are to seek and engage the enemy at your discretion until either the primary objective is achieved or the retreat is called."

"Sir, you're giving us one of the secondary objectives?"

Dante asked. "Isn't that a little important to trust to people you hardly know?"

"Sergeant Caleb earned Sergeant Tsi and General Gai's respect. Is that honor misdirected?"

"No, sir," Dante said.

"You Earthers have extensive experience with close-quarters indoor combat. You're uniquely suited to the task of reaching the modulator housing. I have confidence in you."

"Thank you, sir," John said, though he didn't necessarily agree with the colonel's assessment. He was the only one of the group who had much real combat experience at all. "Consider it done."

"I already do. Private Kiaan, is the Mengin ready?"

"Yes, Colonel," Kiaan said.

"Then let us not waste any more time."

Chapter 36

The transports lifted in near perfect unity, twenty-four ships rising from the stone surface of the cavern, the light humming of the Inahri or Axon technology reverberating across the space. The Mengin was the only ship in the group that was slightly off, ascending more slowly than the rest before coming into position at the back of the line.

John kept his head craned to the left, looking out the forward viewport. The squadron of alien ships was an impressive and imposing sight, unlike anything he had ever seen before. While he had watched squadrons of F-15s drop firebombs on cities to burn thousands of trife, they had rocketed past the target zones, there and gone in the blink of an eye and a wall of flame.

"Zhu Company, this is General Goi." The general's voice came over John's comm, stiff and calm. "You have my honor and respect in your undertaking. I trust you will show the Relyeh that the Inahri need no masters."

"Chi Ban!" a few hundred voices cried back.

"Good hunting, my brothers and sisters."

"Chi Ban!" they shouted again.

"Here we go," Kiaan said through the Earther squad comm. "Hold on tight."

John took a moment to glance at Paige and Dante as the transports all began to accelerate toward the illusory wall ahead of them. It was harder to make out their faces through the blue tinted glass of the battle helmets, but he could tell they were nervous—Dante more so than Paige. The second woman seemed to enjoy being a soldier, despite her anxiety. There was a hint of excitement in her eyes. The sheriff? She probably wished she had never gotten involved with Caleb Card and his Guardians in the first place.

The transports slipped through the projection and out into the open air. Looking back out the forward viewport, John could see every move Kiaan was going to make before he made it by following the lead row of ships. They ascended sharply ahead, each successive row matching the maneuver as though they were wired to the lead column's flight path. And maybe they were right now. Kiaan's hands rested on his legs instead of working to control the ship.

They didn't go too high, sticking close to the terrain and gaining velocity, a trio of blue circles flaring at the backs of the transports. They skirted the river north for a few kilometers and then angled back toward the mountains.

"Sergeant Wash," Colonel Jax said. "I'm sending you updated positioning data from our Dancers."

"Yes, sir," John replied.

A symbol on his HUD blinked a moment later, and he opened it with a thought. A new schematic of the city-ship appeared, showing a ten-second lapse of enemy movements from the last dataset.

"They're fortifying their position, sir," he said. "And it

seems like the rest of the engineers are gathering at the modulator housing."

"Yes. They're increasing their energy on preparing for the modulator. Let us hope that doesn't mean they've already captured it."

"Yes, sir."

John's thoughts turned to Caleb. He was more than a commander to him. Over the last two years, he had become his best friend. More than his best friend. They were like brothers.

He hoped his brother was okay.

"Looks like the bad guys know we're coming," Kiaan said, bringing John's attention back to the forward view. The lead transports were breaking away from the group, splitting along the flanks and turning back. Kiaan lifted his hands at the same time, and the Mengin shuddered slightly, switching from automated to manual control.

"Stay on the target," Colonel Jax said. "Follow the others."

"Yes, sir," Kiaan replied.

The Mengin stayed with the bulk of the group, remaining on a straight vector that carried them directly toward the city-ship.

And the oncoming enemy.

John saw them before anyone else in the transport. For all the damage to his face, his eyes were clean and sharp, and he was able to pick out the dark spots against the fading light, growing slightly larger with each passing second. He couldn't get a good count, not when they were probably arranged in perfect rows like the Free Inahri squadron had been moments earlier. It didn't matter. There was no way they were friendly.

"Buckle up," Kiaan said. "This is going to get a little bumpy."

The Inahri reached under their seats, removing a small device, tapping it to activate it, and placing it on their laps. John did the same, grabbing the anchoring device and getting it into position only moments before the first flashes of incoming energy bolts forced Kiaan to bank hard to the left, peeling away from the incoming Relyeh force.

The maneuver pressed John back against the bench seat, the anchor holding him tight and helping with the g-forces. The tight confines also kept them stabilized, each soldier pressing a shoulder into that of the next one as the transport ducked and dodged.

"There's an awful lot of them," Kiaan said, his hands making delicate gestures that guided the ship into different types of evasive turns and tucks. Bolts flashed around them, each one seeming to pass within centimeters of the hull.

"Heavier than expected," Colonel Jax agreed. "Stay focused."

Voices began coming across the comm, calm words spoken in Inahrai that quickly began to step on one another. The Translator Intellect tried to keep up with them, repeating the words into John's comm as quickly as it could, able to mix three voices simultaneously before reaching its limit. The assault force was taking casualties before it even arrived, the enemy ships quickly blasting them out of the sky.

"Sir, permission to engage," Kiaan said, pushing the ship into a sharp descent.

"Negative. Stay on target."

"Sir, I can get them," Kiaan insisted. "I can help."

"No. You need to get us there."

"We might be the only ones who make it at this rate," Kiaan said through the squad comm. "We're down a quarter of our force already, and we've got thirty klicks to the target. I can outfly these jerks. I know I can."

John turned his head toward Jax. "Colonel, Kiaan is a good pilot. If he says he can help, I believe him. We're losing too many ships and too many soldiers. If this keeps up, we won't have anything left to attack with."

Jax hesitated a moment. Then he nodded. "Permission given."

"Thank you, sir," Kiaan said, the transport slowing suddenly enough that John was shoved sideways into the soldier beside him.

"Kiaan, what are you—" John started to ask.

"Hold on, Sarge," Kiaan said.

John watched the nose of the transport flip up and a pair of blue bolts launched from the cannons on either side of them. The first few flashed into empty sky. Then an enemy ship crossed in front of them, four bolts digging into its hull and tearing it to pieces.

"Whoohooo!" John shouted, the excitement causing the inside of his throat to burn and the fabric over it to itch.

The Mengin accelerated skyward, pushing him harder into the soldier on his right. Kiaan threw the ship into a spin before corkscrewing back into a level position, coming out of it right behind another enemy craft. He triggered the cannons, blasting the blue circles at the back of the Relyeh ship. They smoked and sputtered, and the enemy craft began to drop.

"Impressive," Colonel Jax said.

John couldn't agree more. In the span of a few hours, Kiaan had gone from a nervous kid to a confident pilot. Sometimes all anybody needed was someone who believed in them.

Except more than two Relyeh ships were attacking

them. Kiaan's efforts had quickly helped re-steady the odds, but it was far from over.

"Get us headed back toward the Seeker," Jax said. "We still have other work to do. If you get an easy shot, take it."

"Yes, sir," Kiaan said.

The Mengin flipped and rolled, coming out back on course. John looked over to Paige and Dante. Dante looked like she wanted to throw up. Or maybe she already had. Her face was pale, her eyes flat.

"Dante, are you okay?" John asked.

"A little less spinning would be nice," she replied. "I'll survive."

"Sorry, sheriff," Kiaan said.

"It's okay. I'd rather be sick and alive."

"Yes, ma'am."

Bolts continued to flash past the Mengin and the other ships in the fleet, though there were fewer than before. The remaining lead ships managed to distract some of the enemies, leading them away from the bulk of the assault and into more direct dogfights. It didn't make their ingress easy or safe, but it did improve the odds somewhat.

It wasn't long before John saw the city-ship approaching. There were more lights on inside than he remembered from their first pass, but otherwise it looked the same. The clouds had thickened overhead, and a light rain was smacking off the transport, along with streaks of lightning that added to the flashes of the enemy bolts.

The flashes increased an instant later, red blasts of energy suddenly erupting from the ship itself in heavy ground fire that slammed into two of the transports before they had a chance to react. A pair of fireballs lit the sky, and John could see the soldiers falling out of the suddenly vaporized craft, tumbling toward the ground below.

"Shit!" Kiaan said, joining the other Free Inahri vessels

in fresh evasive maneuvers. A red bolt seemed to hit the front viewport, so big and so bright John was momentarily blinded. The Mengin shook, rocking violently and then beginning to drop.

"Hold on," Kiaan said.

John could hear the pilot continuing to curse beneath his breath, and then the Mengin broke its fall. It still shifted left and right, the anchor pressing hard on John to keep him in place. His eyes began to clear, and he could see they were almost to the target, despite the target's best efforts to keep them away.

The approach didn't get any easier as they closed the last few kilometers. Red bolts from ahead joined blue bolts from behind, while lightning and rain added to the chaos. Ten of the Free Inahri ships were gone, almost half of their original assault force. Colonel Jax seemed unbothered by any of it, calmly passing out orders in Inahrai over the comms, his head still but his eyes moving, watching all of the data projected into his helmet. John was impressed with the way the officer managed to ignore all of the action around him to focus on the task.

There were still a few transports ahead of them as they passed the edge of the ship, the hull rising from the muck. John watched the other ships drop quickly, falling into different channels within the city and lighting up the area around them with cannon fire as they laid cover in preparation for landing. Each one that made it down announced their success and that their units were moving out. John winced when one of the announcements was cut off midsentence, a ball of flame appearing to the west side of the Seeker at the same moment.

"Approaching the target," Kiaan said. "Colonel, I don't know if we can stay on the ground. We're sitting ducks there."

"Drop the squads and then get us back in the air," Jax said, agreeing with the assessment. "This ship is the most important ship in the group. Do you understand?"

"Yes, sir," Kiaan replied. "I have our target in visual, coming in hot."

Blue bolts flashed from the Mengin's cannons, lighting up the surface of the Seeker and giving John brief glimpses of enemy soldiers behind fortified positions, firing large rifles at the fast-approaching transport. They quickly ducked and covered as the bolts slammed against their positions, crouching behind the Axon alloy, which absorbed most of the blow.

"If the Relyeh had the modulator installed, the Seeker's plasma batteries would have shredded us already," Hori said.

"Dojun, Earther, get ready," Colonel Jax said.

John deactivated his anchor and stood at the same time as the commander of Dojun squad. Dojun would exit the transport first, putting down a dense layer of covering fire to allow the Earthers to get out and start moving forward, toward an entrance hatch already marked on their shared schematic. It was nearly a hundred meters past the enemy fortifications, meaning they would need to quickly break through to get inside.

They were going to break through. He would see to that.

"Earthers, line up and prepare to disembark," John said. "Intellect, you're coming too."

The Intellect unfolded itself from the cargo area, standing upright.

"Touchdown in five," Kiaan said. "Four. Three. Two."

The hatch on the side of the transport slid open. A bolt immediately launched through it, catching one of the Dojun soldiers in the shoulder, the heavy weapon piercing his battle armor. He cried out, returning fire with his remaining hand as he slumped back into his seat.

"Go!" Kiaan said, the Mengin bouncing slightly as it hit the Seeker's hull.

Dojun squad charged out of the side of the transport, opening fire as they did. One of the squad was hit immediately, grunting in pain but continuing ahead.

"We're up," John said, lifting his rifle and leading the Earthers to the hatch.

"Good hunting, Sergeant Wash," Colonel Jax said.

John reached the hatch, his helmet already displaying the targets hiding behind cover and firing at Dojun squad, first out of the transport. Their fire was thick, keeping the enemy units on the defensive for the moment at least.

He had spent his last two years on Earth in the middle of the worst combat he could imagine.

This was nothing.

Chapter 37

"Follow me; don't slow down," John said as a red bolt hit the side of the hatch right next to his helmet. He leaped from the transport, charging forward to the nearest cover, where two members of Dojun Squad were already waiting.

Dante and Paige came out behind him, rushing to his position with Goshun, Hori, and the Intellect close behind. The enemy fire seemed to stop momentarily when the Intellect emerged from the craft, apparently surprised to find the Free Inahri had one in their service. It only froze them for an instant, and then they began shooting again.

"Intellect, defend yourself," John said. He felt a slight vibration across the base of his neck where the control band rested, confirming the message had been received. The Intellect raised its right arm, and the enemy bolts started flashing harmlessly against a sudden shield.

The Relyeh were in deep trouble if they had neglected to bring any anti-Intellect weaponry.

They hadn't. The red bolts were joined by a flash of white a moment later. The Intellect barely managed to avoid it, ducking behind cover just in time.

The Mengin hummed more loudly behind them and then began to rise and turn. A few of the enemy soldiers tried to hit it as it retreated, and Paige caught one of them in the helmet with an ion blast, punching through the faceplate and killing him instantly.

"Nice shot," John said. He scanned his HUD, getting a glimpse of the enemy's position. "Dojun, concentrate fire." He marked the targets for the other squad, the Intellect translating for him. "Earthers, we're heading up the right flank. Stay tight and move as fast as you can. On my mark."

"Roger," Paige and Dante said.

"Chi," Goshun and Hori replied.

Washington watched the enemy ahead of them as the Dojun squad continued firing. The left flank ducked away, unable to stay up without risking being hit. The right side adjusted its fire to chase back Dojun, giving the Earthers a small window.

"Go!" John shouted, rising and pushing forward, the exoskeleton straining to move his bulk. He charged ahead, an imposing figure for the smaller enemy, who hesitated at his sudden appearance.

He began shooting, his first bolt hitting the enemy in the shoulder, his next hitting them in the chest. The strikes beat through the battle armor, leaving deep scores as the target ducked out of sight. He took a glancing hit off his side, the shooter dropping when another bolt from Paige scored a direct hit on their faceplate.

JOHN RAN FULL THROTTLE, the suit catching up to him and augmenting his steps. His long strides covered ground in a hurry, taking him further ahead of the others as he raced for the first enemy fortification.

The enemy saw him coming, adjusting their fire too late. He shouted as he leaped toward the barrier the defenders had erected, firing down at them as the suit carried him over the fortification and into their midst. He took one of them out before he even hit the ground, coming down and immediately shoving a second, the force of his mass throwing the soldier back and into the wall hard enough to take them off their feet. He fired his rifle into the enemy point-blank, the ion burst piercing soldier's battle armor and killing him.

He spun, swinging a hard fist and catching a second soldier in the helmet, the force of his blow cracking the faceplate and sending the enemy sprawling. A warning in his HUD gave him a split-second to duck away from an attack from his rear, which ended when Paige caught the attacker in the temple with her blaster. John sprang up toward a visibly frightened Relyeh Inahri, grabbing him by his arm and throwing him back and to the ground.

The Intellect sprang from nowhere, landing on the downed soldier who struggled to rise. The end of the Intellect's hand formed into a blade and it stabbed downward through the stricken enemy's faceplate, stopping his struggle.

"Watch the flank!" Dante shouted, first to fire back to the left side of the path. Their advance had caused the enemy to be more bold, and they were suddenly under heavier fire.

"Cover!" John shouted, ducking against the corner of the nearest rise, joined there by Dante a moment later. They both shot back at the encroaching enemy, helping Dojun Squad catch them in a deadly crossfire.

They were stupid to come out of cover. It was terrible tactics, driven by what? Fear? Desperation?

John's HUD flashed, picking up a new target coming at

them from their intended entry point. It was bigger than any of the battle-armored soldiers they had faced so far and moving fast.

"Abomination!" Hori shouted, the fear evident in his voice. "Take cover!"

It came around a bend in the channel a moment later, splashing through gathered puddles, partially obscured by the intensifying rain. It wasn't the way Colonel Jax had described it—like an oversized suit of battle armor. Not like that at all. Oversized was an understatement. It was nearly seven meters tall and almost too wide to fit in the space between the city-ship's sloping towers. It wasn't shaped like a human at all. Dozens of limbs connected to either side of an oblong center, where the glass of a cockpit was visible in the shape of a sharp slash down the center. Small extrusions like eyes surrounded the cockpit, casting red, green, and white light ahead of it into the street, while the appendages themselves reached out for anything they could grab propelling the machine forward at a ridiculous rate.

It came forward a few meters, and then a pair of doors swung open on its underside, four barrels dropping out with them. Two of the barrels began to fire projectiles at John and the others.

Large shells whipped through the rain and began ricocheting off the city-ship's alloy hull, creating small sparks as they were redirected, flying around the battlefield at odd angles. It made them all the more dangerous.

"Down!" John shouted diving and rolling behind cover as rounds exploded past his helmet. One of Dojun Squad's members was too slow. The heavy caliber shells tore right through the Inahri's battle armor and cut the organic material inside to ribbons. "Hori, how do we fight that thing?"

"We don't," the Inahri soldier replied.

"That isn't an option right now," John snapped back. "I need an answer."

"We need to get in close," Hori replied. "We need to get onto it. There's usually a weak spot on the back near the power plant. Damage that, and it will blow."

All they had to do was get onto it. John ducked his head out, watching its many limbs flail around it as it continued its approach. It was a hundred meters away and closing fast.

No problem. John quickly brought up the city-ship's schematic, checking the area around them. "Sergeant," John said, talking to Dojun Squad's leader. He didn't know the man's name. "Take your squad around the structure to this mark. Earthers, I want you to come around here. Get behind it. I'll draw its fire and lead it into position."

"Sergeant, that's suicide," Paige said.

"Not exactly. Do it. Now!"

The Abomination was still approaching, though it had lost its targets and stopped shooting. The battle armor's sensors were reading more soldiers coming up from the rear, reinforcements from inside. They weren't going to have much time to do this, and if the thing's controller realized what they were doing…

The pilot wouldn't. The Inahri didn't engage in this type of combat very often, and this was precisely why Colonel Jax had deployed him here.

"Intellect, with me," John said, bringing the artificial intelligence to his side. "We're going out there. I want full shields, as much as you can manage."

He closed the schematic and leaned out from cover. The thing was almost on top of him, even more imposing from close in. Would the Intellect be able to prevent him from getting blasted to nothing?

He was about to find out.
He stepped out into its path.

Chapter 38

The Abomination seemed to hesitate a moment, as if John's sudden presence was a projection cast by the Intellect standing between him and the giant machine.

The hesitation didn't last.

The machine started shooting again. Bullets whipped toward John, but rained down, captured by the Intellect's flare of shield energy.. It only took seconds for nearly a hundred rounds to fire, all of them captured by the shields.

John's heart started to race. Was that fear? He looked at his HUD, surprised to find his squad wasn't even close to being in position. "Earthers, what's the holdup?" he asked.

The Abomination continued its advance, closing within twenty meters. It sent another volley John's way, the Intellect capturing the assault. The Axon AI was able to stop the bullets, but it couldn't help him against the dozen flexible arms, each one easily large and powerful enough to crush him, battle armor or not.

"Sarge, we're in trouble," Dante reported. "We're pinned down and taking heavy fire."

"Roger. Dojun, it's on you." There was no reply. "Dojun?" John checked his HUD. The entire squad was missing. Shit.

"Intellect, cut left toward the tower."

The Intellect obeyed him immediately, breaking to the left with him, protecting him from the Abomination's assault.

"Earthers, one of you needs to get behind this thing," John said, ducking behind the tower. The gunfire stopped right away, though he could hear the machine still coming for him. "I don't care who. I don't care how. Just do it, or I'm going to die."

He had always assumed he would be okay with that outcome. Marla was waiting for him, and he had fought the good fight. Now that the possibility seemed so present, he realized he wasn't quite ready to go. Not yet. Not while the people of Metro needed the Guardians. Not while so many lives were at stake.

His plan might have failed.

That didn't mean he would.

It didn't mean he would have time to plan, either. A long, octopus-like arm shot past the corner, the clawed end grappling with him. Another appeared a moment later, and then a third came over the short tower, grabbing the wall a few meters above John's head.

John fired his rifle into one of the arms, testing it. The force of the blast put a dent in the alloy. It was something, but not nearly enough. He turned to run again, finding more cover twenty meters away.

Only the cover wasn't vacant. Red bolts started lashing out from the position. John ducked and rolled, two of the bolts hitting his battle armor without punching through it. He came up facing the enemy soldiers, aimed and fired, hitting one of them and knocking him down. Beside him, the Intellect joined the fight, extending its right hand and firing. The invisible projectile slammed the second soldier, clearing a path for him.

But it was too late.

The Abomination's bulbous body came around the side of the tower, gun barrels swinging into position. John managed to get himself behind the Intellect as the machine began firing again, sending a spray of shells into the AI. Its shields failed, bullets ripping into it and leaving John within a centimeter of his life.

"Hold on, Sarge," Kiaan said.

John glanced to his right in time to see the blue bolts of the Mengin's cannons whip across the sky and into the side of the Abomination. Two of its limbs tore off, throwing it off-balance enough for its attack to suddenly go wide, its shells ricocheting off the side of the tower and past John.

The Mengin whined past, a second Relyeh yun behind it, giving chase. There still wasn't much time.

"Intellect, set your self-destruct. Twenty seconds."

He didn't even know if the AI had a self-destruct until the control ring vibrated, acknowledging the request. He bent over and picked up the battered humanoid, slinging it effortlessly over his shoulder as he charged the Abomination, ticking the seconds away in the back of his mind.

Could he get it in position and get away in time?

The Abomination was recovering, and an arm shot out to grab him. John rolled beneath it, almost losing the Intellect on the way, springing back to his feet. He made it to the bottom of the machine's massive body, still a few meters off the ground.

"Intellect, when I throw you, grab on," he said.

The control ring buzzed again. John smiled. He dropped the ion rifle, getting a two-handed grip on the AI. The Abomination was trying to back up to reach him, its weakness exposed. Another of its arms swept across its body, and John jumped, planting his feet on it for a little extra height. He bounded from it, using all the strength in his legs to gain another two meters. It put him close enough to the Abomination's body that he didn't even need to throw the Intellect. The AI grabbed the bottom of the Abomination's arms, fingers already morphed into claws to dig in and hold on.

John's internal count hit twenty as he fell away. The heat of the Intellect's detonation swept over him as he tumbled, hitting the ground hard and rolling away. Debris and flames licked at his armored body. The smaller explosion was followed an instant later by a larger one, the power plant breached and stability lost. Burning fluid splashed down on and around John as he got to his feet, putting his heavily-armored hand over his less armored faceplate and running blindly away.

"Whooooohoooooo!" Kiaan shouted into the comm. "I can see that fireball from up here, Sarge."

"Earthers, status," John said, still stumbling away from the remains of the Abomination.

"Still pinned, Sarge," Dante replied. "Gorush is down."

"Roger." John could see the HUD behind his hand. He found his squad a hundred meters north, still short of his mark, which had a group of Relyeh soldiers covering it. If the Dojun squad hadn't folded, those troops wouldn't be there.

He eyed the tactical, finding another route. The enemy would see him coming on their sensors, but it wouldn't matter if he went in hard.

He reached for his rifle, left hand grasping air before he remembered dropping the weapon. He rested his right hand on his sidearm. It wasn't powerful enough to break through the battle armor.

He shifted his left hand again, to the pair of xix on his back.

"Earthers, get ready. Paige, keep doing what you do so well. I'm going in hot."

Chapter 39

John didn't know how fast he could run in the Inahri battle armor. Not until he actually attempted it. He had always been quick on his feet despite his size. It had served him well during his college football days, and it served him well now.

He charged along the surface of the Seeker, in a narrow channel between two of the short towers which he assumed where embedded weapons positions like the one he had entered with Caleb. His feet skipped lightly across the ground despite the weight of the armor, the speed of his motion keeping him in the air for the majority of the time. His velocity was measured in the top right corner of the HUD, but it was printed in Inahrai symbols. He watched them go by to make sure he didn't see the same one flash twice, meaning he was slowing down. As long as his momentum increased, as long as he moved fast, he would have a chance.

Judging by the way the ground blurred beneath him, John guessed he was moving close to thirty klicks per hour, an impossible foot speed without an exosuit to keep him upright and in motion. He glanced at the tactical, noting the marks coming into better focus ahead and watching as half of them began to spin to cover the rear.

John held an xix in each hand.He tapped them together activating the energy flow. He remembered his nanna's knitting tips as he moved them across one another, quickly creating a web of energy.

Bolts began whizzing toward him. He raised the xix in front of him, catching a few of them with the weapon, which captured the energy and stored it.

"Earthers, five seconds," he said, closing on the edge of the line. When the first volley didn't drop him, two more of the Relyeh Inahri turned to join the attack. "Three seconds."

He brought the xix together and thrust each of them forward. Two bolts of lightning stretched out from the weapons, striking two of the enemy soldiers. Arcs of energy ran along their battle armor, which shut down momentarily in response.

"Now!"

John dove forward, sliding on the chest of the armor as the Earthers ahead of him came up from their cover and opened fire, multiple bolts pounded the two frozen Relyeh, piercing their protection and knocking them down. The other Inahri realized what was happening and began to turn again. At the same time, John rolled up among them, xix swinging and smashing into them. Electricity took their battle suits offline, and then Paige, Dante, and Hori finished the job.

It was over in seconds, leaving six Relyeh Inahri dead at John's feet. "Clear!"

The other Earthers came out of hiding, rushing toward his position. John bent over one of the dead soldiers and took their rifle, his eyes landing on the face A woman.

Young. Eyes open in surprise. Mouth twisted in pain. A wave of nausea washed over him, and he turned his head away.

"Damn," he said out loud, trying to breathe away the upset. He had no problem killing trife. This was something else. He never thought he could be military before the trife. He could never picture himself hurting another human being.

"Sarge, are you okay?" Paige asked, reaching him.

"Give me a minute."

"What's wrong?"

"I never killed another person before."

"You didn't kill her. I did."

"With my help. I don't want to be angsty about it. But it's a new experience. It's not me, you know?"

"You're a good man, Wash," Dante said. "Kind and generous, and above all loyal. This is the first time for all of us. I don't like it, but it has to be done. We didn't come across the universe to die like this, and it's either us or them."

John nodded. "Yeah. Thanks, Sheriff." He smiled. "I'm okay." He glanced at the HUD, bringing up the schematic. "It looks like we cleared a path. Let's not linger here."

He glanced at Paige, who was looking down at the dead Inahri woman. He caught a hint of sadness in her expression, but it vanished as she turned back to the squad.

"Let's move," she said.

"Form up, I've got point," John said. He looked at Hori, remembering the loss of the Intellect. The Inahri had no idea what he was saying. He switched to the hand signals they had practiced, getting the remaining Inahri soldier to the rear of their wedge formation.

They moved briskly across the city-ship, headed for the entry point still a hundred meters distant. The Relyeh had burned all of their assets trying to hold them further back, leaving the entry point undefended in the process. There was no way the enemy commander ever expected they would overcome the landing, an Abomination and a dozen soldiers with only two squads.

"Kiaan, how are you doing up there?" John asked, finding the Inahri's network had much, much better range than Space Force comms.

"Holding steady at the edge of the cloud cover," Kiaan replied.

"Za Wash," Colonel Jax said, overriding the comm. He started speaking in Inahri. Without the Intellect, John had no idea what he was saying.

"Sir, I don't understand," John said, bringing the squad to a halt.

He looked at Hori, who started speaking back to Jax in Inahrai , hopefully explaining that they had lost the Intellect.

"Chi Cox," Hori said. "Chi Cox. Chi Cox." He turned to John, pointing to their route and then to him. Then he pointed to where the bulk of the transports had landed and shook his head.

John wasn't sure what to make of it, but it seemed like the soldier was trying to tell him the fight wasn't going well.

"Retreat?" he asked, pointing the way they had come.

Hori shook his head.

"Still going in," John said. "Got it."

"Sarge," Kiaan said. "I think he's trying to tell you the battle isn't going well. I can see from here, we've taken heavy losses already. The assault is pulling back about three hundred meters west of you, and the enemy looks like they're reinforcing their positions there."

"Buying us time," John said. "Primary objective is a no go. Secondary is still in play." He looked at Paige and

Dante. "It's up to us to make sure this isn't a total failure."

"Then let's do it," Paige said.

"Already am." John moved forward again, more determined than ever.

Chapter 40

"What the hell were you thinking?" Caleb hissed, glaring angrily at Riley.

"He was about to tell the Inahri where Joe is hiding," Riley replied, equally angered. "It isn't my fault their soldier saw me at the last second and pushed him out of the way."

"It's your fault they know we're here now. We could have gotten to Joe first. We could have gotten him out of there before the Inahri got to him. Tsi and I were on our way here when you screwed it all up."

They were in the split across from Law, having hurried to the area after Kizi reported the sighting of the Relyeh Inahri soldier in an Intellect Skin. After Riley had already taken the shot at the Governor, and two Free Inahri had been forced to engage before Riley had compounded her bad decision by pulling them away.

Now the entirety of Law was on alert, the sheriffs and deputies pulling back to the office and moving into defensive positions around it. Worse, every indication was that the main Relyeh assault team was on its way into the city to deal with the problem and to ensure that they didn't interfere and get the energy unit first.

As Caleb had expected, Riley had managed to do the wrong thing and make everything more complicated.

"We don't have time to stand here and argue," Tsi said. "The enemy is coming. We have to get to the modulator before they do."

"Understood," Caleb replied. "But we need to get into Law without getting into a fight that'll leave half of the officers in Metro dead, and possibly us too. And we need to do it now."

"What was your original plan, Card?" Riley asked. "You must have had one for me to screw it up."

"Tsi and I were going to enter as Sheriff Zane and Beth Stone," Caleb said. "But we need to get everyone inside now, or we'll be going down there to die."

"There's another way out," Riley said. "You know I have access to it. We stick to your original plan. I got a scan of Deputy Bashir before the fight. Two officers bringing in a pair of wanted kids and Beth Stone. It can work."

"Why would Beth Stone be walking with a collar?"

"Right now, I think if it's out of the ordinary that makes it more believable."

"Surprisingly, I think I agree with you for once."

Riley smiled. "Then let's stop wasting time."

Caleb projected Sheriff Zane from his Skin. Kizi and Awak took the two kids from the upper blocks, while Riley projected Deputy Bashir and Tsi projected Beth Stone.

It was crazy, but it just might work.

"Kizi, Awak, you first. Riley and I will hold you from behind. Tsi, walk beside us like you're in charge."

"Chi," the Inahri replied.

Kizi moved in front of Caleb, and Caleb put his hand on the Inahri's shoulder, leading him out of the split with Bashir beside him. The officers assigned to guard the office noticed them immediately, watching with an equal measure of relief and doubt as they crossed the strand.

"I found these two in the hospital and figured I would bring them over," Caleb said as Sheriff Zane. "I heard the Governor was looking for them."

"Sheriff, the Governor's got Law on lockdown. Nobody in or out," the deputy replied.

"I'm sure he didn't mean me," Caleb said.

"And I know he didn't mean me, deputy," Tsi said as Beth.

"Ma'am," the deputy said. "How are you feeling? I heard—"

"I feel fine," Tsi said. "I want to see my husband."

"Uh. He isn't here, ma'am."

"I know he isn't here. But he will be here soon, and I want to see him. Are you really going to make me wait outside?"

The deputy looked at the other law officers with him. None of them seemed like they wanted to deal with the wrath of any Stone.

"No, ma'am. You can come inside. Sheriff, you too. And Bashir. You're part of Law, I know he didn't mean you. But those two can't come inside."

"What do you expect me to do with them, deputy?" Caleb asked. "They ran from Law. Are you suggesting I just let them go?" Caleb glared at the deputy, expecting him to back down. He hesitated a few seconds and then gave in.

"If you're vouching for them, I'm sure they can't do any harm. They're just kids."

"I'm going to throw them in a cell, deputy. I can assure you, they won't be any trouble in there."

"Yes, sir."

"Let's go," Caleb said, giving Kizi a slight shove forward. The deputies moved aside, letting them through the broken sliding door leading into the Law Office.

The office was nearly overflowing with officers, all of them tense and on edge, waiting for Governor Stone to arrive. They had no idea who or what he was bringing with him. They had no idea what he was looking for. All they knew was they had been told to regroup there, armed and ready for something.

"Sheriff Zane, Mrs. Stone." One of the other sheriff's approached. "Adam, how are you feeling? I heard you got clocked pretty good."

It took Caleb a second to realize the sheriff was talking to him. "I'm fine now. Thanks."

"I'm good too," Tsi said.

The sheriff flushed. "Mrs. Stone. Of course, I was about to ask—"

"Forget it," Tsi said, cutting him off. "I'm going to wait for my husband."

"In the back office," Caleb finished for her, pointing to the rear. The door to Dante's office was right beside the door leading back to the cells, and to the garage where they could access the armory. He shook Kizi slightly. "Me and Bashir are going to drop these two off in a holding cell. We're keeping them here until morning since they don't seem to understand the meaning of curfew."

The other sheriff laughed. "Sounds reasonable to me. Say, do you have any idea what all of this is about? The Governor had us looking for Joe King, now he's got us holed up in here. Does it have to do with the aliens that attacked us?"

"I don't know any more than you do," Caleb replied. "If you'll excuse me."

"Of course. Just figured I'd ask."

Caleb pushed Kizi toward the back of the office, making it to the rear without any other interruptions, and then leading them through the door to the garage.

"Hurry," he said, keeping the projection up as he broke into a run. They went around the corner and into the garage, finding the armory sealed.

"Stone didn't want them to know about the armory," Riley said. "But Joe didn't leave him much choice."

"He's trying to do the right thing," Caleb said. "Unlike some of us."

"You have no idea, Card. All I've tried to do is the right thing. For all of humankind, not just one ship of colonists."

"You might have convinced me of that two hundred years ago. I don't believe it now."

"I don't care. Move the crap out of the way so I can activate the platform."

"Joe wouldn't have been able to unplug the power. It should be active."

Riley went to the control panel, which lit up when she tapped it. "I guess you're right. I think that confirms he's down there."

"It does."

They assembled on the platform, which started to descend.

"I feel like we keep dancing in circles around one another, Card," Riley said. "We're back where we started again."

"I keep hoping the next time you'll decide not to be a bitch and screw us all over," Caleb replied. "What are the odds of that?"

Riley smirked but didn't respond.

It wasn't the answer he wanted, but it was the answer he expected.

She was going to do something he wouldn't like. He just had to figure out what.

Before it was too late.

Chapter 41

The platform was only halfway down when Caleb heard the first signs of commotion above. It started as muffled shouting from further back in the Law Office, and quickly escalated to deeper vibrations of a number of running feet, all of them charging toward the garage.

"I think Governor Stone just arrived," Riley said.

"I think the shit's about to hit the fan," Caleb replied. "We can't wait for this thing to hit the ground. Let's go." He ran to the edge and jumped, falling three meters to the armory floor. The Skin absorbed most of the landing, keeping him on his feet.

He pulled his sidearm, quickly sweeping the large room. It hadn't changed much since the last time he was in it. Some of the guns and suits of combat armor were gone, but the vehicles were all there and in the same positions. The Governor had been busy, but not too busy.

The rest of the group joined him a moment later, leaving the platform to continue its descent.

"Can you stop that?" Caleb asked Riley.

"Already on it," she replied, rushing toward the terminal. She was cut off when red bolts began sweeping down from above, one of them hitting the terminal and shutting it down in a shower of sparks and a burst of smoke."Shit!"

"Joe!" Caleb shouted. "Joe, are you in here? It's Sergeant Card." He heard heavy boots slam onto the platform. The enemy was coming fast. "Get behind the APCs," he said to the others, followed by "Joe!"

He dove behind one of the armored vehicles as a series of bolts whipped around him, missing him by a hair. He came up and spun, getting off a couple of quick shots at the first target he saw that wasn't a Law Officer. The Relyeh Inahri was wearing bulky battle armor, worn and scarred as though he had seen a lot of combat. They took the rounds off the armor, adding two more scuffs to the collection.

"Joe!" Caleb shouted again. "Damn it, where are you?"

"Keep them back!" Tsi hissed into the comm.

"There's too many," Awak said.

Caleb got a quick count through the outlines projected in front of him. Nine Inahri and a dozen officers. Why were they helping the enemy?

He pulled back behind the APC, following a red bolt as it flashed past and hit the wall behind him. The hatch next to the strike was sliding open, though he didn't see any feet beneath it.

"We can get out the second exit," Caleb said. "Fall back to the hatch. Fall back!"

The Free Inahri moved, backing toward the hatch and keeping the attackers honest with dense cover fire. Caleb saw one of the law officers go down.

"Don't shoot the humans, damn it!" he snapped.

A hiss at his back got his attention. He turned his head in time to see a trife poke its head around the open hatch. It took him half a breath to remember the docile creatures he had found hiding out down here. What was it doing?

It vanished a second later, retreating.

Riley was right behind it.

Where was she going?

Caleb broke for the hatch. He couldn't let her get ahead of him. There was no telling what she would do if she found Joe first.

Bullets whipped past him. A few of them hit him, the Earther ballistics unable to pierce the material but the force still affecting his balance. He slowed and twisted, quickly grabbing his stunner and firing off three quick rounds. A trio of officers shuddered and collapsed.

One of the Relyeh Inahri broke free, charging toward him with reckless abandon. It was the one in the worn armor. The one he had shot. He could see the man's face through the tinted faceplate, twisted in anger.

Caleb rolled to his feet, eying the soldier and the hatch. The other Relyeh Inahri were closing in, the Free Inahri trying to retreat. Awak was missing. And where was Tsi?

They had to get through the hatch. They had to get to Joe.

He had to slow the enemy down.

"Tsi go through the hatch and to the left. Find Valentine. Find Joe. Don't let her get the energy unit. I'll hold them…"

He trailed off as the Inahri soldier leaped toward him, a dense boulder launched like a rocket. Caleb threw himself aside, rolling and getting back to his feet as the soldier hit the wall, using it to bounce off, his body leaving a dent in the bulkhead. He came at Caleb swinging, arms moving in a quick left-right combo that kept Caleb reversing. He couldn't begin to match the strength of the armor, but he was more agile in the Skin.

He ducked a jab, coming up and slamming his replacement hand into the battle armor's chest while asking the Skin to direct a blast of energy there. Unlike during the trial, the Skin was fully active, and it responded to the request, hitting the soldier with enough force to throw him back and put another deep score in his rusted armor.

Caleb was momentarily free. Tsi ducked through the hatch behind him. Kizi was close. The Relyeh Inahri were right behind them. They didn't shoot at him. Why?

Old Rusty was getting back to his feet, preparing for round two. That was why. The fight wasn't personal to Caleb. It seemed personal to whoever the soldier was.

The Inahri started toward Caleb again, a little more cautiously this time. Kizi passed behind them, making it to the hatch.

The enemy shot him in the back. Three red flashes that cut through the Intellect Skin and burned deep into his flesh. He cried out, falling into the frame, turning as he did. He hit the ground, firing back at the Relyeh, the closer range giving the ion pistol enough power to pierce the faceplate of one of the soldiers. That Inahri collapsed, but there were too many more.

Caleb looked back at Old Rusty. Then he looked past him. The law officers were there, staying away from the Inahri. Staying away from the worst of the fighting. They looked confused. Sad. Frightened. He spotted Governor Stone among them. The Governor seemed like he had aged ten years in a few days. His hands were shaking. His eyes were dull. Did he know how much he had screwed up?

He flicked his eyes back to Old Rusty. "Who are you?"

"Za Harai," the soldier replied. Somehow, he had understood the question. "Your death."

Chapter 42

The four trife that had gone ahead of Joe came scampering back, hissing wildly as they neared him. He could hear the fighting clearly from his position. He had heard Sergeant Card calling his name.

"He's a friend," he tried to say to the trife. They moved in front of him, blocking his path, refusing to let him go.

Maybe they were right. It wasn't as though Sergeant Card had come alone. There was a firefight raging up ahead. The sergeant had arrived just in time, or perhaps just a little too late. Whoever won the battle was going to be the one to find him.

Whoever won the battle would be the one to take the energy unit.

"Let's go back to the others," Joe said. He turned and started to run, the trife gladly flanking him.

"Joe!"

Joe had only made it a few steps. He came to a stop and turned at the sound of Sergeant Card's voice. The trife stopped with him. They spun, moving in front of him to protect him and hissing at the man walking down the corridor.

"Sergeant Card," Joe said. "It's okay," he told the trife. They stopped hissing, watching the sergeant intently as he approached.

"Joe." Sergeant Card's eyes scanned him. "Where's the energy unit?"

"Safe," Joe replied.

"No, it isn't," he said. "We don't have a lot of time. The enemy is coming. We have to get the energy unit out of here. We have to keep it away from them."

"Right. I can bring you to it. I'm so glad you're here, Sergeant. They killed Carol."

"I know. I heard. I'm sorry, Joe. It's on us to make sure she didn't die for nothing. You did well hiding the unit. We can get it out of here."

"How? There's only one way out."

"No. There's another exit. I have access. Take me to the unit, and we'll get it away from the Deliverance. They don't care about the people here. They only care about the unit. Metro will be safe."

Joe stared at Sergeant Card. There was something off about him. Not that he knew the sergeant all that well, but he hadn't reacted at all to the sight of the trife. He didn't seem surprised the creatures were there with him, and that didn't seem right. Sergeant Card had said the aliens could make them see things. Was he seeing things now? Was Sergeant Card standing in front of him?

Or was it someone—or something—else?

"Joe, we don't have time," Sergeant Card said. "We can't hold them back for long. We have to keep moving."

Joe looked past him, toward the fighting. Someone was coming. Sergeant Card glanced back too, a worried expression on his face.

"Damn it, Joe, come on. We need to move. Now!"

The aggressiveness of the sergeant's tone brought him back to the present. There was no way for him to know if this was real or not. If this was Sergeant Card, then they could get the energy unit to safety if they hurried. If they didn't hurry, the enemy would catch them. If this was the enemy, then he was already caught.

"This way," he said, turning and running again, assuming Sergeant Card would follow.

The trife stayed at his side, with him while he ran back down the long corridor and around the corner, back to the server room, to the energy unit and the queen. He reached the door and opened it. The sergeant had caught up to him and was right on his heels.

He entered the room. The embryos the queen had laid were already nearly fully grown, another dozen trife occupying the room and feeding from the immense power of the energy unit. He couldn't believe it. Only a few minutes had passed.

Sergeant Card came in behind him. He heard him gasp from the doorway, finally reacting to the sight of the creatures.

"Joe, what did you do?" Sergeant Card hissed.

"It's here," Joe said, moving deeper into the room. The queen turned her head, small, dark eyes landing on the sergeant. Her mouth opened, revealing rows of sharp teeth. "It's okay, Mamma," Joe said. "You're going to help me get the energy unit someplace safe."

"Joe, you can't be serious," Sergeant Card said. "These things are dangerous. Letting them have a queen? Letting them reproduce? You're out of your damned mind."

"I know they caused a lot of trouble on Earth," Joe replied. "These ones are different. Don't ask me how or why. But they won't hurt me. They won't hurt anyone." He went to the queen. She lowered her head so he could put his hand on it. "See?"

"Give me the energy unit. Now."

Joe's eyes narrowed. He didn't like the sergeant's tone. "Mamma's coming with us."

"That's not an option."

"It won't hurt you. See?"

"That isn't the point. Do you want this world to be for humans or for trife, Joe? Do you have any idea how fast these things can multiply?"

"I think I do."

"No, you don't. We lost most of Earth within six months, Joe. It was over inside of two years. There are millions of trife on Earth, and that was after we killed billions of them. They were engineered to overwhelm planets. To destroy the native intelligent life."

"We aren't native," Joe said.

"You're an Engineer. Use your damned head."

Joe stood over the energy unit, beneath the trife queen. This couldn't be Sergeant Card. He didn't need to know him that well to know he didn't act like this.

"Who are you really?" he said. "Am I hallucinating?"

Sergeant Card looked surprised. Then he vanished, fading away and leaving something completely different behind.

The queen shrieked loudly at the sight of the black humanoid figure, while Joe backed up toward her a step, seeking her protection. The thing had no ears, no eyes, no mouth, and only a small protrusion to serve as a nose. It was clearly female or designed to be shaped like a female. So close to human, but not quite.

It reached up, grabbing at the top of its head and pulling the black material away. A real human head appeared from beneath it, the second reveal in almost as many seconds.

"I guess I shouldn't have told you to use your head," Riley said. "Smart, Joe. Real smart."

"Doctor Valentine? I thought you were—"

"Dead? You haven't been keeping up with current events. Give me the energy unit." She raised her sidearm, pointing it at him.

"Mamma will kill you if you kill me," Joe said. "What do you want with it, anyway?"

"I want it away from the trife, for one."

"I thought you wanted an army, Doctor. Isn't that what all this was about? Fighting the enemy out there with a force powerful enough to destroy it? Using the trife against their makers? Mamma made a dozen little demons in a few minutes with the energy unit."

"Originally, yes. It's too late for that."

"Why?"

"Look at my face, Joe."

He did. Patches of thick skin covered her cheeks and forehead. She looked terrible.

"I'm changing. Becoming a monster. I went to Research. I took the serum. It isn't working. I don't have the skills. I don't have the technology. I brought samples, but I need help. I don't want to die. The enemy I was hunting isn't the enemy I thought it was. We can't stop the Hunger, Joe. And if you can't beat them, the only way to survive is by joining them."

"What? The Hunger? I don't understand."

"Give me the energy unit. Join the Relyeh. Save your life. That's the only option that makes sense."

"Sergeant Card—"

"Sergeant Card is dead," Riley said. "And if he isn't, he'll wish he was soon enough."

"What happens to Metro in this scenario, Doctor?"

"Metro will be taken in by the Relyeh. It's a hard life, but it's life."

"As slaves?"

"That's a matter of perspective. It's still better than burning out and fading away. It's still better than being forgotten."

"Is it?"

Riley's head twitched. The trife reacted too. They heard something in the corridor.

"We're out of time. Give me the energy unit. We don't have to be enemies. I don't have to kill you."

Joe glanced at Mamma, and then back at Riley. Sergeant Card had called her right from the beginning. She couldn't be trusted, under any circumstances. She had no real side but her own. Maybe there had been loyalty at first. Maybe there was a time when her goals were as selfless as she claimed.

That time was over.

"No," Joe said.

He had barely started speaking when he felt a sharp pain in his chest, the smell of his burned flesh entering his nose. He gasped and fell back, suddenly unable to breathe.

Mamma screamed over him, her shout ringing in his ears. The large trife reached out for Riley, slashing at her with long claws.

Riley evaded the assault, pulling a dark blade from her belt. She slashed it through the trife's narrow wrist, severing the claw and causing the queen to bellow in pain. The other trife reacted, ready to pounce on her.

Riley rushed forward so fast Joe could hardly follow her movement. She came to a stop over him, ignoring the trife that slashed at her arm, the material she was wearing deflecting the blows. She reached out almost casually, shooting the trife in the face before crouching in front of Joe. The queen hissed again, head dipping and snapping.

Riley swung her gun hand out, intentionally sticking it in the queen's mouth. The queen froze.

"Be a good girl and don't move," Riley said. "I'll grow a new arm. Will you grow a new head?"

She used her free hand to grab the containment box, picking it up and tucking it under her arm. Then she started backing away, pulling her hand from the queen's mouth but keeping the weapon trained on the trife. She made it to the door, her head whipping to the right. To whoever was coming down the hallway.

"I've got it," she announced. She looked back at Joe. "I'm sorry for killing you. You didn't give me any choice." She put her wrist to the control panel of the hatch. It slid closed, the LED on the inside turning red.

Joe slumped. His heart rate was slowing. He was getting cold. He looked up at the queen. "I'm sorry."

She looked down at him. He saw concern in her eyes. And anger. She rose up and charged the door, using her remaining hand to tap the control panel. It didn't open. Her scream echoed in the room. She backed up and threw herself against the hatch. It didn't budge.

She was still throwing herself into the door when he died.

Chapter 43

Caleb stood in front of Sergeant Harai while five of the other Relyeh Inahri passed through the open door behind him, following Tsi and Riley in search of Joe. Caleb hadn't slowed them as much as he was hoping and he wanted to follow, but there was no way Harai was going to let him.

He hoped he was wrong about Riley. That she was going to do the right thing in the end. That even if she had her own desire for the energy unit, she would still get it out of here. Off the Deliverance and away from Metro. She could help the colony and still help herself.

Either that or he hoped Tsi kicked her ass.

He didn't think that would happen. Tsi was good, but Riley wasn't human. Not really. She had changed herself, and then Hal had changed her. She was a genetic mess. A gross distortion of DNA. She had gambled and lost everything she was and they were all paying the price.

His eyes traveled past Harai, to the colonists behind the Inahri soldier. Two other Relyeh were still with them, keeping an eye on them. Even if he managed to take out

Harai, which he wasn't entirely confident he could do, he would still have them to deal with.

Unless…

He spotted Deputy Bashir in the group, standing beside Governor Stone. Caspar was there too, off to the side. Not all of Law were completely loyal to the Governor. Maybe less of Law would be loyal to him now.

"Tsi, good luck," Caleb said. "I'm going offline."

He didn't wait for her to respond. He reached for the mantle of his suit.

"Well," Harai said. "Are we going to stand here all day? Show some honor in your death."

Caleb pulled the black material away from his face, the HUD going with it. The situation looked different through his naked eyes. In a way, more hopeful. In another, more desperate. He didn't pay any attention to Harai. The soldier wanted an honorable fight. One on one. He was eager for it. He could wait.

He noticed Bashir and Caspar. Their faces changed when they saw it was him. They were surprised, but also pleased to see him, despite the dire circumstances. Even Governor Stone reacted with a sense of relief, a spark of hope as if Caleb could save them.

"Don't just stand there," Caleb said.

It was all he said. Sergeant Harai thought he was talking to him. Bashir, Caspar, and the others in Law took it that he was talking to them.

They were both right.

Harai charged forward, moving quickly in the heavy battle armor. Caleb was ready. He came forward too, meeting the soldier.

Behind them, all hell broke loose.

Caspar pulled his sidearm, pressing it against the side of the nearest Inahri's helmet and pulling the trigger before the enemy could react. The bullet cracked the face-plate, piercing it without enough force to kill. It hit the soldier in the side of the face, drawing blood and his attention.

Bashir raised his sidearm too, pointing it at the other Inahri and firing. The round was ineffective, but it sent a message to the others. *Don't just stand there.* They all began to react, drawing their guns as their fear turned into a weapon against the invaders.

The Inahri soldiers turned on the Law Officers.

Caleb didn't see the rest. Harai stole his attention, his huge metal fist nearly clocking him in the jaw before Caleb could spin away. He shifted his feet and threw his replacement arm up to smash into Harai's forearm. The force knocked him back and he slid across the floor. Using the momentum, he somersaulted back to his feet. Harai rushed him, barreling forward like a freight train. At the last moment, Caleb slipped aside.Stepping in behind the soldier, he raised his gun to shoot, only to have a dozen spikes launch from the back of the soldier's armor and into his chest, piercing his Intellect Skin and leaving him with a number of small stab wounds.

Harai spun back around, smiling at his deception. "Didn't see that coming, did you Earther?"

Caleb sent a wave of shield energy along the Skin, which pushed the tiny spears from his flesh and out onto the floor.

"Cheap trick," he said. "Where's the honor in that?"

The statement angered Harai. He growled as he went on the offensive again, throwing punches and pushing Caleb back. Ducking and dodging, Caleb was able to keep up with the attack, his more agile Skin allowing him to avoid the assault...at least for now.

He spared a glance over his shoulder, noticing that one

of the Inahri soldiers was down, and the other was about to be mobbed by the eight remaining lawmen.

He needed to buy them a little more time.

He sidestepped a hard right cross, moving under Harai's guard and punching him with his replacement arm. Harai hopped aside, regaining his balance quickly despite the bulk of his armor. He caught Caleb's follow-up punch, metal hand wrapping around metal hand.

"Too slow," Harai said, squeezing Caleb's hand like a vice.

Caleb could feel the metal compressing, his fist being smashed down, his mechanical fingers crushing and breaking. He didn't feel pain from it, but he knew he was taking critical damage.

It didn't matter. It was only metal. It was only a hand.

Harai hung onto Caleb's mutilated hand, using his other hand to throw another heavy punch at Caleb's head. Caleb used Harai's grip to swing away from the punch. He reached down, grabbing the blade from his belt and jabbing it down as hard as he could into Harai's chest.

The blade was made to cut through battle armor, and it did its job, sinking through the protection and into Harai's chest near his heart. The sergeant gasped, letting Caleb's hand go and stepping back. Caleb released his hold on the blade. Blood and fluid for the exoskeleton began leaking out of the wound.

"Didn't see that coming, did you?" Caleb asked.

Harai grabbed the blade and pulled it out, dropping it on the floor. He fell to his knees, looking up at Caleb. "You're still going to die," he said.

Caleb turned around. Both of the Inahri soldiers were down, the officers standing over them. Bashir had claimed one of their rifles. Governor Stone held the other.

Caleb heard motion to his left. He looked toward the

open hatch again as Riley returned to the room, the containment box for the energy unit tucked under her arm.

"Card," she said, seeing him. "You're still alive?"

"Disappointed?" he asked.

"It's temporary."

She entered the room.

The five Relyeh Inahri soldiers entered behind her. They weren't holding her at gunpoint. They were following her. One of them had a wounded, unconscious Tsi draped over his shoulder.

"Why?" Caleb said.

Two of the Inahri broke away, hurrying to Harai. They began removing his battle armor.

"You," Riley said, looking at the officers. "Drop your weapons."

"You're a traitor," Governor Stone said.

"Who is?" Riley asked. "You betrayed the people whose job it was to protect you, Governor. Maybe if you hadn't, you wouldn't be here. Now, drop your weapons. You might have taken two soldiers in an ambush but believe me, you won't stop five."

Governor Stone glared at her, furious. "She's right. Drop your guns. All of you."

"I'd rather die," Bashir said.

A bolt of energy lashed across the room, hitting Bashir in the chest and killing him. The officers dropped their guns as Caleb's head whipped to the source of the shot.

Sergeant Harai.

The Inahri was out of his armor and back on his feet. His soldiers had spread some sort of clear paste over his wound, stopping the bleeding.

"Didn't see that coming, did you?" Harai said to him with a feral smile.

"I saw the betrayal coming. I was hoping I could stop it."

"Call it what you want, Card," Riley said. "I'm saving the lives of everyone on this ship. Except maybe yours."

"Where's Joe?" Caleb asked.

"And his," she added. "Sorry. He didn't want to give up the modulator. He was a brave idiot." She walked past Caleb to Harai. "I believe this is what you came for?"

"It is," Harai said.

"I want to make a deal."

"You aren't in a position to deal."

"If you have any honor in you, I am. I captured it and brought it to you willingly. I expect to be rewarded."

"How?"

"I want to meet with Arluthu."

"That isn't possible."

"Make it possible."

Harai smiled. "I like you. I'll see what I can do." Riley held out the energy unit. Harai took it. Then he looked at Caleb. "I like you too. You owe me another fight. Dax ti."

Two of the soldiers approached on either side of Caleb, grabbing his arms. He spent a moment trying to resist, but his replacement hand wasn't up to dealing with battle armor.

"Sha qide," Harai said, motioning to Tsi. He glanced at Caleb, smiling. "Kill the rest."

"No!" Caleb said, straining against the soldiers again, turning his head to the law officers in time to watch the other three Inahri soldiers begin to gun them down. They collapsed one after another like dominoes, including Governor Stone. "Damn you, Valentine!" he shouted. "Damn you!"

"It's already too late for that," she replied. "There's another way out of here," she said to Harai. "Follow me."

Harai nodded. "Zo bae." The remaining Inahri soldiers came to attention on either side of the open hatch. The sergeant glanced at Riley. "Lead the way."

One of the soldiers grabbed Caleb's arm and yanked him toward the hatch. Caleb looked back over his shoulder, taking in the sight of the dead officers bleeding out across the floor. His gaze stopped on Governor Stone. The Governor's eyes were open. He was still alive.

It didn't matter. There was nothing he could do. Not against so many.

Then they were through the hatch, the massacre vanishing from sight. Whatever happened next was out of his control.

For now.

Chapter 44

"Clear!" Dante said.

"Clear!" Paige said.

John and Hori joined them at the junction. Both directions were clear. Not that they needed to announce it—the battle armor's HUD would have lit up if there were any threats detected—but it was good practice for the two colonists-turned-Marines.

They had entered the city-ship ten minutes earlier, through a non-obvious passage in the ship's shapeshifting alloy large enough for the Abomination to have passed through. That entrance took them into a chamber similar to the first one the Guardians had entered the first time they were on the ship. Tendrils hung from a high ceiling, nonfunctional without an Intellect to control them. The massive room was empty when they entered, though the evidence of the Relyeh's war preparations were evident in scraps of waste and empty crates piled in the corner.

Unlike the first room, this one lacked a teleporter. It had another passage out of the north side instead, leading deeper into the ship toward the modulator housing. Based on the position, it was either a few decks above or below the main reactor, where the Guardian Intellect had shown them the collection of trife the Axon had secretly brought to the planet with them. It was hard to tell which without a better understanding of the city-ship's layout. The schematic was helpful, but the Seeker was bigger than massive. It made the Deliverance look tiny by comparison.

Earther squad was still following the path Colonel Jax had outlined, making their way through the ship as fast as they could without being reckless. They were the only unit that had made it into the ship, which was sure to make them a target. The assault force outside was doing its best to keep the Relyeh occupied, but John knew it was only a matter of time before the enemy caught up to them.

They turned left at the junction, following the line on their HUDs and the shape of the corridor on a downward slope. They were closing on the target, with only a tele-porter hop between them and the area adjacent to the housing. From there, it was a quick jaunt along a short passage to the modulator housing itself.

"Stay alert," John reminded the others, keeping his rifle steady on his shoulder. It was easy for inexperienced fighters to get too comfortable when the enemy was absent for a while.

Comfortable meant sloppy, and sloppy meant dead.

They continued along the passage. John kept one eye on the corridor ahead and the other on the overlay, watching for the armor's system to identify and mark incoming targets. At first, he had figured the enemy didn't expect them to overcome an Abomination. He didn't blame them, either. He was alive because of luck, not skill. But there was plenty of time to pull in reinforcements by now, and he couldn't accept that the Relyeh didn't know they had entered.

He kept the idea that they were heading for an ambush in the back of his head. Better to be prepared and be wrong than to walk right into a trap.

"I don't like this," Dante said as if reading his mind. "Where are they?"

"Good question," John replied. "I'm getting a little antsy too."

"You think maybe Caleb got the energy unit?" Paige asked. "It could be they lost interest in getting the ship ready."

"I hope that's true. I'm not counting on it."

"Betting against your friend?" Dante asked.

"Only because Riley Valentine is involved. She's going to pull some shit. I hope Cal cuts her down before she can."

"Roger that."

The passage continued across the center of the city-ship, but Earther squad didn't need to go nearly that far. They hooked left at the next adjacent passage, which led them a short distance to the teleporter. John and Paige entered the room first, scanning both sides before calling it clear.

"Paige, Dante, cover the door," John said. "Hori, I assume you know how to work this thing?" He pointed at the teleporter's control terminal.

"Chi Za," Hori replied, walking over to it. He activated the projection and tapped on a few of the symbols. Then he pointed at the platform.

"Ready?" John asked.

"Chi Za," Hori replied.

"I hate these things," Paige said, climbing onto the platform.

"How can you hate them?" Dante asked. "You can't even feel—"

The teleporter activated in a flash of white light. When it dimmed, they were somewhere else.

The room they landed in was pitch black, so dark it took John's battle armor a few seconds to begin to compensate, and even then it left the room in a black haze. A glance at the schematic told him they hadn't gone where they were supposed to go.

"Hori?" John said, turning to the Inahri soldier. Hori raised his hands. A confused expression shadowed through his faceplate.

"This isn't the modulator housing," Dante said.

"We need to try again," John decided, stepping off the teleporter platform and looking for the terminal.

He didn't see one.

"Uh…" He looked around the room, thinking he had missed it. The others did the same.

"What the hell is this?" Paige said. "There's no terminal. Does that mean we're trapped here?"

"Stay calm," John said. "This has to be why the Relyeh didn't attack. They guessed where we were headed and they altered the teleporter controls instead. They sent us somewhere else."

"Somewhere with no escape," Paige said.

"No. There's no reason to think they Inahri would put a teleporter in a room with no exit and without a way to use the teleporter again. The Relyeh didn't have time to install one in some random place either. But we did go where they wanted us to go, wherever that is." He rechecked the schematic. However the system worked, it was struggling to position them in the city-ship.

"Which means if there is a door, whatever is on the other side is going to suck," Dante said.

"I think we can count on that," John replied. "But

you're honorary Marines now. You don't get scared. You get prepared."

"Roger, Sarge" Dante replied. "How?"

"Check your guns, check your nerves, remember who and what you are, and why you're here."

"Roger that," Paige said.

"Good. Let's find our way out."

John walked over to the wall in front of the teleporter platform. He looked down at the floor, having learned the easiest way to spot the otherwise invisible passages was to pay attention to the pattern in the metal. The grain of the brushed alloy always seemed to change direction near portals.

"It's here," he said, finding the pattern on the floor. "See. No reason to worry." He put his hand on it. All it took to open the hatches was to get close to them.

Nothing happened.

"You were saying?" Paige said.

John leaned forward, pressing on the sealed metal. It didn't liquify and shift out of the way. It remained solid and immovable.

"Shit."

Chapter 45

"I was right," Paige said. "We're trapped."

"No," John countered. "Temporarily contained. I don't get trapped."

"Call it whatever you want, Sarge. Our people are out there dying and we're contained, temporary or otherwise."

"Less bitching, more fixing. Help me think of something." John turned back to the teleporter. "That thing must get some decent juice to it. Maybe we can use it to power the hatch."

"You're assuming it's not moving because it's dead," Dante said.

"Unless you have a better assumption?"

"Not at the moment, Sergeant."

"Kiaan, do you copy?" John said, trying to raise the pilot on the comm. "Kiaan, do you copy?" Nothing. "We must be out of range. Down too deep."

"According to the schematic Jax passed us, we're almost as low as we can go," Dante said, her eyes twitching as she followed the map on her HUD. "This looks like waste control."

"Waste control?" Paige said. "We're in the garbage dump?"

"I doubt the Axon dump any of their garbage," John said. "It's probably all recycled. Reused. It's good to know, but how do we get out?"

"Through that door," Dante deadpanned.

John looked at the hatch again. "It won't—"

He was cut off when it moved aside, creating a rounded portal through the wall.

"I don't know if that's better or worse," Paige said.

"The Relyeh sent us here," Dante said. "They opened the gates. What's going to come through?"

John heard an all too familiar hissing echo through the newly opened hatch. "Trife." He raised his rifle. The demons began to appear on his HUD, the armor's sensors registering their movements. "A lot of them."

"I thought the Intellect shut down all the trife on the ship?" Paige said.

"The ones within range of the signal," Dante replied. "And the ones who had the embedded systems. I bet these are the descendants of the originals."

"And the Relyeh sent us down here to deal with them," John said. "Either we clear out what's left of the trife or we die. They win whichever way it goes. Smart."

"Then I guess there's only one thing to do," Paige said. "Clear out the trife, and then clear out the Relyeh."

"Sounds good to me," Dante said.

"Knuckle up and let's do this, Earthers," John said.

"Roger that," Paige and Dante replied. Hori didn't understand the words, but he seemed to understand the sentiment. He pumped his fist and smiled.

The squad moved through the open passage, into a short corridor attached to a connecting doorway. John could hear motion on the other side, the trife moving into position, likely planning to ambush them the moment they stepped through.

"I'll go out first," John said. "Draw their interest. You pick them off from back here."

"Sergeant, you don't always have to be the diversion," Dante said.

"I'm in charge, which means I do," John countered. "I've watched Caleb do it too many times not to follow his lead. I'm going to haul ass to the middle of the room. They'll jump me from all around. You shoot as many as you can as fast as you can, understood?"

"Yes, Sarge."

John started ahead. He had dozens of trife already painting his HUD, which was struggling to light them up individually. He assumed they were normal trife, Earth trife, though he doubted that was the case. They were more likely the semi-armored version the Axon had created and used to test the Inahri. They were probably bigger and stronger, and able to punch through the heavy battle armor he was about to rely on to save his life.

"Here goes," he said into the comm.

Then he broke down the corridor, charging to full speed and heading for the open passage. His feet shook the metal floor, the sound of his advance echoing loudly, alerting the trife to his approach.

He burst into the room, still running, heading for the center and...

He came to a quick stop, heart rate jumping. This wasn't waste control.

It looked like a damned obstacle course.

There were platforms and false walls, inclines and ropes, blockades, barriers, tunnels, chasms, and other complex terrains and challenges, all of which appeared to have been constructed to pit Inahri against trife. Worse, there were bodies. Heavily decomposed bodies spread across the site, the remains of prisoners the Inahri had sent to this place to do battle. They were in various states of brokenness and decomposition, some splayed out on the floor, others impaled on almost randomly placed sharp objects, and a few piled in the corner as if someone had tried to clean up the mess before dying themselves.

It was shocking and chilling, and it threw John off his guard.

It was the opening the trife waited for—the moment of shock that so often brought their targets to a halt. They hissed and rushed him, launching their ambush from everywhere at once.

John recovered quickly, tracking the abundance of targets as they poured over him. He chose the path of least resistance, raising his rifle directly ahead and opening fire. He hit three trife in the first two seconds before he even had a chance to observe them. They were larger than Earth trife, but not as big as the trife they had encountered in the jungle. They didn't appear to have the alloy plates fused into them, which was a good sign.

But there were hundreds of them, and that was bad.

Four of them hit John almost at the same time, claws slashing down and scraping along his alloy battle armor. John turned as they hit, trying to keep them off balance and managing to toss two of them away. He held his rifle one-handed, using the other to grab a third and throw it from his body.

"Whenever you're ready," John said.

Paige, Dante, and Hori started firing into the scrum, blue and red flashes striking the trife and bringing them down. John grabbed another and crushed its neck, tossing it to the floor. Another trife came at him from behind, scraping at his back before Dante brought it down.

John fired on the trife ahead of him. He was beginning to feel invincible in the battle armor. Their claws scraped against it, trying to get through and failing, barely managing to leave light scratches. Was the battle armor what the Inahri had come up with to challenge the trife? Looking at the corpses around him, he didn't see any of the bulky exosuits. Had everyone who entered this place with one survived?

He might have been impressed, but he already knew the perils of relying on powered armor. Eventually, the power would run out, and then the wearer would be at the mercy of the demons as though they had never worn armor at all. He had seen it happen to good Marines trapped in bad situations. He didn't want to wind up like them.

He shifted and fired, adjusted and fired, turned and fired. He took down trife after trife, throwing off all comers as Earther squad decimated the enemy ranks. He also continued wading through the scrum toward the center, keeping the demons distracted and away from the shooters at his back.

It seemed too good to be true. It seemed too easy. But then, every trife he shot left him with one less round in his rifle. Every demon he killed was one less the Relyeh Inahri had to worry about. And every second his team spent down here was a second they weren't topside, seeking out the engineers prepping the modulator housing and slowing down the Seeker's reactivation and launch. The Inahri outside were dying to give him time to complete the mission.

He needed to hurry up and complete it.

He shoved aside another trife, kicked a second, and punched a third. He kept moving for the center of the room, where a short wall led to a small bit of higher ground. He waded through the attacking demons to reach it, scaling the wall while the trife scratched at his feet. He used the height to scan the large chamber. He saw more dead Inahri nearby, surprised to see they were wearing battle armor like his, only it was torn as though they had run into a buzzsaw.

Something here was able to break through the thick armor. But what?

It didn't matter. He spotted an open archway at the far side of the room, the control terminal for a teleporter visible through it. The end of the challenge came when the Inahri made it from one side of the course to the other. There were a few barriers in the way, not to mention dozens of trife, but damn it, the Earthers were going to make it.

"Dante, Paige, Hori, I've got eyes on the exit. Form up on me, and we'll make a break for it. Watch your tails."

"Roger, Sergeant," Dante said.

John refocused on the exit. It seemed clear and open. It couldn't be that easy, could it? Despite the number of trife in the room, the whole thing hadn't been that difficult to manage. Was it simply because they were better equipped than the Inahri slaves who were forced down here to fight?

He wanted to believe that was the reason, but it didn't add up. Neither did the armored dead in the corner, closest to the exit. There was a trick to this—something he was missing.

The other Earthers fought their way to the platform, easily overpowering the trife in their battle armor and killing nearly fifty more on the way. John quickly scanned the room, checking all of the platforms, checking the shadows, and looking at his HUD. They had thinned the ranks considerably in less than a few minutes.

"Easy peasy," Paige said, climbing up beside him.

"Too easy peasy," John replied. He didn't trust it. Not with his experience. It suddenly occurred to him that there was one direction the battle armor wasn't well-designed to look in.

Up.

Chapter 46

John could move his head to look up, but the helmet didn't move with it. The armor used the sensors and the HUD to help target anything that was directly in front. If the armor couldn't see it, then he couldn't see it either.

He remembered the jungle. The trife that appeared out of nowhere. They didn't register on any of their sensors. They were invisible until they chose not to be. He grabbed at his helmet, pulling it off his head.

"Sarge, what are you doing?" Paige asked.

He didn't respond, arching his head back to look directly up over the platform.

The trife queen was suspended nearly twenty meters up, dangling from a mess of tendrils, using them as support for herself and her brood. She had secreted some kind of hard material across them, creating a surface she and her dozens of mates could grip and use in their reproductive process.

Only the queen wasn't in the middle of reproduction. The area had been maxed out on the number of trife it could support before the Earthers had entered. Instead, she was looking down at them. Watching them.

Preparing to strike.

"Shit," John said. "Get down!" Dante was the closest to him. He got his arm around her as he dove from the platform, losing his helmet in the process. The queen and her consorts dropped from the sky, plunging toward them.

John hit the ground with a hard clank, Dante beside him. He didn't hesitate, rolling to his feet and getting his fist in the face of the first trife that tried to bite his unprotected neck. He heard a scream and looked back in time to see the queen catch Paige in the back as she tried to leap away, a claw the size of the smaller woman's torso tearing through the metal of the armor and then through flesh and bone.

She crumpled to the floor.

"No!" Dante shouted, bringing her rifle to bear on the queen. She started firing, sending a heavy stream of energy into the trife.

John turned, bounding two steps to Dante's back and slamming one of the trife with his shoulder, spinning and punching another. Three of them jumped at him, and he cried out in a fury, knocking them all to the ground. He grabbed Dante's xix from the back of her armor, activating them.

"I've got your back, keep shooting that bitch!" he shouted.

Dante fired round after round at the queen. She cried out in pain and leaped down from the platform, landing in front of Dante. Her consorts joined her.

"Need a little help up front," Dante asked.

Hori began shooting from the left flank, sending blasts of energy into the trife. Two of the consorts went down in a hurry. The queen made a quick snapping noise, and a group of consorts broke for the Inahri soldier.

John swung around to Dante's side as the other consorts closed in. He sidestepped a slash from dark claws, driving his xix under the demon's arm, energy arcing through it and leaving it a steaming corpse. He tapped them together and then flung the energy at a second creature. It shuddered in place as it died.

The queen rushed Dante, who cried out in fear, backing up but still shooting. A trife jumped on her back. Then another and another. They couldn't pierce her armor, but if enough got to her, they could drive her down and suffocate her.

Hori saw them and started shooting. The consorts were approaching him from behind, taking the long way around, but he didn't see them coming. Or maybe he did. He focused his firepower on the queen, and on the trife trying to reach Dante, leaving her clear to fire. John watched as two of the consorts jumped Hori, one grabbing at his helmet with a powerful claw, the other taking him from behind. They knew exactly what they were doing. One dislodged the helmet while the other cut his head almost entirely away from his body.

"We can't win this," John said. "We have to run."

"What about Paige?"

"She's gone. I'm sorry."

"No. My HUD says she isn't."

John looked at her. He couldn't bear the thought of leaving anyone behind. How were they going to manage this?

"Okay, I'll take Miss Nasty. You get Paige."

"Are you crazy?"

"Yeah. I'm also not afraid to die, and I've got these." He tapped the xix together.

Dante didn't argue. She shifted her focus to reaching Paige as John stepped in front of the queen.

"One of you bitches took my boss' arm," John said. "And one of you took my voice and half my face. I owe you for that."

The queen hissed in response.

"Let's go," John said.

She did, shooting toward him like a rocket. He tapped the xix together, creating a web that he spread in front of him. Her claws hit it, her charge still enough to force him back as she cried out in pain..

He reversed, driving forward with the xix. She spun away, and he cursed as her tail smacked him in the chest, throwing him to the ground. He rolled over, getting up just in time to catch another claw on his xix. He glanced over. Dante was kneeling next to Paige, shooting at the consorts trying to reach her. What was she doing? They were out of time.

He blocked another claw and then tried to circle the queen. Her tail lashed at him again, and this time he ducked below it before rolling forward and getting almost under her body. He saw the delicate area between her legs and jabbed the xix up into it, causing her to scream so loud it hurt his ears.

She reached down for him, and he rolled back out of the way, staying agile despite the armor. The queen continued to howl, in pain and plenty angry.

John was on the right side of the fight, the exit directly behind him. Where the hell was Dante?

He looked to where Paige had fallen. She was still there. Damn it. Had Dante left her? Had she died? He noticed her sidearm was beside her helmet, and her helmet had a fresh hole in it.

Damn.

"Sarge, let's go!" Dante shouted, appearing in the teleporter room. "It's charged and ready."

"Where are we going?"

"Modulator housing, maybe? I'm not sure."

John backed up. The queen was approaching more cautiously, limping slightly. Dark blood ran between her legs. She didn't try to attack again. John continued to retreat until he was through the archway to the teleporter.

"Paige?" he said.

"She was paralyzed. She wanted it that way. She told me to—" Her voice broke.

"Roger that," John said.

They reached the teleporter, stepping onto the platform.

They were out in a flash.

Chapter 47

The teleporter brought them to another small teleportation room. John glanced at Dante, waiting for her to identify where they were on the HUD.

"This is the place," she said.

He nodded. "See if you can reach Kiaan. We need prep for immediate pickup."

"What about the engineers?"

"We'll see what we can do in the time it takes for the Mengin to circle back."

"Roger, Sarge." She cut the external mic, her mouth moving inside her helmet. John turned his attention to the closed hatch leading out of the room. Did the enemy know they had made it out alive?

Some of them, anyway.

He felt the clenching pain of losing a team member tight in his gut. It always hurt, but this one was more personal. This one was his, not Caleb's. It was his lead. His team.

"Sarge," Dante said. "We have a problem." Her face was pale. "Actually, we have a lot of problems."

"What is it?" he asked, keeping his voice low.

"We're too late. The Free Inahri are on full retreat. Everything they had left has already pulled back."

"You're saying we're trapped here?"

She nodded.

"Tell Kiaan to get his ass down here for pickup."

"I did. Believe me, I did. Sarge, he said Colonel Jax is holding him at gunpoint. If he tries to come back, they'll kill him."

John couldn't believe it. What the hell was going on? "And leave himself without a pilot?"

"Jax is a pilot. Or was. He knows how to fly the transport."

"Damn it. So our allies just hung us out to dry?"

"It gets worse."

"How can it get worse?"

"Kiaan said they got an emergency communication from the compound. The Relyeh attacked their base. It's destroyed. Completely destroyed. Even the civilians..."

"What? How?"

"It gets worse," Dante said, her eyes tearing up.

"How the hell can it get worse than that?"

"Kiaan said Caleb was with them." She could barely keep her voice going. "Caleb was helping them."

"No," John said, shaking his head. "No way. It had to be a projection. A trick. Caleb wouldn't change sides like that. He isn't made that way."

"I want to believe that too," Dante said.

"Then believe it."

"The Free Inahri don't trust us. They think we betrayed them. I'm worried they'll go after the Deliverance."

"They don't have the resources to hit the Deliverance. Especially if the Relyeh are moving against them." John paused to think. "Okay. Screw them, Sheriff. We deal with one thing at a time. First order of business is to take out the engineers. We still have to slow the Relyeh down."

"Why?"

"Because the way I see it, there's only one way out of this. We have to get the colony off this planet. Between the Relyeh, the Inahri, and the Axon, this place is worse than Earth by a long mile."

"How are we going to do that?"

"I don't know. If we don't, we're all going to wind up dead or worse. We need time, and the only way we can get it is to do some damage and slow the Relyeh down."

"They're going to be waiting for us."

"Maybe. If we die, we have to hope the real Caleb is out there, and he's thinking the same way I'm thinking. I'm willing to bet he is."

Dante's face told John she was terrified. He was scared too. It wasn't a feeling he was accustomed to, but the stakes were too high now.

She nodded. "Okay. Standby." She looked at her HUD. "The housing is through the hatch, to the right down a short corridor, through another hatch. I don't have readings past the corridor. The coast is clear right now. Since we can't see them, I don't think they can see us either."

"A little bit of good news."

"We're still going in blind, Sergeant."

"I've never let that stop me before. I wish I had some explosives."

"Me too."

John stared at her a moment. "I've got an idea. Let me borrow your helmet."

"Why?"

"Just hand it over. That's an order."

She did as he said. He snapped it into place, the display

adjusting to his system. He navigated through the menus. He couldn't read any of them, but he remembered the instructions Hori had given. He found the self-destruct and set it to five minutes. It started counting down, and he disconnected the helmet and gave it back to Dante. Then he quickly started loosening the connectors keeping him in his armor.

"What did you just do?" Dante asked in response to the activity.

"We've got five minutes. Then this thing is going to blow."

"Sergeant—"

"Not your decision," John replied. "Time's wasting. Knuckle up sheriff. If these are the last five minutes of your life, how do you want to die?"

"Doing my duty," Dante replied.

"Me too. It's been an honor, Sheriff."

"You too, John. You're a good man."

"I've done the best I can. Let's move."

Dante leveled her rifle. John tapped the xix together, forming an energy web between them.

"For Metro," she said.

"And for Caleb," he added.

The hatch opened ahead of them.

They attacked.

Chapter 48

It briefly occurred to John, as he was charging down the short corridor toward the modulator housing area, that he and Dante were running directly into another trap, and rushing headlong to their deaths.

In that same moment, he also realized he didn't care. As long as he damaged the housing, as long as he slowed the Relyeh's attempt to get the Seeker back online, he would consider his mission accomplished and his death worthwhile.

Dante was still with him. She had to feel the same.

The hatch required pressure and proximity to open, so John threw one of the xix at it, hitting it and causing it to move aside. The weapon ricocheted off with a loud clang, hitting the floor and bouncing up to where he recovered the fumble with practiced ease. He burst through the open curtain without slowing, taking in his surroundings as he barreled in.

Dante loosed a shot past his head, hitting a target that appeared on her sensors before he saw it. An Inahri in a white uniform, who was walking directly toward him. An engineer, he guessed. The shot quickly caught the attention of the other engineers, who were spread across the area.

John took in the surroundings in as fast as he was able. He had emerged onto a grated metal catwalk at least ten meters over the area below, which appeared to be composed of dark, bowl-shaped material. He could easily imagine the bowl collecting the energy passed out by the QDM. He glanced up, noticing the same shape above. The catwalk split ten meters ahead, winding around a central pillar he took to be the housing and extending out to the walls, where thick conduits and computer terminals were arranged, along with a few monitoring stations. There was a second entrance on the opposite side of the room, allowing the housing area to be used as a passage across the ship.

He quickly counted eight engineers and four soldiers. Two of the engineers were working at the central pillar, which spread from the center into dozens of smaller spike-like cylinders aiming at the bowls above and below. It was surrounded by a visually chaotic arrangement of parts. The four soldiers were at each of the corners around the pillar, and they began leveling their rifles at John before he had finished his sweep of the room.

He didn't slow or hesitate, continuing toward them at full speed. The battle armor shook the entire catwalk. It was too narrow for him to maneuver much as he headed for the housing, tapping the xix together. He spread them out ahead of his face, catching the bolts the soldiers fired at his chest and face.

But their aim adjusted quickly to the weapon, and they shifted their fire to his knees and feet, sending blasts of energy into the lower part of his armor. He smelled the burning metal and felt the heat of the bolts as they bombarded him, piercing the armor and trying to stop him before he reached the platform.

Dante fired back at them, sending rounds of her own into their midst, hitting their armor without punching through. They didn't redirect their attack, not immediately concerned with her. Not when the large Marine was rapidly approaching.

John saw the shot that pierced his knee. He watched it flash by and then felt the sudden burning in his leg, followed by the loss of feeling that caused him to stumble. He was close. So close. He pushed off with his good leg, throwing himself at the nearest Inahri soldier, leading with the xix.

He tumbled into the enemy with enough force to knock the soldier down, driving the xix into the man's helmet with enough force to crack the faceplate. He struck him twice more. Still moving — rolling with his momentum to keep from being shot in the head—he came up in front of another Inahri and jammed the xix into his helmet from both sides. He sent energy arcing through the material and into the soldier's head, dropping him immediately.

"Two minutes!" Dante shouted. She kept shooting, and the third Inahri soldier fell.

The fourth came around the pillar, trying to get an angle on John. He limped in the other direction, using the housing as a barrier. He had two minutes to finish this and find cover.

"Dante, the engineers," he cried out.

Dante shifted her attention. She hesitated to shoot the unarmed workers, but only for a second. She knew what was at stake. Red bolts struck the unarmored Inahri one after another, dropping three of them in a hurry.

The soldier got around the pillar, outpacing the injured Marine. John stopped, ducking low and spinning on his good knee, forcing himself forward and staying upright on willpower alone, driving his xix into the soldier's chest. It was enough to disable the battle armor for a second. That was all the time John needed.

He grabbed the soldier, straining and grunting as he lifted the armor and heaved the Inahri over the side and to the bowl below. The soldier hit hard, the black material cracking as he rolled over and started to get back up.

John slumped against the pillar, his knee finally giving out. He grabbed at the buckles of his armor. Dante arrived beside him, assisting him.

"I'm hit," he said. "Knee is busted. I can't run. You should leave me."

"Bullshit. We're leaving together."

"Sheriff—"

"I already did that duty once today. That's enough for a lifetime."

"Roger that."

They got the armor open. Dante helped John lift himself out of it. She would never have had the strength without her exosuit.

The door opposite them slid open, revealing a squad of Relyeh Inahri soldiers. Dante fired at them, her shots making them hesitate just long enough for John to finish abandoning the battle armor and pull himself up on her arm. He glanced down at his knee, wincing when he saw the swelling and blood. It wasn't in good shape.

"Get behind me," Dante said.

"Sheriff—"

"Get behind me!"

Washington did as she said, ducking behind her armor as best he could. She backed away, keeping a steady stream of fire on the enemy. They shot back, rounds hitting her armor and leaving deep scuffs and scores. It was only a matter of time before one of them broke through.

But time was something they wouldn't have.

"Dante, take the xix!" John said.

"I can't hold them both in one hand."

"Pass me the rifle. You can use them for a shield."

The exchange of weapons was awkward under fire, but they managed. John used his height to fire over Dante's shoulder, while she used the xix to block the incoming assault.

The Inahri soldiers reached the modulator housing, glancing curiously at his armor. One of them must have realized what they were trying to do, because the soldiers stopped shooting, two of them grabbing the armor and heaving it over the edge, away from the housing.

It exploded in mid-air, sending shrapnel everywhere. Hot metal blasted through the soldiers' armor, sank into the pillar and struck the xix's web, threatening to kill them. It also battered both collectors bowls, creating more cracks in the parabolic shapes. Would it be enough to slow the Seeker's repair?

It would have to be.

The detonation left two of the Inahri soldiers badly wounded, and the other three shaken. Dante continued pushing John back until they were through the hatch. Then she turned around, helping support him while they quickly stumbled away.

Chapter 49

The Relyeh transport met Caleb and his captors in the hangar of the Deliverance, already resting on the stained and scuffed metal flooring when they arrived. Riley had let the Inahri out through the secondary exit, using her identification code to open the sealed hatch and guide them the short distance from the hidden armory.

The soldiers remained silent during the trip, including Sergeant Harai. He remained out of his battle armor, clothed in a robe not all that different from the Free Inahri dress, while one of his men carried his scuffed and beaten battle armor. The metal suit had some kind of personal value to the sergeant. It had to, considering its condition.

Caleb spent the walk glaring at Riley's back, wishing he had something to sink into it. She could say what she wanted about handing over the energy unit. She could claim she had saved the colony. He knew it was bullshit. They would come back for the colony later.

It seemed Harai had more important business to deal with first.

The Inahri sergeant walked briskly and with purpose,

the body language and movements of a man on a mission. His silence was evidence of his eagerness. There was no time to waste with words.

The Relyeh transport was nearly identical to the one Caleb had been brought to the Free Inahri compound in. The main differences were in the color of the outer shell, which ran a deeper shade of gray and the shape of the wings which, on the Relyeh version, were a delta configuration.

They shared the same interior. Same cockpit. Same seats. Same cargo area. Caleb expected the soldiers to drop him there, but instead they shoved him into a seat beside Riley and across from Harai.

"Welcome aboard the Mogu," Sergeant Harai said in crisp English. How was he able to speak their language so well?

The rest of the Inahri finished getting settled. The outer hatch closed, and the transport vibrated slightly as it lifted from the hangar floor, rotating in mid-air before accelerating out and up.

"Why do you want me alive?" Caleb asked.

"He thinks he's special, Sergeant," Riley said before Harai could answer.

"Please. My name is Ohno Harai. Sergeant Ohno Harai. And you are?"

"Your death," Caleb replied.

Harai smiled. "I might have been a little overdramatic. The heat of battle pulls me up sometimes. Please, Earther. Your name."

"Sergeant Caleb Card. United States Space Force Marines."

"Military, obviously," Harai said. "And a fellow sergeant. A leader of men."

"Caleb was part of a special forces team on Earth,"

Riley said. "The best in the world."

"You're a disgrace to them," Caleb said.

"I knew you were special," Harai said. "The way you fight. I haven't been challenged like that in years. You nearly killed me." He said it like it was something to laugh about. "You would make a powerful member of Arluthu's army. We're going to war, Sergeant Card. We could use someone like you."

"You expect me to say yes after you just gunned down a dozen innocent people in cold blood? They dropped their weapons."

"They betrayed my trust," Harai countered. "They showed no honor in turning on us. But you knew they would. It was well played. Casualties of fate."

Riley was looking out of the cockpit viewport. She shifted her attention to Harai. "Sergeant, why are we going south?"

"Very astute. Doctor Valentine," Harai said. "We have some business to attend to before we return to Arluthu's Citadel." He leaned over and patted the energy unit, which he had placed between his feet.

"The Seeker?" Caleb asked.

"Yes. The Free Inahri put up an honorable fight. They did try very hard."

"What happened to them?"

"Most of them died. A few of them ran. They won't get far." He gazed at Riley. "You can help us with that."

Caleb glared at her. "Haven't you helped enough already? You know what they plan to do with the energy unit, don't you?"

"Yes, Card. You like to speak to me like I'm an idiot. Does it make you feel like less of one? The Relyeh will use the modulator to launch the Seeker and take it back to Axon space. I imagine many Axon will die."

"That isn't possible," Harai said. "There aren't many Axon remaining, and even we don't know where their homeworld lies. But we're going to find it. We know they have a portal there."

"A portal?" Caleb asked. "Like a teleporter?"

"Similar. It takes more power and is longer range. It opens a quantum wormhole between destinations. Between planets. Between galaxies. From the beginning of the Hunger to the end. The Relyeh want the portal technology very badly."

"And you're going to give it to Arluthu," Caleb said.

"Not exactly. We Inahri don't know how the portals function. We know how to operate them, but that's all, and it isn't enough. You need at least two portals to make a connection, and the Seeker is only one. The Axon, they treated us like children before they treated us like slaves. They tried so hard to make us into them. They gave us technology and asked us how to use it for war. And still we would be their slaves if not for Arluthu."

"So you're his slaves instead. Nice upgrade."

"With Arluthu, there is opportunity to be more than a slave. To end beyond where you begin. Isn't that all we can hope to ask for? A chance to succeed? We respect Arluthu, and he respects us. And I respect you, Sergeant Card. You will make a fine challenger, whether you choose to do it willingly or not."

"Not."

"We shall see. But it makes no difference. Doctor, will you help me again?"

"I don't know. What's in it for me?"

Harai smiled and tapped the energy unit. "For this, an audience with Arluthu. I understand you want a cure for your disease. It can be arranged."

"How do you know you can cure me?"

"Arluthu can cure you. I'm sure of it. The Hunger mastered genetics hundreds of ens ago."

"I want more."

"For the small favor I intend to ask? I don't know how much more I can promise. I'm only a sergeant. I have superiors too."

"Small favors can have huge returns."

"What is it you want?"

Riley glanced at Caleb. "I want the trife gone from Earth."

"Trife?"

"Uluth. The creatures Arluthu sent to our homeworld to destroy our civilization. I want them destroyed. All of them. If the Relyeh are masters of genetics, then they can make a disease that kills them, the same way they made a disease to kill us."

"Why would Arluthu destroy your people and then agree to help you save them?"

"Because the Axon are more valuable."

"That is true, but we already have what we need for that."

"Thanks to me."

"Yes. You already bargained the modulator."

"I have something else to bargain, beyond what you want me to help you with."

"How do you know?"

"I know about the portals. I know how to direct them."

Harai's smile grew. He was intrigued. "Really? You are a most valuable and honored guest if that is the case."

"You're lying," Caleb said.

"I'm not."

"How can you know anything about Axon portals? You didn't know anything about the modulator before David activated it."

"We found a portal with the ship," Riley said. "A portable portal. From what we gathered, the Axon deploy them ahead of their ships and pass through them to fast travel to other parts of the universe. I spent two months with the team working on it. Of course, we never had enough juice to turn it on, but the science team had a good idea of what it did and a solid theory of how it did it."

"Did you bring it with you?"

"No. We sent the portal out to Area 51. Last I heard, it was on the Pilgrim with the team researching it. But that was two hundred years ago."

"That part might be true. I'm still not buying that you know how Axon tech works."

"Because girls can't do advanced mathematics?"

"No, because you're a manipulative, lying bitch."

Riley looked like she wanted to punch him. Instead, she turned back to Harai. "That's the deal. Can you make it happen?"

"I can't promise with complete certainty, but both myself and the Advocate will do our best to convince our Relyeh commander and Arluthu himself."

"Advocate?" Caleb asked.

Harai nodded, grabbing his right sleeve and pulling it up, revealing a worm-like creature wrapped around it. Caleb was sickened by the sight. "What the hell?"

"This is my Relyeh Advocate," Harai said. "It's what allows me to speak to you in your tongue. It is part of me. A symbiote."

It reminded Caleb of a giant leech.

"We are losing time, Doctor. What is your decision?"

"What's your question?" Riley replied.

"The Free Inahri base. We have been searching for it for many cycles. You know where it is."

"I do."

"Guide us to it, and our deal is made."

"Riley," Caleb said. "You can't. There are innocent civilians there."

"Innocent Inahri civilians, Card," Riley corrected. "Why do I care about them?"

"Are you kidding? Is there not a single ounce of humanity left in you?"

"We don't kill the innocent, Sergeant Card," Harai said. "We aren't monsters."

"See, Card. They don't kill innocents. You heard Sergeant Harai. I give up the Inahri, and they help us get the trife off Earth. That seems like a good deal from where I'm sitting."

"It's been two hundred years. How much do you think is left to save? And even if you did save it, what happens when the rest of the Relyeh arrive? They'll just take the planet back again."

"You're never satisfied, are you Card? Everything I do is wrong to you, even when it's right. I came here to avenge Earth. I'm going to save it instead."

"And destroy the colony in the process."

"It's worth it."

"No, it isn't."

"So try to stop me. Oh, you can't. Because you're a prisoner, Card. Because you're on the losing side. Give up on the colony. Give up on the Deliverance. You'll be happy you did. I know I am."

"I'm not like you, Valentine. I care about others. I care about honor, respect, and duty." He looked at Harai. "I'll keep fighting you until I'm dead."

Harai bowed his head. "And I honor you for that, Sergeant. Doctor, we have a deal. Show us the way."

Chapter 50

Caleb couldn't do anything to stop Riley from leading Sergeant Harai to the Free Inahri base. Surprised she had captured so many of the details so perfectly, especially the location, he listened while she described where it was, what it looked like, and how to find it.. Then again, she had taken the same gene editing formula as David, and it had made him exponentially more intelligent than before. There was no reason to think her outcome was much different.

The transport circled for nearly thirty minutes while Harai communicated with the Relyeh base, wherever it was, and had reinforcements sent up to meet them in the proximity of the Free Inahri compound. Sergeant Harai didn't speak to Caleb again, and thankfully neither did Riley. They planned and plotted together, leaving him to sit and listen.

Soon enough, there were four Relyeh transports in the area instead of their one, all of them loaded with soldiers from Harai's company, which was commanded by an Inahri he called Cox Ae, which Caleb figured meant either

Major or Colonel. Not that it mattered. He only heard the sergeant respond with "Chi Cox" multiple times. Yes, sir.

The transport accelerated suddenly, turning south and gaining velocity. Caleb assumed the other transports did the same behind them.

"It's time," Sergeant Harai said, looking at Caleb. "We're launching an attack on the Free Inahri compound, and I want you to be part of it."

"I'll die before I attack them," Caleb replied.

"That won't be necessary." He smiled, lifting his sleeve and revealing the Advocate again. It unrolled itself from his arm as he did, revealing dozens of small punctures and bruises along Harai's biceps and shoulder. Hundreds of legs carried it across his chest and down into his lap, where it stopped to look at Caleb.

Caleb wanted to vomit. The Advocate had a pair of black eyes on the front of it, too intelligent for something that looked like the cross between a slug and a millipede. It made a series of high-pitched tones he took as speech before bunching itself, preparing to leap the chasm between Harai and Caleb.

Riley reached over unexpectedly, grabbing his replacement hand and quickly tapping in the code to deactivate it on the control ring. His prosthetic fell limp, the weight pulling him slightly to the side.

The soldier next to Harai stood, grabbing Caleb's left arm. He held it out, while Caleb gritted his teeth, trying to figure out how to keep the Advocate away from him. The Relyeh jumped, crossing the aisle and landing on his lap. It was lighter than he would have guessed but even more disgusting up close.

It got even closer, hundreds of legs gripping his flesh and climbing out toward his arm.

"What the hell is it going to do?" Caleb asked.

"Convince you to do the right thing," Harai replied. "Believe me; the Advocate is very convincing."

Caleb looked down at it, struggling to move. There was no way he could overpower a battle-armored soldier.

The Advocate stopped directly in front of his face, large black eyes taking him in. It made a sound like a laugh before crawling the rest of the way to his arm and quickly wrapping around it. He felt the burn of dozens of needles jabbing into his muscle, the creature attaching itself to him, hooking itself up in a method he didn't understand.

He turned his head, looking at the creature. He couldn't see the front of it anymore, only its body wound around his arm and moving subtlety up and down as though it were breathing. He looked back at Harai, confused.

Sergeant Caleb Card.

The voice was no voice at all. It was more of a feeling. A suggestion. And yet it registered clearly in his mind.

United States Marines special forces. Sister Margaret, deceased. Parents, deceased. College dropout. Suppression of many emotions. Loss. Sadness. Guilt. Pain.

Caleb closed his eyes. It spit his entire life back at him, too fast for him to keep up. He felt every emotion, going through them full-bore within a span of seconds. All the time, the pressure of the suggestion continued to build in his mind, a confusion that began to overwhelm him.

"Stop," he said.

No.

It continued. He didn't see his life flash in front of his eyes, but he experienced it again all the same. Joining the military, the arrival of the trife, the death of his parents and sister, joining Space Force. The Vultures. Losing Banks and Habib. Boarding the Deliverance. Sho. Everything, all the way up to the present in the space of a handful of seconds.

I know you, Sergeant Caleb Card.

To Caleb, it felt like someone was at his back, watching everything he did. Reading his every thought and emotion.

Because I am. My name is Ishek. I am an Advocate, sixteenth in the Advocate Descendancy of our Lord and Master Arluthu, Ancient of the Relyeh. I have seen you, Caleb Card. You will make a fine host.

"Fine host for what?" Caleb said out loud.

I wish to experience the downfall of the Free Inahri. I wish to place a hand in their destruction. As you have seen, I have no hands of my own.

Ishek laughed, a human laugh in Caleb's mind.

"What does that mean?" he asked.

We are the Relyeh. The Hunger. The Darkness of the Universe. The Ancients of Ancients. All of space and time will one day be ours. All intelligent life will fall under our domain. We conquer all. Devour all. That is our purpose. Our reason to exist. Yet it is rare we have the opportunity to fulfill the obligation so personally. I savor the occasion. I relish you as well, Caleb Card. You who have stood against our uluth. You who have overcome the challenge of our nature with strength, and whose pain is a bounty to feast on.

"You still haven't told me what you mean."

I'm going to kill, Caleb Card. I'm going to slaughter the Inahri, one by one. And I'm going to use you to do it.

Chapter 51

The Relyeh transports took only minutes to reach the Free Inahri base. Caleb stared out the forward viewport window, watching the approach to the projected waterfall that protected the compound. His heart raced as they closed on it. The Advocate, Ishek, had been silent since its final murderous statement, but its presence was omnipotent in his mind, overseeing every thought, every movement, every breath.

He tried to control all of those things, to keep himself as closed-off to the Advocate as he could. Somehow, it was going to use him as a tool to slaughter the Inahri. He would try to fight it, but in the back of his mind, he already knew resistance was futile. It was only speaking to him now, but the sense that it could do much, much more was ever-present.

"Prepare to disembark," Sergeant Harai said, standing up. He was speaking in Inahrai , the Advocate translating to English so Caleb would understand.

The rest of the soldiers in the transport stood. So did Riley.

"If it moves and isn't ours, you have permission to kill it," Harai said. He motioned to one of his soldiers, who went to the back and retrieved an Intellect Skin for the sergeant. Harai stripped and quickly put himself into the Skin before turning to Caleb. "I prefer battle armor, but you made a mess of mine."

He moved to the hatch, turning and facing forward. Caleb looked back out the front of the transport. The waterfall was only a hundred meters away and closing fast.

Three more heartbeats and they were through.

The transports entered the Free Inahri compound, facing a stiff line of fire as they did, the Inahri Dancers having spotted them coming with only minutes to spare. Blue bolts lashed out at the transports, flashing against the cockpit glass and smacking harmlessly into apparent shielding. The transport dropped hard toward the ground, hitting so violently Caleb expected its landers to crumple beneath the impact.

The hatch slid open beside Harai. "For Arluthu!" he shouted, jumping out of the craft ahead of his soldiers.

"For Arluthu!" they shouted back.

"For Arluthu!" Caleb found himself crying out, through no intention of his own.

"For Arltuthu," Riley said. She turned to him, reactivating his replacement arm and getting to her feet. "I'll stay close to you."

"I don't want you anywhere near me," he replied.

"I'm not talking to you," Riley said.

Caleb's body betrayed him then, his legs working to bring him to a stand, his arms bringing his Intellect Skin back up over his upper body and sealing it closed, lifting the mantle over his head and then carrying him to the rear of the craft, to the open hatch. One of the soldiers handed him a rifle as he reached it, bowing his head reverently.

"For Arluthu," the soldier said.

Then he was out of the transport, joining the Relyeh Inahri in a charge toward the Free Inahri rebels, aiming and firing his rifle at them, completely out of control. He could sense the Advocate's excitement in his mind, the bloodlust and thrill of the fight. He tried to push against it, to find his limbs and regain motor control. It was as though the Advocate was stopping all of his brain activity from reaching the rest of his body, capturing it and replacing it with a will of its own.

No Advocate was controlling Valentine's actions. She charged ahead with the other Relyeh, firing into the rebel forces, helping to bury the weak defense in an avalanche of offensive destruction. The Free Inahri fell one after another, the assault against them barely slowing, their defenses shattering beneath the onslaught. Sergeant Harai barked orders to his team over the comm, the Advocate following them, letting Harai lead Caleb into the compound toward the central ring, a path of death in their wake.

This is better than I ever imagined.

The Advocate decided to speak to him. Caleb didn't know why.

"Go screw yourself," he replied. His hands were already responsible for killing one Free Inahri soldier. But it was only his hands.

I believe it could be better still.

Caleb's hands opened, the rifle falling to the ground.

"Sergeant Harai," he found himself saying. "I want to get closer."

"Good idea," Harai replied. "Inahri, let's make this more personal." The sergeant stowed his rifle, speeding up the charge toward the corner of a building, where a pair of unarmored Free Inahri were shooting at them. He raised his forearm, energy shield blocking their assault until he reached them. He grabbed one, throwing him easily out into the open before taking the other and placing his palm against his chest, a flare of energy from the Intellect Skin burning into the Inahri's heart and killing him.

The first Free Inahri struggled to his feet. Caleb rushed toward him, grabbing him as he rose. His replacement arm locked around the man's neck at the elbow and squeezed, his spine cracking easily beneath the force. Caleb wanted to close his eyes. He wanted to look away.

He couldn't do anything.

More.

The Advocate dropped the dead Inahri, searching for another.

"More," Caleb said to Harai over the comm.

"Yes."

The sergeant found another target, grabbing a woman and pulling her out into the open, kicking her leg out from under her and leaving her on the ground. Caleb walked over to her, standing over her while she looked up at him with tears in her eyes.

"No, damn it," Caleb said helplessly.

Yes.

He kicked her in the face, and she crumpled to the ground. He leaned over her, reaching for her neck.

A dark blur hit him from the side, the impact taking him away from the woman. He rolled with his attacker, coming to a stop beneath the Free Inahri, finding himself looking up at General Goi.

General? The Advocate was pleased to know who it was fighting. It's amusement echoed in Caleb's senses as it pulled the mantle from Caleb's head.

General Goi froze over Caleb. "Sergeant Card?"

The hesitation gave the Advocate time to punch Goi in

the side of the head with the replacement hand, still stuck in a balled fist. The blow knocked the General away, but he rolled with the punch and bounced up, raising his hands and falling into a martial posture.

Caleb stood, shifting into a Marine fighting stance. How did the Advocate know how to fight?

I know everything you know, Caleb Card. And more. So much more.

General Goi grabbed a pair of xix from his back, tapping them together to activate them. "I trusted you."

"You trusted Valentine. I told you not to. You didn't listen."

"You betrayed us with her."

"I did..." The Advocate choked off the last word, changing the meaning completely. Caleb could sense its joy at the harm it caused. Whatever the Relyeh were, wherever they had originated, they were evil. Pure evil.

Not evil. This is our birthright. This is our universe. We use it as we will.

Caleb reached for his hip as Goi rushed in, creating a web with the xix to throw at him. He grabbed his sidearm, raising his replacement hand and using it to catch the blow from the weapon. He blocked the xix, holding them shoulder-high while his human hand finished drawing the ion pistol, firing it into Goi's stomach.

The general stumbled back, the xix falling from his hands. The Advocate controlled Caleb's hand, firing the pistol again, and again, and again. General Goi's body nearly disintegrated beneath the blasts. The Advocate didn't stop.

"Stop!" Caleb roared. The Advocate did. Had he managed to break through?

He is dead enough.

The Advocate turned away from Goi. The rest of the

Relyeh Inahri had continued, but Riley was standing nearby, ready to intervene if needed.

"His blood is on your hands, Valentine," Caleb said. "All of their blood is on your hands."

"They mean nothing to me, Card," she replied. "Nothing. This victory will be a victory for Earth. For Earth. Not Essex. Not the Deliverance. For our home."

A wave of sadness washed through Caleb.

She is a fool.

"I guess we agree on something."

When she sees the true might of Arluthu, she will forget your world. She will understand it belongs to the Hunger, as she also does.

Caleb couldn't argue with that. Riley's greatest folly was that she kept thinking she was in control. She had lost control before the Deliverance ever left Earth. She just wasn't capable of seeing it.

"The enemy forces are retreating into the caverns," Sergeant Harai said. "We've broken them."

"Do any survive?" Caleb asked.

"Yes."

"Then our mission isn't complete. We will kill every Inahri in this compound. There will be no more resistance to Lord Arluthu."

Come, Caleb Card. I hunger.

Chapter 52

Two hours of sneaking cautiously through the Seeker put John and Dante in the nearest hangar in search of a vehicle that might get them out of the area and hopefully back to the Deliverance. They had managed to avoid the Relyeh forces who were gaining an ever-increasing presence in the ship. It was easy to correlate a positive hit from a battle armor's sensors if everyone was an enemy. It got more difficult when the pings could be either friend or foe.

The hanger was relatively small, located part-way up the side of the central tower. It was also nearly empty, containing a few smaller delta-winged craft that could have passed for jet fighters and a single dark transport similar to the one they had arrived in.

The presence of the transport forced them to rush from the open hatch to squeeze behind a stack of long, silver cylinders—John assumed they were battery cells—stacked in the corner. The hangar's interior entrance was a few meters to their right, where they could see anyone coming through.

They crouched there, hoping the pair of soldiers inside

the transport's open hatch didn't bother to put their helmets back on to check their sensors. Otherwise, they were as good as caught.

"What do you think is going on in there?" Dante asked.

John shook his head. "No idea. A squad meeting maybe."

"What should we do?" Dante said.

"Hopefully, they'll all head out soon. Then we can take the transport."

"We don't know how to fly it."

"I'd much rather take my chances flying that thing than trying to walk out of here. I watched Kiaan. It didn't look that hard."

"Famous last words."

"Let's hope not."

Ten minutes passed before anything happened, and when it did, it happened fast. The soldiers in the transport jumped out of the open hatch, quickly pulling their helmets on and standing at attention on either side, rifles across their chests. John started to worry that the guards would notice them on their sensors. But if they had, they weren't showing any evidence of it. Maybe the batteries were screwing with the signals? He and Dante should be so lucky.

The entrance to the hangar slid open, and two more guards moved inside, taking up a matching position beside the others.

Then a third person climbed from the transport, an older man in a purple robe. He looked important. He took a couple of steps past the soldiers and came to attention himself, eyes locked on the hangar's entrance.

"Someone really important is coming," Dante whispered in John's ear.

He nodded. He didn't care who it was as long as they

all left quickly, and on foot, before somebody noticed them on their sensors.

A few more minutes passed. All of the soldiers held their posture and positions without showing any sign of impatience. Or knowledge that they were being watched. The hangar door slid open again.

John would never have believed what came through if he weren't there to see it.

He assumed it was a Relyeh. A real Relyeh. It was large. Almost three meters, and at least two-hundred kilos. Wide and thick, with the vague appearance of a slimy, clothed frog. Its limbs were soft but dense, with protrusions extending from the joints which rounded up and vanished beneath a resplendent black hooded robe. Its head was as alien a thing as John had ever seen. Its skull was massive and round, its face tiny in the center of it. Dozens of small, narrow tendrils dropped from beneath a pair of large black eyes, either replacing its mouth or covering it. They wiggled like worms along the neckline of the robe, leaving a stain of ooze behind. Its ears were a pair of long slits along the side of its head, and it's nose a pair of slits at the base of the tendrils. It walked upright but slightly bent, using one of its menacing hands as it moved to help it stay balanced.

The Inahri in the purple robe moved forward to meet it. They stopped near the middle, two meters apart. The Relyeh spoke in a weird series of layered tones, like a brass quartet playing random notes all at once. The Inahri nodded, seemingly able to understand the language. He spoke back to the Relyeh in Inahrai.

They exchanged words back and forth for nearly a minute. Then the Relyeh reached out and put his huge hand on the man's shoulder, immediately leaving a stain on the purple robe. The Relyeh turned, walking out with the Inahri. John couldn't tell what any of the alien's strange, tendrilled reactions meant. He could see that the Inahri 's face had shifted from arrogant confidence to anger. What was that all about?

The four guards trailed behind the pair as they headed out of the hangar. John continued to wait until the hangar door closed behind them and a few minutes had passed without activity. Then he stood up straight, moving from behind the batteries.

"This is our chance," he said. "You getting anything?"

"Negative," Dante replied, emerging beside him. "We're clear."

"Still clear?" he asked.

"Yes, Sergeant."

"Let's go."

Dante helped support John while they crossed the hangar to the transport. John's heart began to race, a feeling of relief rushing through him. They were going to make it.

The elation only lasted a few heartbeats. They were still a few meters from the transport's open hatch when a dark form appeared, coming around the corner and dropping to the hangar floor. A second form was right behind it, joining the first.

"Shit," John said, looking at the pair of soldiers in Intellect Skins. "I thought you said it was clear?"

"There's nothing on my sensors," Dante said. "They must be jamming me somehow."

"I guess we have to fight."

"I guess so."

John pulled away from Dante, balancing on his good leg and bringing his rifle to his hip to fire one-handed. The two enemy soldiers split apart, one coming at him, the other charging Dante.

Dante quickly grabbed the xix, activating them as the Inahri soldier neared. John got his finger to the trigger, squeezing off a pair of rounds at his attacker. The bolts died against the Skin's shield, and then the enemy was on him. He grabbed the muzzle of John's rifle, yanking it easily from his unarmored, weakened grip. John tried to get into a fighting stance, but he stumbled when he tried to put weight on his knee. The enemy soldier grabbed him, spinning behind him and putting his head in a choke hold.

A Marine choke hold. What the hell?

A couple of meters away, Dante cursed as the Relyeh soldier finished disarming her, using the first xix they had captured to send a charge through the battle armor, freezing it long enough to grab the second. She stood in front of the disarmed sheriff, tossing the xix behind her and reaching up to pull her mantle off.

"Today is not your lucky day," Riley Valentine said as she revealed herself, shifting her gaze between Dante and John. "Take your helmet off."

Dante hesitated.

"Take it off, or Washington dies."

Dante removed her helmet, tossing it to the side.

"Hello, Wash," Caleb said, leaning his head in next to John's ear.

"Cal?" John said, confused. Kiaan had told them what Caleb had done. He still couldn't believe it. "What are you doing, Sarge?"

"What you should be doing," he replied. "Joining the winning side. You can't fight the Hunger, John."

"Sarge, tell me you didn't kill those innocent people at the Inahri compound."

Caleb's voice lowered. "I did kill them, Wash. And do you want to know something else? I enjoyed it."

John's heart pounded harder than it ever had before. How could that be? This wasn't the Caleb Card he had spent the last two years serving under. It didn't matter what Caleb said. He refused to believe it.

"I'll get you out of this, Sarge. Whatever happened, I'll help you fix it."

"There's nothing to fix," Caleb replied. "You should be more worried about yourself."

Caleb put more pressure on John's neck, using it to spin the larger Marine around as the hangar door slid open again. The man in the purple robe approached them at a quick walk, a smile spreading across his face.

"I knew it," the man said in perfect English. His eyes traveled from John's face to his knee. "I take it you're the ones who damaged the modulator housing?"

"Screw you," John said, causing Caleb to tighten his grip even more.

"You're hardly in a position to make demands," the man replied. "You were probably going for the housing itself, weren't you? You probably had no idea the damage you did to the collectors will be harder to repair, especially since you killed our engineers. You have my respect for completing your mission. How does it feel to have your allies turn tail and leave you behind?"

John didn't answer. He had nothing else to say.

"A soldier who knows when to be silent. I respect that too." The man shifted his attention to Riley. "It looks like it'll be a little while before the Seeker is ready. General Ogg sent a communication to Arluthu. Our glorious Lord has agreed to your petition. We'll depart at once."

"What about these two?" Riley asked.

"You tell me," the Inahri replied. "Who are they?"

"Private John Washington," Riley said, pointing at John.

"He's one of my squad," Caleb said. "He's a better soldier than me."

"He can be of use," the Inahri said. "We'll bring him with us."

"Sheriff Lasandra Dante," Riley said, looking back at the sheriff. "Head of the Law Office in Metro."

"So the people we killed were yours?" the Inahri said. "Their training was lacking. So was their loyalty." He glanced over at the rifle Caleb had pulled from John's hands.

"I'll do it," Caleb said, releasing the choke hold and shoving John forward. He collapsed face-down onto the floor, turning his head to look at a suddenly desperate Dante.

"Sarge, you can't," he said.

Caleb grabbed the rifle, turning back toward the sheriff. Dante hadn't moved. She was too frightened to move.

"I hunger," Caleb said, a nearly inhuman expression passing across his face.

"Caleb?" Dante said weakly.

He aimed and fired in one smooth motion, the bolt passing through Dante's skull. Her head drooped forward, the battle armor holding her upright for a moment before it toppled forward.

"Noooo!" John cried, trying to get to his feet. "Damn you, you son of a bitch!"

He tried to charge the Inahri, falling forward on his bad knee, grunting in pain and getting up again. The Inahri took a casual step back as John fell a second time.

"Yes, definitely a keeper," he said.

Caleb grabbed John from behind, throwing him to the

ground and standing over him. He raised the stock of the rifle over John's head.

"Goodnight, Wash."

The stock came down on John's temple.

Everything went dark.

Chapter 53

Governor Jackson Stone opened his eyes. He immediately knew he was in the hospital. The IV running from the back of his hand to the bag hanging over his head was a dead giveaway. He took a moment, trying to recall how he had gotten there.

Joe.

He closed his eyes and groaned, remembering how he had led the Inahri Sergeant Harai to the Law Office, sure that Joe King had decided to hide in the armory below.

He recalled how Sergeant Card had confronted the Relyeh soldier, and convinced the sheriffs and deputies to fight back against the invaders.

He remembered getting shot.

He shifted his head, looking down at his body. He was under a weighted blanket. He could feel the pressure against his arms and chest, warm and comforting.

But why couldn't he feel the pressure on his legs?

His heart jumped as he tried to wiggle his toes. His eyes shifted to the protrusion of his feet, staring at them when the blanket didn't move. It couldn't be. He tried to bend his knee.

Nothing.

He groaned again, a sound of sadness and loss. He couldn't feel his legs. He couldn't move his legs. The energy unit was gone. Everyone in Law was dead. Beth was...

Beth.

He remembered his wife. She was here, somewhere.

He turned his head, finding the call button dangling from the IV rack. He yanked his hand out from under the blanket and grabbed it, tapping furiously.

Only a few seconds passed before Doctor Rathbone rushed into his room with a pair of nurses in tow.

"Governor Stone," she said. "You're awake." She looked terrified. She knew he was paralyzed. Of course, she knew. She was the doctor. She was afraid of his reaction.

"Beth," he said. "Where's Beth?"

The question took her off-guard. She stammered out a reply. "She's... Uh... Upstairs, Governor."

"Get me a chair and take me to her."

"Sir?"

"Now!"

Rathbone turned to the nurses. "Get him a chair."

They hurried from the room.

"Governor," Rathbone started to say.

"Forget it, Gina," he replied. "Whatever you were going to say. Just answer my questions."

"Yes, Governor."

"The invaders?"

"They left with Doctor Valentine. They took Sergeant Card prisoner."

"How do you know?"

"You aren't the only survivor."

"Joe King?"

"I don't know."

"What do you mean you don't know?"

"Nobody outside of the hospital staff has been down there since the attack. We're still on curfew, sir. We didn't find him in the armory, or the corridors nearby. But one of the rooms is locked."

Jackson exhaled. "Okay. Valentine had the unit. She most likely killed him. But why would she lock him in?"

"I can't guess, Governor."

"Me neither. Where's the damn chair?"

"Coming, sir."

Jackson lowered his head and closed his eyes. "I screwed up."

"I know."

"You weren't supposed to agree with me."

"I'm sorry, Jack. But you really, really screwed up."

"I thought I could handle it."

"Because you're arrogant. It's not completely your fault. Your life has been far too easy up till now."

"I could put you in jail for talking to me like that."

"But you won't."

"Why not?"

"Because if you have half a brain in your head, you've realized by now that you need to start listening to people other than yourself. A lot of good people died today, Governor. And it's your fault."

Jackson felt the accusation in his gut. Sudden, wrenching guilt. It was his fault—all of it. He had thrown the Guardians to the wolves, and now the colony was in silent chaos, as vulnerable and confused as it had ever been.

"My wounds," he said.

"Your spine was melted at the 12th thoracic," Rathbone said. "Completely severed. We can't give you prosthetics with that kind of damage."

"You're saying I'm never going to walk again?"

"Not necessarily. We have some advanced options, but considering the current state of the colony, you might want to be conscious right now."

The door opened, and the nurses came in with a simple wheelchair—little more than a lightly padded seat with a motor beneath and a joystick on the left armrest.

"Help me up," Jackson said. "Get me to the chair. I need to see Beth."

"Governor, your wife…I don't know if this is a good time," Rathbone said.

"Why not?"

"She's still in shock. To be honest, I don't know if we'll be able to help her."

Jackson's heart dropped. "All the more reason for me to see her then. Help me."

Rathbone nodded, and the nurses pulled off the blanket. He was naked underneath, and they quickly removed his catheter and helped him into underwear and a gown before shifting him to the wheelchair.

"Take me to her."

Doctor Rathbone led the way, with Jackson rolling behind her. The doctor was right. He didn't have time to waste on his legs, repairing them or mourning them. The colony was in trouble, and it was his fault.

He had to fix it.

Somehow.

They took the lift up to the next floor. Rathbone stopped in front of the door to her room, facing him.

"Are you sure you want to see her? It's…troubling."

"Get out of the way," Jackson said.

Rathbone stepped aside. Jackson rolled into the room, his eyes tearing up as soon as he saw Beth lying in bed, head shaking back and forth, eyes moist, small groans of fear escaping her.

He went to her bedside and tried to take her hand. She screamed at the touch, pulling it away without looking. It was like a knife to his heart. He looked back to Rathbone.

"There's nothing you can do for this?"

"We can put her in a coma," she replied. "Otherwise, no."

"Beth. Oh, Beth." He stared at her face, so beautiful and so disturbed. "This is my fault, my love. All of it is my fault. I let my pride get the best of me, and look what happened. This planet isn't what we thought it would be. It isn't what we were promised."

He lowered his head into his hands, body shaking as he sobbed.

"It wasn't supposed to be this way. It wasn't supposed to happen like this. We should be in our mansion by the river, toasting our new home."

He straightened up, wiping his eyes, realizing the tears weren't going to help.

"Governor Jackson Stone, one way or another, you will have no choice but to fight. The only decision you can make is who and what you will fight for."

Jackson remembered what Sergeant Harai had said to him during their first meeting. In that moment, he would have given anything to delay his decision. He would have, and did, agree to anything to save himself and Beth. To save Metro. But he couldn't hide from the truth any longer. The truth had put his wife here and massacred his officers.

"We still will — one day. I promise. I can't change the past. I can't undo the mistakes I made. But I'll be damned if Metro is going down easy. I'll be damned if we're going to fade away without a fight. This isn't the home we expected, but this is our new home, and I'm going to fight for it. Do you hear me, love? I promise you that.

"I'm going to fight for it."

Thank you for reading
Destruction

Thank you so much for sticking with the series and picking up Destruction.

If you loved the book, please show your support for the series by leaving a review (mrforbes.com/destruction) and telling potential readers how great you think the series is.

The next book in the series is called Declaration. Give it a look at mrforbes.com/declaration

Thank you so much for your support. If you have Facebook, please stop by my page sometime at facebook.com/mrforbes.author. I'd love to hear from you.

Cheers,
Michael.

Other Books By M.R Forbes

M.R. Forbes on Amazon

mrforbes.com/books

Forgotten (The Forgotten)

mrforbes.com/theforgotten

Some things are better off FORGOTTEN.

Sheriff Hayden Duke was born on the Pilgrim, and he expects to die on the Pilgrim, like his father, and his father before him.

That's the way things are on a generation starship centuries from home. He's never questioned it. Never thought about it. And why bother? Access points to the ship's controls are sealed, the systems that guide her automated and out of reach. It isn't perfect, but he has all he needs to be content.

Until a malfunction forces his Engineer wife to the edge of the habitable zone to inspect the damage.

Until she contacts him, breathless and terrified, to tell

him she found a body, and it doesn't belong to anyone on board.

Until he arrives at the scene and discovers both his wife and the body are gone.

The only clue? A bloody handprint beneath a hatch that hasn't opened in hundreds of years.

Until now.

Earth Unknown (Forgotten Earth)
mrforbes.com/earthunknown

A terrible discovery.

A secret that could destroy human civilization.

A desperate escape to the most dangerous planet in the universe... Earth.

Two hundred years ago, a fleet of colony ships left Earth and started a settlement on Proxima Centauri...

Centurion Space Force pilot Nathan Stacker didn't expect to return home to find his wife dead. He didn't expect the murderer to look just like him, and he definitely didn't expect to be the one to take the blame.

But his wife had control of a powerful secret. A secret that stretches across the light years between two worlds and could lead to the end of both.

Now that secret is in Nathan's hands, and he's about to make the most desperate evasive maneuver of his life -- stealing a starship and setting a course for Earth.

He thinks he'll be safe there.

He's wrong. Very wrong.

Earth is nothing like what he expected. Not even close. What he doesn't know is not only likely to kill him, it's eager to kill him, and even if it doesn't?

The Sheriff will.

Starship Eternal (War Eternal)

mrforbes.com/starshipeternal

A lost starship...

A dire warning from futures past...

A desperate search for salvation…

Captain Mitchell "Ares" Williams is a Space Marine and the hero of the Battle for Liberty, whose Shot Heard 'Round the Universe saved the planet from a nearly unstoppable war machine. He's handsome, charismatic, and the perfect poster boy to help the military drive enlistment. Pulled from the war and thrown into the spotlight, he's as efficient at charming the media and bedding beautiful celebrities as he was at shooting down enemy starfighters.

After an assassination attempt leaves Mitchell critically wounded, he begins to suffer from strange hallucinations that carry a chilling and oddly familiar warning:

They are coming. Find the Goliath or humankind will be destroyed.

Convinced that the visions are a side-effect of his injuries, he tries to ignore them, only to learn that he may not be as crazy as he thinks. The enemy is real and closer than he imagined, and they'll do whatever it takes to prevent him from rediscovering the centuries lost starship.

Narrowly escaping capture, out of time and out of air, Mitchell lands at the mercy of the Riggers - a ragtag crew of former commandos who patrol the lawless outer reaches of the galaxy. Guided by a captain with a reputation for cold-blooded murder, they're dangerous, immoral, and possibly insane.

They may also be humanity's last hope for survival in a war that has raged beyond eternity.

(War Eternal is also available in a box set of the first three books here: mrforbes.com/wareternalbox)

Hell's Rejects (Chaos of the Covenant)
mrforbes.com/hellsrejects

The most powerful starships ever constructed are gone. Thousands are dead. A fleet is in ruins. The attackers are unknown. The orders are clear: *Recover the ships. Bury the bastards who stole them.*

Lieutenant Abigail Cage never expected to find herself in Hell. As a Highly Specialized Operational Combatant, she was one of the most respected Marines in the military. Now she's doing hard labor on the most miserable planet in the universe.

Not for long.

The Earth Republic is looking for the most dangerous individuals it can control. The best of the worst, and Abbey happens to be one of them. The deal is simple: *Bring back the starships, earn your freedom. Try to run, you die.* It's a suicide mission, but she has nothing to lose.

The only problem? There's a new threat in the galaxy. One with a power unlike anything anyone has ever seen. One that's been waiting for this moment for a very, very, long time. And they want Abbey, too.

Be careful what you wish for.

They say Hell hath no fury like a woman scorned. They have no idea.

Man of War (Rebellion)
mrforbes.com/manofwar

In the year 2280, an alien fleet attacked the Earth.

Their weapons were unstoppable, their defenses unbreakable.

Our technology was inferior, our militaries overwhelmed.

Only one starship escaped before civilization fell.

Earth was lost.

It was never forgotten.

Fifty-two years have passed.

A message from home has been received.

The time to fight for what is ours has come.

Welcome to the rebellion.

Or maybe something completely different?

Dead of Night (Ghosts & Magic)
mrforbes.com/deadofnight

For Conor Night, the world's only surviving necromancer, staying alive is an expensive proposition. So when the promise of a big payout for a small bit of thievery presents itself, Conor is all in. But nothing comes easy in the world of ghosts and magic, and it isn't long before Conor is caught up in the machinations of the most powerful wizards on Earth and left with only two ways out:

Finish the job, or be finished himself.

Balance (The Divine)
mrforbes.com/balance

My name is Landon Hamilton. Once upon a time I was a twenty-three year old security guard, trying to regain my life after spending a year in prison for stealing people's credit card numbers.

Now, I'm dead.

Okay, I was supposed to be dead. I got killed after all; but a funny thing happened after I had turned the mortal coil...

I met Dante Samghieri - yeah, that Dante. He told me I was special, a diuscrucis. That's what they call a perfect balance of human, demon, and angel. Apparently, I'm the only one of my kind.

I also learned that there was a war raging on Earth between Heaven and Hell, and that I was the only one who could save the human race from annihilation. He asked me to help, and I was naive enough to agree.

Sounds crazy, I know, but he wished me luck and sent me back to the mortal world. Oh yeah, he also gave me instructions on how to use my Divine "magic" to bend the universe to my will. The problem is, a sexy vampire crushed them while I was crushing on her.

Now I have to somehow find my own way to stay alive in a world of angels, vampires, werewolves, and an assortment of other enemies that all want to kill me before I can mess up their plans for humanity's future. If that isn't enough, I also have to find the queen of all demons and recover the Holy Grail.

It's not like it's the end of the world if I fail.

Wait. It is.

Tears of Blood (Books 1-3)

mrforbes.com/tearsofblood

One thousand years ago, the world was broken and reborn beneath the boot of a nameless, ageless tyrant. He erased all history of the time before, enslaving the people and hunting those with the power to unseat him.

The power of magic.

Eryn is such a girl. Born with the Curse, she fights to

control and conceal it to protect those she loves. But when the truth is revealed, and his Marines come, she is forced away from her home and into the company of Silas, a deadly fugitive tormented by a fractured past.

Silas knows only that he is a murderer who once hunted the Cursed, and that he and his brothers butchered armies and innocents alike to keep the deep, dark secrets of the time before from ever coming to light.

Secrets which could save the world.

Or destroy it completely.

About the Author

M.R. Forbes is the mind behind a growing number of Amazon best-selling science fiction series including Rebellion, War Eternal, Chaos of the Covenant, and the Forgotten Universe novels. He currently resides with his family and friends on the west cost of the United States, including a cat who thinks she's a dog and a dog who thinks she's a cat.

He maintains a true appreciation for his readers and is always happy to hear from them.

To learn more about M.R. Forbes or just say hello:

Visit my website:
mrforbes.com

Send me an e-mail:
michael@mrforbes.com

Check out my Facebook page:
facebook.com/mrforbes.author

Chat with me on Facebook Messenger:
https://m.me/mrforbes.author

Made in the USA
Las Vegas, NV
24 September 2021

30853300R10198